Praise for
New York Times bestselli
Christina Dodd

"Featuring an unforgettable protagonist, who makes Jack Reacher look like a slacker, Dodd's latest superior suspense novel builds on the well-deserved success of *Dead Girl Running*."
—*Booklist* (starred review) on *What Doesn't Kill Her*

"Christina Dodd reinvents the romantic thriller. Her signature style—edgy, intense, twisty, emotional—leaves you breathless from first page to last. Readers who enjoy Nora Roberts will devour Dodd's electrifying novels."
—Jayne Ann Krentz, *New York Times* bestselling author

"Action-packed, littered with dead bodies, and brimming with heartfelt emotion, this edgy thriller keeps the tension high."
—*Library Journal* (starred review) on *What Doesn't Kill Her*

"Dodd's gripping voice will appeal to fans of Sandra Brown, Nora Roberts, Linda Howard and Jayne Ann Krentz."
—*Mystery Tribune* on *What Doesn't Kill Her*

"No one does high-stakes, high-voltage suspense quite like Dodd, and [*Dead Girl Running*] is another guaranteed keep-the-lights-on-late read. Dodd is at her most wildly entertaining, wickedly witty best."
—*Booklist* (starred review)

"Complex, intense, and engrossing, this riveting romantic thriller has a chilling gothic touch and just enough red herrings and twists to keep readers on edge."
—*Library Journal* (starred review) on *Dead Girl Running*

"You can always count on the ingenious mind of Christina Dodd to deliver fascinating, unusual and highly intriguing stories. Dodd is truly a masterful storyteller!"
—*RT Book Reviews* on *Dead Girl Running* (Top Pick)

**Also available from
Christina Dodd
and HQN**

Cape Charade

Hard to Kill (ebook novella)
Dead Girl Running
Families and Other Enemies (ebook novella)
What Doesn't Kill Her
Hidden Truths (ebook novella)
Strangers She Knows

Right Motive (ebook novella)
Wrong Alibi

For additional books by Christina Dodd,
visit her website, www.christinadodd.com.

WRONG

ALIBI

CHRISTINA
DODD

HQN

HQN®

ISBN-13: 978-1-335-08082-0

Wrong Alibi

Recycling programs
for this product may
not exist in your area.

This edition published by arrangement with Harlequin Books S.A.

For questions and comments about the quality of this book, please contact us at
CustomerService@Harlequin.com.

HQN
22 Adelaide St. West, 40th Floor
Toronto, Ontario M5H 4E3, Canada
www.Harlequin.com

Printed in U.S.A.

For Lillian

Thank you for friendship

Thank you for love

Thank you for wisdom

Thank you for Alaska

All God's blessings on your new journey

WRONG
ALIBI

PART ONE

PETIE

1

ALASKA
Midnight Sun Fishing Camp
Katchabiggie Lodge
Eight years ago

JANUARY.

Five and a half hours a day when the sun rose above the horizon.

Storm clouds so thick, daylight never penetrated, and night reigned eternal.

Thirty below zero Fahrenheit.

The hurricane-force wind wrapped frigid temperatures around the lodge, driving through the log cabin construction and the steel roof, ignoring the insulation, creeping inch by inch into the Great Room where twenty-year-old Petie huddled on a love seat, dressed in a former guest's flannel pajamas and bundled in a Pendleton Northern Lights wool blanket. A wind like this pushed snow through the roof vents, and she knew as soon as the storm stopped, she'd be up in the attic shoveling it out.

Or not. Maybe first the ceiling would fall in on top of her. Who would know? Who would care?

The storm of the century, online news called it, before

the internet disappeared in a blast that blew out the cable like a candle.

For a second long, dark winter, she was the only living being tending the Midnight Sun cabins and the lodge, making sure the dark, relentless Alaska winter didn't do too much damage and in the spring the camp could open to enthusiastic fishermen, corporate team builders and rugged individualists.

Alone for eight months of the year. No Christmas. No New Year's. No Valentine's Day. No any day, nothing interesting, just dark dark dark isolation and fear that she would die out here.

With the internet gone, she waited for the next inevitable event.

The lights went out.

On each of the four walls, a small, battery-charged nightlight came on to battle feebly against the darkness. Outside, the storm roared. Inside, cold swallowed the heat with greedy appetite.

Petie sat and stared into a dark so black it hurt her eyes. And remembered...

There, against the far back wall of the basement, in the darkest corner, white plastic covered...something. Slowly, Petie approached, driven by a terrible fear. She stopped about three feet away, leaned forward and reached out, far out, to grasp the corner of the plastic, pull it back, and see—

With a gasp, Petie leaped to her feet.

No. Just no. She couldn't—wouldn't—replay those memories again.

She tossed the blanket onto the floor and groped for the flashlights on the table beside her: the big metal one with a hefty weight and the smaller plastic headlamp she could strap to her forehead. She clicked on the big one and shone it around the lodge, reassuring herself no one and nothing was here. No ghosts, no zombies, no cruel people making ruthless judgments about the gullible young woman she had been.

Armed with both lights, she moved purposefully out of the Great Room, through the massive kitchen and toward the utility room.

The door between the kitchen and the utility room was insulated, the first barrier between the lodge and the bitter, rattling winds. She opened that door, took a breath of the even chillier air, stepped into the utility room and shut herself in. There she donned socks, boots, ski pants, an insulated shirt, a cold-weather blanket cut with arm holes, a knit hat and an ancient, full-length, seal-skin, Aleut-made coat with a hood. She checked the outside temperature.

Colder now—forty below and with the wind howling, the wind chill would be sixty below, seventy below…who knew? Who cared? Exposed skin froze in extreme cold and add the wind chill… She wrapped a scarf around her face and the back of her neck. Then unwrapped it to secure the headlamp low on her forehead. Then wrapped herself up again, trying to cover as much skin as she could before she faced the punishing weather.

She pointed her big flashlight at the generator checklist posted on the wall and read:

Hawley's reasons why the generator will fail to start.
The generator is new and well-tested, so the problem is:

1. LOOSE BATTERY CABLE
Solution: Tighten.

2. CORRODED BATTERY CONNECTION
Solution: Use metal terminal battery brush to clean
connections and reattach.

3. DEAD BATTERY

*Solution: Change battery in the autumn to avoid
ever having to change it in the middle of a major
fucking winter storm.*

If she wasn't standing there alone in the dark in the bitter cold, she would have grinned. The owner of the fishing
camp, Hawley Foggo, taught his employees Hawley's Rules.
He had them for every occurrence of the fishing camp, and
that last sounded exactly like him.

The generator used a car battery, and as instructed, in the
autumn she had changed it. This was her second year dealing
with the battery, and she felt secure about her work.

So probably this failure was a loose connection or cor-
rosion. Either way, she could fix it and save the lodge from
turning into a solid ice cube that wouldn't thaw until spring.

That was, after all, her job.

She shivered.

So much better than her last job, the one that led to her
conviction for a gruesome double murder.

"Okay, Petie, let's grab that metal battery cleaner thingy
and get the job done." Which sounded pretty easy, when she
talked to herself about it, but when she pulled on the insulated ski gloves, they limited her dexterity.

Out of the corner of her eye, a light blinked out.

She looked back into the lodge's Great Room. The night-
lights were failing, and soon she really would be alone in the
absolute darkness, facing the memories of that long-ago day
in the basement.

Good incentive to hurry.

She grabbed the wire battery connection cleaner thingy
and moved to the outer door.

There she paused and pictured the outdoor layout.

A loosely built lean-to protected the generator from the worst of the weather while allowing the exhaust to escape. That meant she wasn't stepping out into the full force of the storm; she would be as protected as the generator itself. Which was apparently not well enough since the damned thing wasn't working.

She gathered her fortitude and eased the outer door open.

The wind caught it, yanked it wide and dragged her outside and down the steps. She hung on to the door handle, flailed around on the frozen ground, and when she regained her footing, she used all her strength to shove the door closed again.

Then she was alone, outside, in a killer storm, in the massive, bleak wilderness that was Alaska.

2

SOME MIGHT SAY PETIE was stupid to put herself in this situation.

She had to agree.

Except…

No, really, she had to agree.

Her forehead light scarcely pierced the dark of the night and the dark of the storm, so she groped in her coat pocket for her big flashlight, clicked it on and waved the beam around.

The left wall of the lean-to had been shattered by a tree branch that had ridden a gust like a battering ram. Everywhere, snowflakes twisted and spun in glittering arcs, and more snow settled against the outside of the generator.

Stupid to feel relieved, but nothing she'd done had compromised the generator. It was that bitch Mother Nature. She was out to kill them all.

Who could blame her?

A snow shovel hung on the external wall of the lodge, clamped at the top and bottom; still it clattered like a skeleton's bones. Petie used the broad scoop to clear her path to the generator. Putting the shovel down, she knelt to release the lock on the door that opened onto the battery.

The wind caught the shovel and shoved it across the slick ground.

On her knees, she hustled after it, caught it before it escaped into the storm, brought it back to the generator and knelt on the scoop. The cold seeped through her ski pants, pants and underwear. *Incentive to finish quickly.* She cleaned the posts, scraping, wiping, scraping, wiping. She reattached the battery cables and pushed "Start."

The generator coughed and chugged on. A light popped on over the door leading to the lodge. More came on inside.

She had fixed it. She had fixed it!

She had saved Hawley's lodge. It would be safe until spring. Probably safe until spring.

Her momentary exultation flickered and died.

Now she was stuck here, alone, for another four months.

Her head bent. She closed her eyes. She felt the pain of piercing cold, of blistering wind, of loneliness and hopelessness that had no end.

Four more months of life barren and lost to exile...unless she did something to change that.

She turned off the flashlight and left it on the ground next to the shovel.

She didn't need them anymore.

She pushed her way through the snow to the broken north wall and faced the full brunt of the storm. Even through her scarf, the wind scoured her face. Snow froze onto her eyelashes. If she walked out there, straight into the storm's violent embrace, she would struggle and struggle, until at last she would lie down and die.

Why not? What did she have to live for?

TSTL. That was what they called women like her. *Too Stupid to Live.*

Truth. She was too stupid to live. She despised herself. Now she was stuck here, forever, alone every winter, without anyone who cared about her.

Why not walk out and die? Why not?

She took the first step.

A gust of wind slammed into her belly, lifted her off her feet, carried her backward and knocked her into the wall. Her neck whiplashed, and her head thumped hard enough to rattle her brains.

The wind disappeared as rapidly as it came.

Petie fell to her knees.

Night enveloped her.

If she hadn't had the hat, the scarf, the hood on her head, she would have been dealing with a concussion. As it was, the memory that floated to the top of her brain was the moment when, at fourteen, she had faced her mother in juvenile detention.

Petie was afraid, horrified, ashamed, but she faced Ioana with her chin defiantly stuck out.

"Evie, I'm an immigrant. I have an accent. You're making it hard for me at work and hard for your sister at school. Someone in the neighborhood sprayed paint on our windows—GO BACK WHERE YOU CAME FROM!"

"Those bastards," Evie had said sullenly. "Tell them to stuff it."

"You do not repent? When you can make me proud, come home." Ioana stuck her finger in Petie's face, and her Eastern European accent was strong and angry. *"Until then, you stay away from your sister. Stay away from me. Life is hard enough without having your kind drag us down."*

"My kind? I'm just like you!"

Ioana had slapped her.

Petie's hand flew to her cheek.

Ioana gasped. Reaching out, she pulled Petie into her arms. "Forgive me. But you're throwing away all your opportunities with both hands. Stop. Think. Live!"

Apparently, her mother and the wind had something in common.

Petie hung her head and cried a few tears, tears that froze instantly into the scarf. She staggered to her feet. She groped her way to the generator, knelt and found the large metal flashlight right where she'd left it and turned it on. She picked up the snow shovel, stood, pointed the beam of light at the ground and stepped carefully across the icy patches and up the steps. Still carrying the shovel, she let herself inside, shut the door behind her, locked it and stood listening to the beastly roar of the storm, now muffled by the protective walls.

She *had* fixed the generator.

The lights *were* on.

The heat *was* running.

She was not going to die here.

She said it out loud, needing to hear the words. "I am not going to die here."

Someday, somehow she would leave the wilderness behind, mend the rift in her family, but most of all, she was going to sometime, somehow find Donald White: conspirator, con man…killer.

She would have revenge—and he would face justice.

3

IN THE LAST EIGHT YEARS, Petie had risen up the Midnight Sun chain of command to become Hawley's camp director. She no longer had to pick up guests from the airstrip and drive them to their accommodations at the fishing camp; however, when Cardinal Electronics CEO Jeen Lee requested Petie perform that service, Petie made an exception.

Now Bradley Copeland and Jeen Lee rode in the back seat of the Land Rover, and with the painful care of someone who spoke Quemadese as a second language, Bradley Copeland said, "When we announce the chip, Cardinal Electronics stock is going to leap. Miss Lee, have you made your moves?"

Presumptuous of him. But if the discussion Petie had overheard from Miss Lee's employees was true, that was to be expected. Bradley was not only the new technological wonder boy, but a conceited young American who effortlessly offended everyone he met.

What did Jeen Lee think of him?

No way to tell. Miss Lee was a woman of indecipherable age, with carefully tended skin, a forehead botoxed and wrinkle-free, dark eyes fringed with lash extenders and generous lips tattooed a dark, glorious red. She ate sparingly, worked out diligently and moved with choreographed grace. The online community officially admired Jeen Lee for all she had achieved in her business life, but if one dug deeper, and Petie had, elements of a darker past emerged. The woman who fronted the prominent tech company operating from Quemada had once been feared for her cruel, swift vengeance against anyone who betrayed her.

She was feared still. Yet she had never been anything but kind to Petie, and Petie had her own reasons for doing the secret thing she had done. Now she had to find the nerve, and the right moment, to tell Miss Lee the truth.

As they bounced along the gravel road, Bradley asked in Quemadese, "The driver—does she understand us?"

"She's American." Miss Lee could not have sounded more bored.

"So am I, and I speak Quemadese."

"So you do," Miss Lee said.

"I'm getting better!" He was defensive. "I have a gift for languages!" And conceited.

"When you are not born on the islands, it is a difficult language, the distillation of more than five hundred years of varied European, African and American cultures." Miss Lee *had* been born on the islands. Located near the equator, from the time of Isla Quemada's fifteenth-century discovery by the Spanish, the primary island and the smaller islands had been a shipping crossroads and a haven for the dispossessed. Since Quemada won its independence in 1977, they had welcomed tourists who enjoyed luxury and natural beauty, and more important for Miss Lee, the islands proved a haven for corporations like Cardinal Electronics.

During the winters, Petie had enjoyed online explorations of Quemada. As the wind howled and the snow blew sideways, she imagined herself in a cottage above a white sand beach, basking in sun and breeze.

Someday…

In a self-congratulatory tone, Bradley said, "It's good for me to be able to communicate in the dialect."

Dialect? Petie wouldn't have phrased it quite like that.

"This driver does look Asian." Bradley didn't know how to say *Asian* in Quemadese, so it came out in clear English.

"Asian. Really." Petie could feel Miss Lee's gaze on her profile.

"Maybe Chinese. It's her skin. Good color, nice texture." His tone was patronizing enough to make Petie's teeth grind.

"I hadn't noticed," Miss Lee said.

"And her hair. Black and straight. But that braid!" He laughed as if Petie's choice of style amused him.

Petie looked into the rearview mirror and met Miss Lee's low-lidded gaze.

Miss Lee shrugged. "American. Lots of different ancestors. Like you. So what?"

Petie had never actually spoken Quemadese to Jeen Lee, but somehow Miss Lee figured out that Petie spoke a little and understood more.

"Miss Lee, industrial spies lurk everywhere."

Bradley's instructional tone irritated Petie, and she aimed the vehicle at a particularly deep pothole and hit it straight on.

Miss Lee swayed with the motion.

Bradley's head hit the window. He grabbed the ceiling strap and said in English, "You! Driver! Watch where you're going. I'll have you fired!"

Fired? Really? Would he try?

Miss Lee seemed not to notice his little tantrum. In Quemadese, she said, "I've been coming here seven summers. This person, this Petie, has been here every year. I've spoken freely in front of her in many languages, and not a hint of my business has been released."

That was true. Petie didn't tell anyone what Miss Lee said about upcoming breakthroughs, but through Hawley, Petie had nonetheless acted on them. As she would act on this one involving their new chip.

Every year, Jeen Lee was the camp's first guest of the season. Last week, she had arrived to make sure the preparations for her team-building retreat had been done to her specifications. When she was satisfied, she took personal time to hike Denali, then returned in time to greet her employees.

Earlier today, as her crew of professionals arrived and dispersed among the camp's rooms and cabins, Miss Lee had introduced two young women as her attendants, Matella and Tziamara. She explained they would care for her needs. The lodge would provide fresh linens, but Matella and Tziamara would make up her rooms—further proof that Miss Lee was a very private person.

As Petie pulled up to the entrance to the Katchabiggie Lodge and stopped, Miss Lee said, "We will speak later, Bradley." She moved smoothly to open the door and get out on the front steps. She seemed always to be practicing tai chi: graceful, controlled, focused.

Bradley slid all the way across the seat, leaped out and hopped.

"Magnificent, isn't it?" Jeen Lee gestured around them.

The snowy mountains cupped the valley and fed the river that rushed with cold, green water. The forest, the part that had shown the incredible brilliance to grow away from the river's reach, stood smugly verdant.

The whole world smelled of timeless conifers and this year's spring: cool, invigorating, glorious in its fresh splendor.

"Great," Bradley said in English. "Is there a casino?"

Petie foresaw difficulties for the resort, and even more for him. "No." She got his bags out of the back. "You have a room in the lodge."

Miska hurried down from the wide porch.

"If you'd place Mr. Copeland's bags in his room, please," Petie instructed.

"Sure!" Miska saluted. This was his first US job, and he was anxious to accommodate her. It was well-known among the staff that Hawley had turned all day-to-day tasks over to her, and she held power over the staff.

"Where are *you* staying?" Bradley asked Miss Lee.

"I have a cabin." The best cabin, with two bedrooms and two baths and a sitting room with a small conference table for those moments when Miss Lee wanted to speak privately to an employee.

Clearly, he didn't like that. If she had a cabin, he wanted one, too, and the demand trembled on his lips.

Miss Lee looked at him, and Petie knew how cool that gaze could be.

Bradley turned to Petie. "Do you have a cabin?"

"Yes. A small, private cabin." She met his eyes. "At the back of the property in the staff housing."

"Oh." Bradley lost interest.

"Mr. Foggo likes to greet his guests in person. If you would follow me..." Petie led them into the lodge, through the Great Room, behind the check-in desk and into Hawley's office.

The first thing one noticed about Hawley Foggo was his height, six foot five, and his weight, which was... Petie didn't care to speculate. All she knew was, every autumn Hawley disappeared from Alaska, and every spring when he came back, his wide face was deeply tanned, and the tan disappeared beneath his starched collar and artfully painted tie. In the winter when she spent too much time alone, she could imagine him sprawled on a beach in the South Pacific, a corpulent island god with a fire hidden deep in his belly.

She really hoped her imagination had run away with her, but knowing the hedonistic Hawley as she did…probably not.

"Jenny!" Hawley stood up from his desk and came around to greet Jeen Lee with arms outstretched. "Did Petie take good care of you and your guest?"

Miss Lee endured his embrace, as she endured his mangling of her name, with serene indifference. "Petie drove me and my guest with perfect competence as always." She stepped aside and, with a beautifully choreographed gesture, presented the young man who stood behind her. "Mr. Bradley Copeland, formerly of Santa Clara, California, now of Quemada."

"Good to meet ya." Hawley shook Bradley's hand enthusiastically. "First time here, right? Wait until you pull in your first twenty pounds of fighting salmon!"

Copeland wore carefully tailored jeans and a starched white shirt. He looked incredulously at Hawley, then slouched, hands in pockets, and drawled, "That sounds…awesome."

Miss Lee's eyes narrowed, and she said to Bradley, "I knew you would be pleased to join your new colleagues in the team bonding exercise."

Bradley straightened up so fast, Petie thought he might have given himself whiplash. "I'm pleased to bond with my new team."

"The whole group of you'll go out tomorrow first thing to catch your first fish." Hawley loved to sell the camp. "Make sure you attend the orientation tonight. Petie runs it, and you'll come away knowing everything about Alaska and salmon fishing. You'll be a pro before you start!"

Bradley cast an unfavorable eye at Petie. "That sounds interesting."

Petie thought he was one of those guys who never needed, or wanted, anything explained to him. "We look forward to seeing your success in this new venue." She was careful not to inject sarcasm into her tone.

She might not have bothered.

Not by a flick of an eyelash did he indicate he'd heard her.

Miss Lee put her hand through his arm. "We should go to our rooms and unpack before our meeting with our people."

"And dinner!" Hawley patted his extensive belly. "You'll have the best chef in Alaska cooking for you at the Katch-abiggie Lodge!"

"Such a…unique…name for the lodge." Bradley couldn't have been more insincere.

"I named it myself. Always makes me chuckle, and isn't that what we're all here for? To catch a biggie?" Hawley gave forth with a peal of laughter.

If Bradley had looked beyond Hawley's loud, bluff demeanor and wide girth, he would have noted that Hawley's eyes were sharp, and his new, perfectly tailored suit was a Brioni.

But Bradley saw no reason to pay attention to others, and he could barely contain his contempt.

"After Bradley unpacks, he'll wish to join the rest of my employees as they plunge into this new adventure," Miss Lee said.

"Of course." Petie held the door for them and shut it firmly behind them. She turned back to Hawley.

"We're going to have trouble with that boy," he said.

4

"**I SUSPECT YOU'RE RIGHT,**" Petie said. "Bradley is a superficial man made acceptable by his brilliance."

"Ain't it always the way?" Hawley returned to his desk and lowered himself into his chair. "Have you decided what to do about Jeen Lee?"

"I'm going to tell her."

"You're makin' a mistake."

"It wouldn't be my first."

"One supposes." Hawley had never asked what events had driven Petie to the camp, or inquired why she stayed, day after day, month after month, year after year, never leaving the vicinity, never calling out or receiving personal calls, never making friends or taking lovers. In turn, she didn't ask him about his similar lack of personal relationships.

Petie liked, admired and respected him. She thought he felt the same about her. But they didn't share confidences.

They did share finances.

Now she followed him to the desk, leaned over and said

softly, "We have an investment opportunity with Cardinal Electronics."

"What did you hear?"

Jeen Lee and her people weren't the only corporate entities that visited Midnight Sun Fishing Camp. Wealthy, successful people came and went, and most seemed only half-aware of Petie as a person, and virtually all of them spoke freely about their successes, their failures and their investments.

During her second summer, she'd realized her opportunity.

If she invested as they invested, she might possibly make... a fortune.

Yet thanks to Donald White, she did not exist in the modern world. She had no identity and no social security number, no way to capitalize on her insider intelligence.

She began to chart the investments she would make, and the lines for profits made a steep ascent. So in the spring of her third year at Midnight Sun Fishing Camp, she went to Hawley with a proposition. She would report the financial tips to him, he would invest her meager salary for her and take twenty percent as his commission.

At first he'd been skeptical, but within those first two months, she had more than doubled her money. Then she got cocky and lost it all. He rumbled a laugh and let her sit on her hands until he paid her again. That was when he started investing, too; her successes had convinced him she knew what she was talking about, and he believed her failure had taught her a lesson. Which it had.

"Invest half my winter's savings." She tapped her lips with her index finger. "And sell all my stock in Kontos Structural."

"*All* of it?" Hawley leaned back and folded his hands over his belly. "For what reason?"

"The prosperity/building cycle is due to end. Sales will

crash within a year. I don't want to take the ride down with the stock prices."

"All of Kontos and half your winter's savings. You're very sure about this."

"I am. Miss Lee wouldn't steer me wrong."

"She didn't know you were listening."

"She doesn't miss much."

"Be careful, Petie, when you tell her, how much you tell her, how you tell her. She'll not appreciate you sticking your nose in her business, and I have never known a female as dangerous as Jeen Lee."

"How many dangerous females have you known?" Petie was joking.

"All females are dangerous." He didn't smile. "It takes a wise man to know that. *You're* dangerous. Try to be wise, too."

"I'll be careful. I wouldn't want to leave you without a camp manager."

"I appreciate your care about my nerves."

5

"**THIS ISN'T A DISNEYLAND** version of the wilderness. This *is* the wilderness." Petie stood in front of the massive fireplace, speaking to the eighteen men and women who sat on the lodge's couches and chairs, and to Hawley, lounging in his oversize recliner in the back. "Do you know what a bear thinks when it comes across a camper in a sleeping bag?"

The new fisherfolk shook their heads.

"Mmm, a taco."

Laughter.

The seasoned fisherfolk, the ones who had come with Jeen Lee in previous years, smiled wisely. They knew what was coming.

Petie asked, "What does a bear think when it comes across a camper with pepper spray in a sleeping bag?"

Heads shaking.

"Mmm, a spicy taco."

Laughter became less amused, more worried.

"Bears have right of way. If one wants your salmon, give it

to her. If one wants your rod and reel, give it to him. If one wants your liver, pray you're long gone or he will take it." Petie had made her point and moved on to the next subject. "A male moose can be almost seven feet at the shoulder and weigh fourteen hundred pounds. Their antlers can have a span of six feet. This isn't the mating season, so they're typically not aggressive, but we don't take chances."

"I'm afraid to go out there!" one of the women said.

Bradley looked up from the phone he'd been told to leave in his room. "Why don't you fence off the river?"

Petie didn't often find herself without words. But his cluelessness rendered her speechless…

Well, not really. She wanted to shout and wave her arms. But speechless was a better choice.

Miss Lee asked, "Mr. Copeland, have you looked out the window? Even once?"

"No, but—"

"Put the phone away," she snapped.

He lifted his lip, much like an aggressive dog called to heel by its master, and slid the phone into his pocket.

A few sidelong glances. A few not-quite-hidden grins.

As if nothing had happened, Petie continued, "While you fish, one of the Midnight Sun Fishing Camp employees is always on guard with a powerful rifle."

"Are they trained in their use?" Arjun Patel was their Brit, recently employed by Jeen Lee's company and commuting between London and Quemada.

Petie subdued a smile. "In the state of Alaska, virtually every citizen is armed, and all of them know how to use their weapons. So yes, if even our employees are not from Alaska, we train them in the use of firearms. Our people are frighteningly competent." Had she reassured them? She thought so. "When and if a bear or moose or wolf appears—"

"Wolf?" Lucas Chu pressed himself into the back of his chair.

"—you'll hear an alarm that sounds like this."

Miska played the melodic chime meant to soothe aggressive wildlife while alerting the guests.

"We'll tell you to get out of the river and off the riverbank, and we'll take you to safety." Petie had scared them enough to make them listen. She cast an unfavorable eye at Bradley. Except him. He was too smart to listen to a woman.

No, not just a woman. He was too smart to listen to *anyone*.

"Also," she said, "the state bird of Alaska is the mosquito."

"Really?" Chu asked.

"No. It's the willow ptarmigan." She smiled at him. "But the mosquitoes are vicious, so shut the doors behind you, and when you go out, use your bug spray."

For the first time, Hawley spoke up. "Petie here has made Alaska sound like a perilous place, but we want those of you who are new to understand the dangers are real. Spend some time speaking with the people who have been with us in previous years, and you'll discover such incidents are rare and brief."

Petie put warm reassurance into her voice. "That's true, Hawley. We have expeditions and activities ready for those moments when some wild creature is catching *your* fish."

"Thank you, Petie. I know we're all ready for tomorrow." Jeen Lee stood up. "Everyone sleep well tonight." She stalked past Bradley, out the front door and toward the isolation of her cabin.

After one moment of hesitation, Petie took a deep breath and retrieved her briefcase from the locked sideboard. She turned and found Hawley at her side.

"Don't do it," he said. "Don't go after her."

"If I don't, I won't sleep at night."

He sighed deeply, stepped aside, and as she followed Miss Lee into the still sunny evening, he clapped his hands together. "I don't know about you all, but all this talk of wild animals made me want a drink. This lodge runs on Hawley's Rules, and one of the most important is—on your first night in the lodge, drinks are on the house!"

A small cheer rose from the group.

Petie caught up with Jeen Lee as she reached the steps that led up to the porch of her cabin. In a firm, calm voice, she said, "Miss Lee, I have something for you."

Miss Lee turned with one of those beautifully choreographed movements. "What would that be?"

"A year ago, I heard your employees discussing the fact that, when he was four, your son was kidnapped."

Jeen Lee didn't move, yet Petie thought she was balanced on her toes like a ninja warrior ready to attack. "Tell me the names of those you overheard."

"I don't remember," Petie lied. She remembered exactly, but she knew by Miss Lee's reaction their unwise words would result in, at the least, their termination. Hurriedly, she continued, "I'm alone at the camp eight months of the year, and one of the skills I've taught myself is to find things."

"Things?"

"Usually stolen things. Antiques, art, that sort of stuff."

Across the compound, a few of the Cardinal Electronics employees wandered out of the lodge, drinks in hand, and stood on the porch.

Miss Lee observed them, then walked up the steps, opened her door and stood aside. "Come in."

Petie stepped into the sitting room where the young women who were Miss Lee's attendants sat at the small table strewn with papers and books. They dropped their pens and stood.

Miss Lee shut the front door behind her. "Matella and Tziamara, we need privacy."

In unison, they left via the sliding glass door that led to the small private yard at the back of the cabin.

Two interior doors opened into the two bedrooms, and inside the cabin, everything had been meticulously stowed; there were no panties tossed on the bed or half-full water bottles.

Miss Lee gestured to one of the burgundy leather great chairs that sat on either side of the fireplace. "Sit down, Petie."

Petie sat.

Miss Lee did not. "Go on."

"It's been over ten years since your son disappeared, and in the world of kidnappings, that's long enough for similar cases to occur." Petie opened her briefcase and handed a photograph to Jeen Lee. "Do you recognize this woman?"

The bright red polish on Miss Lee's nails contrasted with the shadowy black and white of the security-camera image. "She was my son's nursemaid. She committed suicide after the kidnapping. It was a matter of honor."

"That picture was taken last year in Belgium."

Those bright red nails bit into the paper. "Impossible. I identified her body in the morgue."

"Yet here she is. The Belgian child she was caring for disappeared and, upset by the disgrace, this nursemaid committed suicide."

Jeen Lee veiled her dark eyes. "You're saying this is a similar case?"

"I'm saying the nursemaid runs a scam whereby she steals the child of wealthy parents, coordinates the kidnappers' demands and when the money comes through, she sells the child for additional cash. She then pretends to commit suicide to avoid interrogation. When the money runs out, she rises from the dead to commit a similar crime. In the case of your son—"

Miss Lee struck with the swift grace of a serpent. She leaped, gripped a fistful of Petie's hair, gripped her chin and dug those nails into the tender skin at her throat. "Are you saying my son is alive?"

The fist gripping Petie's hair tightened, and tightened again, as the sharp end of Miss Lee's nails threatened to cut into Petie's jugular.

Petie closed her eyes, took two deep breaths, opened her eyes and looked into the frigid depths of Jeen Lee's eyes. "I know your son is alive, and where he is, yet if you kill me you will never know."

"You'll tell me everything."

"You've made a mistake, Miss Lee. I'm not afraid to die."

Jeen Lee's nail bit into the skin, slicing a small opening.

The wound burned. Blood trickled toward Petie's collarbone.

Petie kept her gaze on Miss Lee's obsidian eyes, shiny, ruthless, reflecting a pit of hell Petie recognized. Abruptly, something shifted in Miss Lee's face; it was as if the glacial ice disintegrated beneath a flood of hope. She released Petie and stepped back, hands held up in the universal gesture of surrender. "I wonder what you've lost to be so careless of your own life."

"Everything." Petie dabbed at her throat. "Like you, I've lost everything."

Miss Lee pulled a handkerchief from her pocket and handed it to Petie.

Petie pressed it to the cut. Now that the moment had passed, she knew she would rather not die from the slice of a fingernail across her jugular. "Shall we start again? I heard about your son's kidnapping. I investigated. I found the woman who had been his nursemaid and had committed similar crimes with similar results. I went looking for your son."

"Did you find him? Did you find Hugh?" Miss Lee allowed emotion into her choked voice, or maybe she couldn't stop it.

"Yes. He lives with—is considered the son of—a family of farmers in the United States, in Wisconsin. He attends school. He works on the farm. He appears to be loved." Petie flipped to an album titled "Hugh," and handed her tablet to Jeen Lee.

Miss Lee stared at the first image, a current school photo, stared so long Petie wondered if she had died where she stood. Finally Miss Lee enlarged the photo, scanning the boy's face. "Fourteen. Hugh is fourteen. He doesn't look like me. He looks like his father."

Petie couldn't remark on that; she had no idea who the boy's father was. "His name is now Andriy Kishnir."

Miss Lee looked up in horror; that he would have a new name hadn't occurred to her. "Of course." She flipped through a few more pictures. "Is he… How are his grades?"

"He's a highly intelligent young man with an exemplary school record."

"He looks healthy." Miss Lee darted a questioning look at Petie.

"He seems a normal adolescent. Colds. Flu. I found one hospital stay for a broken elbow. It required surgery. A few visits to the doctor for stitches."

"He was always an active boy. I took him skiing in Switzerland not long before he disappeared. He ripped down the steepest mountains. I feared for him. I didn't realize where the true danger lay…" Her demeanor shifted from mother to businesswoman. "No one ever demanded a ransom. Why not?"

"I don't know that. I focused on finding your son, nothing more."

"Someone paid her to take Hugh and let her keep the

money from the sale. Someone who wanted to disrupt my work."

"Or someone who thought you were too focused on your child."

The breath hissed between Miss Lee's teeth. "I will kill him."

Petie knew who Miss Lee suspected. Petie suspected him, too. Jeen Lee's father, a cold man who had turned his business over to his daughter while watching her every move. He had taught her ruthlessness, and she had learned well. Now he was in his seventies; Petie doubted he would get much older.

"What about Hugh's... What about the people who care for him? Are they...good people?" Miss Lee seemed to be fumbling for the right things to ask. "Wealthy? Moral? Forward-thinking?"

"They're not wealthy. From all appearances, they're moral and forward-thinking. They had no children of their own, and he wants for nothing."

"Does he remember me?"

Ah. The question that Miss Lee had truly wanted to ask. "I do not know."

As if to contain the pain in her heart, Miss Lee put her hand on her chest. "When he was taken, I feared two things. I feared he was dead. I feared he cried for me in the night. At least I now know he's not cold in the grave. Thank you for that." She handed Petie her tablet, picked up a small bag, pulled out her phone and called in her plane. "What is his location?"

Petie handed her the boy's current address.

Slinging her bag over her shoulder, Miss Lee said, "I'll be back. If this is a trick, you should get your affairs in order. If it is not, then I owe you whatever favor you ask."

"You owe me nothing. I did it for myself."

"I will remember." Miss Lee strode from the cabin.

Petie walked to the window.

Miss Lee walked down the steps to Hawley, who stood beside his jeep. He'd no doubt figured he would need to clean up the blood before any of the guests found out about Petie's murder.

Miss Lee spoke to him.

Hawley heaved himself in the driver's seat.

Miss Lee slid into the passenger's seat.

They drove up the road toward the airstrip.

They left Petie standing in the luxurious room and wondering—did Jeen Lee mean she would remember the debt, or remember Petie's comment?

6

THE CINNAMON-COLORED MOTHER bear came out of the forest, lean from hibernation, from giving birth and from nursing her young.

Miska saw her first and sounded the alarm. At first, none of the fisherfolk in waders in the river noticed the loud, melodious chime.

But Petie noticed.

This bear looked hungry, impatient, and she was moving fast.

Rifle in hand, Petie strode quickly to the riverbank and gestured for the guests to come out. As the people looked around and saw the bear, they complied, eyes wide and terrified.

Bears looked a lot bigger when they weren't in a zoo surrounded by bars.

Some guests brought their fishing gear. Some abandoned theirs. Midnight Sun Fishing Camp always lost gear when they had a wildlife run-in. That was, Hawley said, the cost of doing business. Better that than a loss of life, which would reflect badly on Midnight Sun.

More employees—Taylor, Fred, Lucas, Addison—arrived from the lodge, driving jeeps and trucks, picking up guests as they fled the danger. Everyone was aware, everyone was obedient—except Bradley Copeland.

Of course. It had to be him.

Copeland hadn't cared about fishing until five days ago, when his colleague had pulled the biggest salmon ever caught at the lodge, a fifty-two-pound salmon. The celebration and admiration had snagged Copeland's attention, and he'd boasted he could do better. The people born and raised on Quemada didn't scoff at his claims—as some of the world's consummate businesspeople, they had raised tact to a high art—but the Brit and the Canadian hadn't bothered to contain their grins.

When Copeland ruffled up like a banty cock and demanded they explain themselves, Arjun Patel offered a bet Copeland couldn't catch a thirty-pound—he lowered it mockingly, no, a twenty-five pound—salmon before the week was out.

As Copeland realized everyone was laughing at him, he fell into a froth. Him, the golden boy who knew everything, who his mama had raised to be worshipped and admired!

Bradley Copeland reminded Petie of her father.

She really disliked Copeland.

But leaving him to be eaten would be bad for business and…and she didn't like the look of death. She remembered all too clearly the look of death. And the smell. And the horror.

There, against the far back wall of the basement, in the darkest corner, white plastic covered a dark lump of…something. Something that oozed fluid toward the floor drain.

Petie's eyes hurt from the smell and the effort of holding them wide, from never blinking. She took care not to step in the dark pud-dle and reached out, far out, to grasp the corner of the plastic, pull it back, and see—

The sound of the alarm yanked Petie back from the old horror and into the present. The tuneful tones that were meant to soothe the wildlife wasn't working on the female bear.

In the river, Copeland fought to bring his fish to the net and ignored the chime for all he was worth.

For Petie, the world, normally encompassed by snowy mountains, a sandy shore, a loud, icy, rushing river, narrowed to focus on the bear and on Copeland, the oblivious fool who stood braced against the river's flow and the salmon's fight.

The bear waded toward him intent on dining on salmon—and human.

"Get out!" Petie shouted at Copeland again and again. "Get out! She's coming for you! You're in danger!"

Without glancing up, he shouted, "Shoot her!"

Fury surged. Petie's heartbeat roared louder. "I'm not shooting a bear and leaving her cubs motherless for a fool like you!"

"I command you!" Copeland probably thought he sounded imperial.

He sounded petulant. She brought the rifle around and zeroed in on him. "I'll kill you and save you the suffering of being eaten alive."

That got his attention. "I will have you removed!"

The bear was closing on him.

Soon Petie would have to make a decision. Death must come for Copeland—or for the bear. She should not shoot Copeland. She knew she shouldn't. But the cubs...

From behind her, a figure strode past, headed toward Copeland.

At last, Jeen Lee had returned. She wore white. Her makeup and hair were perfect. Without hesitation, she waded into the water and made for Copeland.

Something about her, her focus, the menace that radiated from her, reminded Petie of the mama bear.

Copeland stared, frozen by the sight of the slim, deadly woman.

Miss Lee seized his chin in one hand and his neck in the other and turned his head to face the bear. She spoke to him; from this distance, Petie couldn't hear the words, but whatever they were, they galvanized Copeland. The words and, Petie knew, the pressure of Miss Lee's fingernails over his jugular.

He abandoned the salmon and the gear and bolted toward the riverbank. He fell once, struggled up, fought to get to safety with his chest-high fishing overalls filled with icy water.

Miss Lee swiftly moved downstream at an angle, away from the bear.

Petie stayed where she was until Copeland and Jeen Lee had gained the bank and were in a vehicle fleeing the scene. Then she ran toward the four-wheeler driven by Miska.

The bear reeled in the salmon Copeland had abandoned and ripped it to shreds with teeth and claws.

Petie settled on the seat behind Miska, and they roared toward the lodge.

The world expanded again. There were the snowy mountains, the wide sky, air to breathe, the breeze on her face and, most of all, her heart was still beating. Beating hard, beating fast as it recovered from terror and desperation. She was alive, and sometimes it was important to remember how grand that could be.

When the four-wheeler arrived at the lodge, Petie scrambled off and ran up the steps into the crowd of guests milling on the wide porch. Hawley was already there, passing out wine and liquor, and assuring them they had done exactly the right thing, and telling them the Hawley's rule that applied to this instance—there would be an extraordinary dinner and fabulous entertainment.

Some of the guests were shaking so hard they needed a straw to sip their liquor. A couple were showing photos and videos they'd managed to take as they fled the scene. They gave Petie a round of applause.

Petie said the right things, but she was still livid about Copeland's careless disregard for life: hers, the bear's and his own. "Where's Miss Lee? Where's Copeland?"

"Miss Lee had her driver drop her off at her cabin," Hawley said.

"Copeland stepped out of the jeep, still sloshing, ripped off his waders—" Arjun pointed at the puddle of water on the walk "—and stormed upstairs. No one's seen him. I don't know how that cretin's going to face any of us ever again."

Heads nodded.

From the open front door of the lodge, Copeland declared, "I don't have to face you. I'm through with this uncivilized place and you ignorant incompetents. I'm leaving." He had changed his clothes, but his face glistened with the remains of flop sweat. He pointed at Hawley. "You fire that woman." His finger swung on Petie. "She's insolent. She's incompetent. She made me lose my fish!"

"She saved your life," Arjun said.

"I was never in any danger!" In his few minutes alone, Copeland had convinced himself his humiliation was someone else's fault, and that someone was Petie.

"Since you're leaving, you'll want to pay up your debts," Hawley drawled.

Copeland drew himself up. "What debts? I have no debts!"

"You bet everyone here you'd catch a twenty-five pound salmon." Chuntao, one of Jeen Lee's employees, had clearly studied her boss's demeanor, for she sounded serene even as she threw gasoline on the fire of Copeland's humiliation.

"I don't know you. I no longer work with you. I'll never see you again. I am moving back to the United States where civilization reigns!"

Chuntao had to put her hand over her mouth to cover her smile. "Sir, last I heard, Alaska *is* part of the United States."

"You think you're so smart." Copeland pointed a shaking finger at her, then pointed at Hawley again. "Get someone to drive me to the airport *now*."

Arjun condemned him with a single quietly spoken word, "Welsher."

When Hawley wished, he could appear to be moving in slow motion. In the face of Copeland's demands, he was positively snaillike, all the while keeping his gaze fixed on Copeland's face.

As Copeland saw the big man pacing toward him, he seemed for the first time to recognize his size, strength and wiliness.

Copeland took a hasty step backward.

Too late. Hawley wrapped an arm around the young man's shoulders, hauled him close and escorted him across the porch and down the steps. "I'll take you myself," he rumbled. And, "You're still pretty damp. I hope you don't ruin my suit. It's new, an Armani."

Copeland cast desperate glances behind him, but Hawley thrust him into the front seat of the Land Rover and, dropping the pretense of leisure, hustled around to the driver's side. As he climbed in, he bellowed, "Petie, make sure our guests are happy!" The Land Rover roared away, hitting every pothole in the road.

Arjun said, "With Copeland gone, we're all happy."

Laughter rose, then fell to silence.

Miss Lee strode toward the lodge. Like Copeland, she had changed into dry clothes, but unlike Copeland, she'd taken the time to fix her hair and reapply makeup, or perhaps her staff had done it for her. She stopped at the foot of the porch steps and in her low-pitched voice, she said, "My friends, I'm sorry, but I must remove Petie from among your midst. She and I need to speak about a matter of some importance."

All heads turned toward Petie, whose feet were glued to the boards.

All heads turned to Miss Lee again. "We will be absent for some time, possibly days. I wish that in our absence, you enjoy your stay at Midnight Sun Fishing Camp to the fullest, and if we are still not among you when the time comes to leave, travel safely and I'll see you on my return to the Quemada office."

Someone gave Petie's shoulder a shove.

She staggered forward, then continued through the crowd and down the stairs. "Miska, handle things," she said.

As she set foot on the gravel walk, she heard a voice whisper, "Poor girl."

They were talking about her.

She wasn't worried, though. Miss Lee had had contact with her son, and even if the meeting hadn't gone well, she was a fair woman. She wouldn't blame Petie.

Would she?

7

PETIE AND JEEN LEE walked shoulder to shoulder toward Miss Lee's cabin. They mounted the steps. Miss Lee opened the door and gestured Petie ahead of her.

Petie would have been a liar if she'd said the middle of her back did not twitch with fear.

Miss Lee followed her in and shut the door, walked to the wet bar and brought a bottle of reddish liquor out of the refrigerator. "Drink with me."

"In celebration of your successful meeting with your son?"

"It was a successful meeting. And a sorrowful meeting. A meeting that set my heart at ease. And a meeting that scarred like lightning that strikes a mighty oak. I'm not dead from that lightning, but I will wither, if not this year, then the next, or the next." She poured two small glasses full and offered one to Petie.

Petie took the glass.

"To my son." Miss Lee raised her glass.

Petie clinked it and took a sip. It tasted of fruit and

cinnamon—and its potency took her breath away. "What is it?" she croaked.

Miss Lee sipped also, and smiled. "It is patxaran, from Navarre. It's our preferred drink in Quemada. I bought a brand with a light aroma, hoping it would not be too challenging for you."

Great. She's going to kill me subtly, with liquor. "It's most refreshing."

"Let us sit at the back of my cabin where we can speak and not be observed." Miss Lee picked up the bottle and directed Petie out the sliding glass door and into her own private backyard and screened gazebo. They seated themselves side by side in the comfortably padded wicker chairs overlooking the river, surrounded by the forest and the mountains. Miss Lee snapped her fingers—no small feat with the length of her nails—and her two attendants rushed out from beside the cabin, one carrying a stacked bamboo steamer, the other carrying small plates, napkins, serving ware and sauces.

As they laid the food out on the small round table, Petie stammered, "Where did they...? How did they get the...?"

In Quemadese, Miss Lee said, "Matella and Tziamara, this is Miss Petie. You've met her before. She is my friend."

The two women, both of similar height, with brown hair and blue eyes, bowed and in heavily accented English murmured, "We are honored, Miss Petie."

"Thank you," Petie replied in Quemadese.

They smiled in surprise, then melted back toward the cabin.

"I rescued Matella and Tziamara from the brothels that held them imprisoned. I care for them. They care for me. I protect them. They protect me. I asked that they make international appetizers to please us. Today, we honor Chinese cuisine." Using her chopsticks, Miss Lee selected a dumpling, dipped it in a dark brown sauce and conveyed it to her mouth. "Avail yourself."

"Chef doesn't like people messing around in his kitchen."

"Chef will do as he's told." Miss Lee had no doubt.

Petie had no doubt, either. She was hungry and enjoyed a scallion pancake, a dumpling stuffed with savory pork and cabbage and one of shrimp and mushrooms, and sweet and sour duck. With prudent care, she sampled the sauces and found one so spicy it scalded the roof of her mouth, one so tasty she could have picked up the bowl and drunk it all, and soy sauce.

As she ate, she sipped the patxaran and felt herself mellow. She looked up to see Miss Lee smiling as she refilled Petie's glass. As if Miss Lee had spoken, Petie answered her. "I haven't eaten food like this since I was a child and visited China with my father." That seemed naked and revealing, and she added, "You wouldn't offer food and drink to someone you intended to kill later."

"No. There's blood on my hands, but yours will not stain me."

Petie understood what Miss Lee was saying about the blood on her hands. When Petie wasn't busy with the guests, she had been watching the news for signs of Miss Lee's meeting with her son. She'd seen nothing of that, but within twenty-four hours of Miss Lee's discovery of the nursemaid's treachery, the woman had died a horrible death. For six more days, Petie caught no hint of Miss Lee or her passage, then yesterday, she'd read the reverent obituary—Miss Lee's father died on his small, private Quemada island. Miss Lee had made the necessary statement of respect—and now she was here.

Petie took a sip of her drink, placed her chopsticks beside her plate and plunged into the conversation. "Your son didn't know you?"

Miss Lee blinked but nodded. "I explained to his...his

parents who I was, and they agreed that…that Hugh and I should meet alone."

Petie suspected it was not so simple, but she could hardly accuse Miss Lee of intimidating the elderly couple.

"When we met, they hadn't told my son who I was. He seemed not to recognize me. Even when I introduced myself, he seemed uninterested in speaking with me. Brusque. But I persisted over several days and several meetings, and at last he admitted he did remember me."

"Ah." Heartbreak was looming.

"He believed I had sold him for some minor infraction. He said when the nursemaid took him, she told him so. What other explanation could there be? Through his child's eyes, I was completely powerful, a goddess dedicated to his protection. If he was gone from me, it must be because I wished it." Miss Lee's voice broke.

"I'm sorry. That's…awful." An understatement.

"Yes. I solemnly assured him I had mourned his loss every day, that I had been tricked by a powerful man into thinking him dead, and now I wished nothing so much as to once again be a parent to him." Miss Lee drank her patxaran.

Petie filled her glass to the brim.

"He is not an adult, but he has grown up. He listened to my words. He looked back at that time. He gazed on my face. He believed me." Miss Lee drank. "He spoke gently, as if I were a person to be pitied. He said his life was with his parents who had loved him and raised him and his friends. I offered to help with his further education, and he agreed to that and thanked me. He also agreed to visit me annually in Quemada, and he admitted he would enjoy skiing again. We will go to Switzerland together." Miss Lee put her hand over her face, but when she lifted it away, her eyes were dry. "The loss of my son is punishment for allowing my father to think he could manipulate me. I should have known better than to trust him. I knew that he was better than anyone." She looked at Petie. "I sent an assassin to the nursemaid. But I killed my father myself."

Petie nodded. "He took your son. He made you a shell of yourself. Miss Lee, I do indeed understand."

"I thought you would. You will call me Jeen now." It was a startling pronouncement from a woman of Jeen Lee's stature. "If we are not friends, we are at least not strangers. We know each other's secrets."

Petie wanted to back away. "We do?"

"You know mine. Perhaps I do not know yours in its entirety, but I have guessed a few things…Miss Evelyn Jones."

8

PETIE HEARD JEEN LEE'S cool voice utter her real name, *Evelyn Jones*, and it felt like sticking her finger into a light socket. She jumped so hard, she bit her tongue. She pressed her back against the cushion and tried to get her breath. "How did you know?"

"It wasn't easy, and I wasn't sure." Jeen leaned forward, her eyes glowing like black coals. "Not until this minute."

With shaking fingers, Petie raised her glass to her mouth and tried to drink. She couldn't. Not without splashing patxaran down her shirt. She put it back on the table. "For years, I was governed by the fear that someone would spot me. That they'd come for me. With time, I had relaxed. Now you—"

"Your facial structure has so changed, not even recognition software could make a positive identification." Jeen gestured for silence and leaned back again.

Matella and Tziamara returned with a second course of appetizers. As they opened the stacked bamboo baskets, the dumplings, the spareribs, the octopus smelled delicious, but Petie's stomach rebelled, and she said softly, "I don't think I can eat right now."

"We have all the time in the world," Jeen replied.

To Petie's surprise, Tziamara put her palm on Petie's head and said something in a dialect Petie didn't recognize.

Jeen smiled and agreed.

Matella spoke angrily, picked up Petie's hands one after another, then put her hand under Petie's chin and tilted her face up. She scowled at Petie's forehead, then turned to Jeen with what was obviously a question.

Jeen agreed again, then to Petie she said, "To keep my image as I wish, my young attendants have learned the skills of hair styling and grooming. They have, I fear, grown bored with me. Tziamara wishes to cut your hair. Matella asks to… improve your complexion and soften your hands. Will you let them practice on you?"

Alarmed, Petie took the end of her long braid and protectively pulled it over her shoulder. "I style my hair so it's easy!"

Tziamara laughed, a light chime of amusement. "Miss, this is not a style." She closed and stacked the bamboo baskets. "I promise, when I am finished with you, it will be easy."

"When you wish to follow us, we have set up our stations in the sitting room. They await only your presence." Matella hurried to open the door for Tziamara.

Astonished, Petie turned to Jeen.

Jeen chuckled at her expression. "I know. It's an odd thing, to have your true self revealed and, at the same time, to have the commonplace occur."

"Cutting my hair is not commonplace!"

"Obviously not." Jeen looked down, collected her thoughts, then looked up again. "Until you said that, as a child, you had visited China, I thought you must be Barbara Husvich."

Another name from so long ago. Jeen knew everything. *How?* "Barb Husvich didn't survive. I almost didn't survive. You really didn't know me?" Petie begged for reassurance. "The software didn't recognize me?"

"In that instance, you have little to worry about." She paused. "But in the matter of Bradley Copeland, you are not so lucky. He is brilliant, vindictive and he hates you. He blames you."

"That salmon would have won him the bet. It was easily forty pounds."

"Then I'm glad he lost it." Miss Lee spoke in a slow, even tone. "I regret to inform you, but you have won yourself a dangerous enemy."

"I know. But what can he do to me? I've already lost everything. I'm already condemned to exile."

With a swift, efficient movement, Jeen slapped a bug in midair. She showed Petie the smear of black and red that stained her palm. "Creatures like Copeland can always find a way to do harm." She stood. "The chill of nighttime grows in the air, the mosquitoes have come out, and we should go in."

Petie gazed longingly at the gate that would allow her to escape from the inevitable and traumatic remembrance of her past. But Jeen—and the truth—waited, and she knew the time had come at last.

She stood and walked ahead of Jeen into the cabin.

PART TWO

EVIE

THE BEST GIRL FOR THE JOB

San Jose, California
February, ten years ago

EVIE SAT BEHIND HER counselor's desk, took several long breaths, then picked up the old cordless phone and dialed the number she'd been sent.

"Hello?" The man's voice was deep, warm, kind, reassuring.

"Hello, this is Evelyn Jones. I'm calling for Donald White?" To her horror, her voice wobbled.

"This is Donald White."

"Um." Not *um*. Sound sure, like her counselor told her. "I've called to interview for your position of bookkeeper?"

"Right, Evelyn." She heard a keyboard tapping. "I've brought up your résumé. According to this, you have no experience."

"No experience, but a week ago, I graduated from bookkeeping school. I was top of the class. I tested top in analytical statistics, process and computer programming. I'm qualified to do whatever you require of me."

"I know you can. I've reviewed your scores, your profile.

But frankly, I'm reclusive, and in addition, it's winter and I live in a small town in Alaska. You're a young woman from sunny California. I'm more worried about whether you can survive the isolation, the cold, the dark, the storms."

"I can. San Jose is not all that. Parts of it are not so good." The streets at night, the gangs, the knives, the parts the tech people never saw and pretended not to know about. "To go somewhere and start fresh is a dream of mine."

"You're young to be talking like that. Eighteen years old, right?"

"Next week, and I, um…" She didn't have to say this. It wasn't on her record. Her counselor told her not to say a word. But she wanted to make a fresh start. An honest start. "I've had lots of time to study. I'm currently in a juvenile detention center."

Silence.

"I was involved in a drive-by shooting, a fatality. I wasn't the gunman—" the gunman had been Ramous, cold, indifferent to the suffering he'd caused "—or the driver, but I was considered an accessory to the crime. I've been here for a couple of years." She cleared her throat. "Actually, four years."

More silence.

Her counselor was right. She shouldn't have said anything. "I guess I don't get the job, huh?"

"Since you're going to be handling big sums of my money, your honesty is to be admired. Where before I only knew how good your grades were and that you understood the basics of finance, now I feel as if I can trust you. Thank you. That made my decision for me."

What did that mean?

"What's your full, legal name?"

Why was he asking for her full name? "Evelyn Angelina Jones."

"Do you have legal identification? A driver's license?"

Why did he want legal identification? "I'm taking my driving test the day I get out. Next, um, Friday."

"Perfect. You'll fly into Anchorage. Can I buy your plane ticket for Sunday? Or is that too soon?"

"Sunday is great." Evie began to feel exaltation—and terror—bubble in her veins.

She had the job.

She had the job!

"Don't you want to visit your family for a few days before you fly up?"

"My family doesn't live here anymore." She bit down hard on her tongue before she babbled out more information. Evie wasn't taking any more chances, and besides—she didn't want to talk about her mother and her younger sister, and how they'd moved to Rockin, Alaska, and left her *here*, and how much Evie missed them.

"Tell me your address. I'll send a car to take you to the San Jose airport."

"Okay." A car. Like…what? A cab? A limo?

"On the other end, I'll pick you up at the Anchorage airport. We'll come right back to Rockin. I'm sorry to tell you, I'm going to require a lot of work from you right from the get-go."

"I'm not afraid of hard work." She wasn't. She wanted a new life, she wanted to be part of her mother and sister's life again, and she'd do whatever was needed to get it.

"You're a girl after my own heart. Now I must be frank. My home is on the outskirts of Rockin, and it's isolated. We'll be living alone while we organize my finances. Are you going to be okay with that? You'll have a lock on your door, and you can introduce yourself to the police if it would make you more comfortable."

"No!"

"I thought you might say that." He sounded smug in a way she didn't care for. Then in a voice as comforting as a baked potato with all the fixings, he added, "I'm not a pervert, but if you ever feel vulnerable, that option is always open to you."

"Good to know." And not in a million years did she need more law enforcement hanging around. She didn't like them. She didn't trust them.

Of course, she didn't really trust anybody but her own self, so that was no news flash. "I'll take your word and assume you're a good guy." She tried to sound humorous, but she was pretty sure he heard the grim tone in her voice. "But I will use the lock on my door, and I do know how to defend myself." Because in San Jose JDC—the C stood for *Craphole*—she had learned more about fighting and surviving than she'd ever learned on the streets.

"Message received. I'll be at baggage claim with a sign with your name on it. I look forward to meeting you on Sunday. We can really make this work for me." Donald White sounded pleased with himself.

After they hung up, Evie sat in a gratified daze, too.

She was going to Alaska. She was going to Rockin. She would be close to Mama and Marya, and when she had established herself as a reliable employee who could earn a living, she'd go to her mother and—

A knock on the office window. She looked up at her counselor, Regina Griffin. Regina wasn't that much older than Evie. She'd been on the job most of the time Evie had spent here, and she was the one who'd convinced Evie that when she got out, she could be something. She could be a success.

Now Evie gave her a grin and two thumbs up.

Regina unlocked the door to her office and came in. "You

got it?" She didn't save many of the juveniles, so Evie was a special victory for her.

"Yes!"

The two joined arms and jumped up and down in unison.

Regina broke the embrace. "The salary is good. He's paying your health insurance. Remember, don't say anything more than you have to. Don't tell anyone you were in JDC."

"In goddamned prison," Evelyn corrected.

"Don't swear. Don't let anyone see your gang tattoo. No one needs to know you were with the Mongols. Remember to check in with your parole officer. Stand up straight. Look around and figure out how to be like everyone else, and then be like everyone else. Evelyn..."

Evie grabbed her shoulders and looked into her eyes. "Stop worrying. I'm a smart girl, and I've learned my lesson. And I'm going to Alaska!"

"Are you scared?" Regina sounded breathless. "You'll be all alone out there with an older man you don't know."

"No." Evie's grin spread all over her face. "The worst is over. I'm out of here. I've got a job. I'm going on an adventure. At last, everything's going to be perfect. I can't wait to get there and tell you all about it."

Regina's smile faded a little.

"What's wrong?"

"Nothing." Regina's faded smile twisted. "Just that things change."

"And about time. I love change!"

"Right. Right! You're right. I'll take a page from your book and love it, too."

DON'T TALK

EVIE HADN'T FLOWN SINCE her father divorced her mother, dumping his blond, cool, Slavic immigrant wife for a brunette, fiery, Mexican immigrant wife. He left his first family without a backward glance, leaving her mother furious, her little sister confused and Evie devastated.

She had been his favorite.

Now he had a son, and he didn't care about her.

That was why she had gone looking for trouble. And found it on a street filled with blazing gunfire and a tragic death.

Incarceration worked as it should. She hated that she had joined the gang, that she'd been anywhere near the tragedy, and she mourned for the death of a child. She hadn't been the killer, but the burden of guilt would weigh on her forever, and she swore she'd never again be so heedless.

The Anchorage airport wasn't as overwhelming as San Jose's, and the guy holding the sign for *Evelyn Jones* was tall, spare and old, around her father's age. His hair was ash-blond, his eyes were calm green and he had a droopy mustache. He looked like the movie version of a dull chauffeur. Evelyn figured he probably *was* the chauffeur, until she stopped in front of him and held out her hand. "Hi, I'm Evelyn Jones."

He smiled with so much charm she was forced to reevaluate her impression about him being dull. Accepting her hand, he shook it. "I'm Donald White. Welcome to Alaska."

Okay. He'd said he was going to pick her up himself, and he had. No big deal, right? "It's good to meet you, Mr. White."

He made a face. "Call me Donald."

"Um…"

"Let's get your luggage."

She lifted her backpack. "This is it."

"Not planning on staying?" His voice turned crisp and his eyes darkened.

She shrugged. "It's what I've got."

He didn't seem to understand. "Where's your coat?"

"I'm wearing it." Blue denim, and perfectly adequate for almost all California weather.

"That's a jacket. You can't wear a jacket here in the winter." He frowned. "Fine. We'll stop on the way to Rockin and get you a coat."

"No. Please! I'll be fine. Please. I don't need to spend money on a coat." Because she'd arrived with one hundred dollars and a firm warning to make it last until her first paycheck, and she'd already spent eight dollars on a really expensive rip-off of a lunch on the plane.

He lost that granite expression and smiled again. "Come on, then. Follow me."

She did, out to the parking garage.

He was right. It was cold, with a wind that whistled through the columns and the lines of cars and bit her to the bone. "How cold is it?" she shouted over the wind.

"Warm day," he shouted back. "Five degrees, wind chill of minus fifteen."

God. She'd heard about such temperatures, but she had never imagined she could shiver so hard she thought she would break apart.

Then he stopped by a car. A car so amazing, she forgot the cold and stood with her mouth open.

He handed her the keys. "Since you're going to be doing my errands, let's see you drive this bad boy."

She stared at the keys. She stared at him. She stared at the car.

The bad boy was a black Jaguar XJ 757.

When she'd been with the Mongols, she'd been regaled with tales of Jaguar heists and how stupid they were, because cops always stopped Jags looking for drug dealers. Stealing an expensive car, she'd been told, was the best way to do a prison stint. Better to stick with a boring car: a Camry, a Prius, even a Santa Fe.

"Mr. White, I can't…"

"Donald." He opened her door and gestured her in. "It's just a sedan. Go on."

"Sure." As the seat enfolded her with comfort and the scent of rich leather filled her nostrils, she told herself, *It's just a sedan. Just a sedan.* But her inner self responded in reverent tones, *It's a Jaguar.*

As soon as she started the car, Mr. White got in and turned on her seat heater, and the warmth stopped her shivering and added to the sense of luxury.

Driving out of the airport involved city streets; she was busy watching the signs, listening to the guidance system, figuring out which lane led to Glenn Highway going north out of town. At this point, the Jaguar was merely a car that handled well, and when one guy in a Ford F-150 pickup tried to race her, she gracefully allowed him to win.

Mr. White—Donald—seemed to be utterly unconcerned; while the car was giving her directions, he was typing on his phone.

She headed north, moving through Anchorage traffic. They crossed the water—Donald told her it was Knik Arm.

She nodded—who cared what it was called? She turned north onto Alaska Highway 3. After they passed through Wasilla, traffic thinned, then they were headed toward Rockin. Ahead of them were mountains, real mountains, and they passed lakes and rivers and a wild, weird, varied landscape of frost and ice. She had been expecting snow piled everywhere. But no; white swirled on the wind and glittered in the sun, but the road was dry and the hard ground was brown and green, and off to the side of the road, she saw her first-ever frozen pond.

Donald complimented her on her driving, then asked, "Have you traveled much?"

"Not in the last few years. I mean, naturally. But when I was a kid, yeah. My family went all kinds of places."

"Where?"

"Around the States a little, but my mother is from Belarus, in Eastern Europe, so we visited there once when I was six."

"Your mother's an immigrant?"

"Yes." Evie didn't say more. She couldn't. Her mother had never told her anything about Belarus except that she'd lived in an orphanage and out of all the men who applied for her hand, she'd chosen their father to marry.

At one point, after the divorce, Evie had bitterly told her mother she shouldn't have picked a man who would rather buy a subservient wife than court an independent woman.

Her mother had said, *Evie, I'm going to give you good advice. Don't talk about what you don't understand.*

Evie still didn't understand what she didn't understand. But people could get ugly about immigrants, so she explained, "My mother's a US citizen now. She did it in the minimum, three years. She's very proud of her citizenship."

"Uh-huh. Where else have you traveled?"

"When I was ten, I visited China with my father. My grandmother lives in Liaoning Province. We spent two weeks with her and a week touring the country."

"Your father is Chinese?"

"Half Chinese. His father was European-American and met his mother at Yale, where she was an Asian archeology professor visiting from China." Evie tensed, waiting for the questions…

How could a girl with such a distinguished and educated family background end up in JDC? Why wasn't Evie enrolled in a distinguished university, graduating early, getting her historical or tech degree? Or languages? She was good with languages. Or…

Or. Or. Or.

She could feel Donald White studying her. "That explains a lot," he said.

"About?"

"About your appearance."

"Oh." Her mother was petite, fair and curvaceous, with thick blond hair that grew to a luxurious length.

Her father was tall, skinny and tanned, with thick black hair that sprang over his brow and gave him a distinguished look.

Evelyn was like an egg scramble: a little bit of this, a little bit of that. Dark eyes, slanted over Eastern European cheekbones, and heavy eyebrows that needed to be waxed or plucked or whatever. Pale skin that burned and peeled every time she hit the beach. A flat nose, not much for boobs or hips, big ears. But she'd picked up a couple of really good things from both parents: she was tall, and the world was easier for tall people. Her hair was shiny black, thick and long. She'd shaved her head when she joined the Mongols, but when she got into JDC, she let her hair grow. She braided it, and more than once a swift swing of the head had knocked an assailant away. The longer it grew, the thicker the braid, the better weapon it became. No one in law enforcement knew, unless they were at the receiving end of a slap, and no one could make her cut it off.

Having Donald White stare at her made her uncomfortable, so she said, "Tell me about where we're going."

"Rockin is, um, small. Unprepossessing. Population one-thousand plus people in the borough... You know what a borough is?"

Evie had done her homework. "A borough is what they have in Alaska instead of counties."

"Right. In town, the buildings are old and mostly decrepit. Some people in Anchorage use the area as a weekend home destination—three-hour drive, houses on the lakes and rivers. It's close to Denali." He sounded impatient. "You know about Denali?"

"Denali is the tallest mountain peak in North America."

"Big tourist attraction for people who like to hike, fish, do the wildlife thing." He didn't sound like he was a fan. He glanced behind the car. "On this road right now, there's not much traffic, so open her up." The car, he meant.

He was her boss, and she had been tempted anyway, so Evie obeyed.

My God. She'd never imagined driving a car like this. The Jag handled like a car that wanted attention. That wanted speed. That understood how to hug the corners. No wonder that one Mongol gang maverick had ignored all the advice and stolen a Jag. She now knew that however much time he spent in JDC, it was worth it.

Evie guided that baby right into the curves. The engine roared, the tires gripped the road, she grinned as she drove. This was the most fun she'd ever had in her life...legally.

A flash caught her eye. More flashes. Blue and red flashes. And the wail of a siren.

An Alaska state trooper was pulling her over.

GAINFULLY EMPLOYED

"OH, NO," EVIE WHISPERED. She took her foot off the gas and pulled into a turn out. "I'm so sorry, Mr. White."

"Donald. You didn't do anything wrong. You were barely speeding. The cop stopped you because he can't believe anyone is driving this car. Up here, it's all SUVs, pickups and all-terrain vehicles."

From the tone of his voice, Evie deduced he liked law enforcement as little as she did.

Donald pulled her wallet and license from her backpack and some paperwork from the console. He handed it all to her. "Here. Give him this and let me handle the rest. Remember, he's freezing and he's pissed, so no matter what, smile and give him the admiring-a-man-in-uniform look."

Evie was watching the rearview mirror. "Her. It's a female trooper."

"Even better. Remember—you always wanted to be a cop."

"Okay." Evie lowered the window as the officer stalked up to the car. As the frigid air rolled in, Evie caught her breath and offered the paperwork. "Hello, ma'am. Is there a problem?"

The trooper's jacket said *Officer Johnson*. "Five miles over the speed limit when it's frozen solid and all you have to do is slip a tire to go spinning off the road, and I'll have to get a tow truck out here to bring you in!"

Donald was right. The trooper was cranky, looking at the car, fender to fender, in total disbelief. She thoroughly examined the paperwork.

Impulsively, Evie said, "It's cold out there. Do you want to sit inside with us? At least if you're going to write a ticket, you might as well be comfortable."

At Evie's invitation, Officer Johnson stepped back and put her hand on her gun.

Uh-oh. Somehow she'd decided Evelyn really didn't belong in this car.

"You'd better get out," Officer Johnson said.

For the first time, Donald leaned across the console, looked up at the officer and, in a voice as smooth as hot fudge, he said, "Please don't make her get out. She's my niece from California. I just picked her up at the Anchorage airport, and this jacket is all she's got in the way of cold-weather gear. Much more exposure and she'll be frozen solid." He smiled that same smile that had made Evie like him right off the bat.

Officer Johnson enjoyed a little thaw herself. But she was a sensible woman, and she proved it with her next question. "If she's your niece from California, what's she doing driving this car? In this weather?"

"She's up here to help me with my work. She's going to get the groceries, go to the bank, grab fast food, that kind of thing. I wanted her to practice driving with me in the car. It's the only responsible thing to do."

"He's a really responsible uncle." Evie hoped that helped.

"The car is registered to a Michele Jameson." So Officer Johnson had looked it up before she'd come to the window.

"She sold it to me in the same transaction as the house. I can't believe that hasn't been updated yet." He pulled an indignant-citizen frown. "Can you advise me? What should I do to expedite the process?"

"It probably means she hasn't transferred the title." Officer Johnson kept a suspicious eye on them and checked her tablet.

He thought about it. "You're right. It must've slipped her mind, I'm sure. Her husband is an antiquities expert. He's being held hostage in Magara, for ransom. It was in the news. You've probably heard about it. She sold me the house, took her son, Timothy, and went to live with her parents while she raises the money to free him. I'm contributing, of course."

Evie found herself relieved that Donald White was such a good guy.

Officer Johnson didn't seem impressed. In fact, her eyes narrowed, and she got that cynical-cop look.

"I'll give Mrs. Jameson a call," Donald White said. "We'll get this straightened out ASAP."

"You do that." Officer Johnson must not have found a stolen-car report on her tablet, because she handed the paperwork back to Evie. "I should give you a warning ticket."

Donald leaned over more. "Please don't. Evelyn's license is new. I'll personally make sure that from now on she's more cautious."

"Make sure you get the insurance updated, too." Officer Johnson bent down and looked them both over as if memorizing their faces, then stepped back. "You're free to go. Young woman, keep your foot light on that accelerator, and steer into a skid."

"Thank you." Relief made Evie sag. "I will. Thank you!"

The trooper waved them on.

"That went about as well as could be expected." Donald sounded pleased, but he looked behind them as Evie pulled back onto the road. He faced forward. "Figures. She's going to follow us to show off her big-cop muscles."

Evie drove with excessive caution down the highway.

After a few miles, Donald laughed. "You're going so slow, she got bored and turned off. Go on, bring it back up to the speed limit."

Evie did as she was told. "This week, I, um, have to go in and report to the local cops."

"Why?"

"Because someone has to make sure I'm gainfully employed and not committing any more crimes."

"That's stupid." He waved the news away. "I'll call and talk to them."

"Would you?" She was lavishly grateful. "I hate being anywhere near cops. They either got into the job because they want to help simpleminded, misguided folks or because they're bullies and with a badge they can officially pick on everybody." Maybe she was being unfair about the good ones, but she was ugly right about the bad ones.

"The bullies get off on making people miserable," he said, "so you have to learn to spot the do-gooders, get them on your side, and you can manipulate them to do whatever you need."

She glanced at him in surprise. He sounded like he'd been through the system. Which was interesting because if he had, he was living proof you could move on, get rich and own a Jag.

They passed the city limits sign: *Welcome to Rockin, Alaska. Population 1,643.* So more than the thousand Donald White reported. Yet she saw no town, no buildings, just the same frozen landscape and trees.

It was as if her mother's damning gaze found her. Evie let off the gas and let the car slow to the official speed limit.

"Good for you," Donald White said. "You're aware of your surroundings and the lawful speed limit. You are exactly who I want doing my business for me. Now—turn here, I'll show you where I live."

Evie turned off the highway onto a narrow paved road that wound through bare deciduous trees and tall evergreens that shook sparkling bits of ice onto the pavement. She had a small panic attack when she saw an oncoming car; the ditch was right beside the road, and she'd already slipped once.

Donald muttered, "You're doing fine," but he bent down his head to rest on his knees, so she figured he was assuming the crash position.

As they passed, the lady waved, but Evie kept a tight grip on the steering wheel. "We made it past her okay," she told Donald.

He straightened. "Left on this driveway."

The twisty driveway led away from the road far enough that Evie wondered if they would ever arrive. Then there it was—the house: all brick, two stories, three-car garage. Lots of windows. "Wow," she said. "Nice place."

Donald pushed the opener on the dash, and the middle garage door rose. She pulled in carefully.

One of the other garage bays held a brown SUV. In the other, someone had set up a workbench with power and hand tools.

He leaped out, hustled to the keypad beside the door where a red light blinked and input a number.

"Wow," she said again. A security system. She got out and stood awkwardly.

"Come over here, and I'll show you how it works." Donald stepped back as she approached.

She tensed. This was it. He had her in his house, and he was going to jump her. She prepared to fight—and he said, "The code to set the alarm is pound, 37, capital A, 83, star, 47. Got that?"

She recited it back.

"Good memory," he approved. "Now set the alarm."

She did. A beeping started, and the red light blinked furiously.

"Once you open any door—the garage door, the front door, whatever—you've got a minute to disarm the alarm. It's the same sequence except it ends with 48."

"Pound, 37, capital A, 83, star, 48." She typed it into the keypad.

It stopped beeping and blinking.

She beamed.

"Get your stuff and come in." He opened the door to the house and walked in. Over his shoulder, he said, "Your bedroom is up the stairs, the first on the left. When you get unpacked, come down, and I'll show you what your job will be."

TOO SMART

EVIE CAME DOWN THE stairs from her luxurious bedroom to meet...no one. Her boss was nowhere in sight. She hovered in the entry, wondering what to do and where to go, and finally followed the light to a small, windowless den that opened off the corridor. There Donald White slumped on a stiff-looking love seat, surrounded by papers and photos, a computer in his lap and a tablet in his hand. The light came from a display cabinet filled with treasures: a graceful Asian jade vase, a marble goat/man, a reclining gold Buddha. Inside, everything glittered and shone, and the exhibit drew Evie over to stare. "Wow. Mr. White—"

"Donald."

"Donald, what is all this stuff?" Evie clasped her hands behind her back. "They're so pretty."

"Pretty?" He sounded offended. "That's a trite word for works of extraordinary skill that have survived the ages. They're awe-inspiring."

She'd never used that word, but she'd never seen anything like this stuff. "Awe-inspiring, then. How old are they?"

"Older than you."

"Are these Mr. Jameson's?"

Donald suddenly loomed behind her. "What makes you ask that?"

She stepped to the side and faced him. "You told the cop Mr. Jameson was an antiquities expert, and that he was being held captive in that country, and that this was his house, so I thought maybe you bought them with the—"

"Magara. Right." Donald didn't change posture or expression.

She realized she could breathe again.

"These are mine," he said. "Come on. I gave you the first-floor office."

He led Evie down the corridor to a room with walls covered with built-in oak bookshelves and leather-bound books. The desk was mid-century modern, a wide sweep of unembellished wood. The computer was miniature; the monitor was curved and massive. She wanted to say *Wow*, but she'd said it too many times today.

He gestured to the leather desk chair.

Evie seated herself and marveled at the comfort.

On the file cabinet behind the desk sat an Egyptian bust of some guy, or maybe it was a woman, with wings and a beak. "That's awesome. What is it?"

"It's a fake."

"Really?" Evie leaned closer and studied it. "It looks really old."

"It's believed to be almost two thousand years old."

"I don't understand." She figured two thousand years was a long time ago.

"The statue was discovered in Rome when they excavated

the floor of a home. A Roman soldier had lived there. It's speculated that he brought home a souvenir from Egypt—that statue. He may have thought it was real, created hundreds of years before *him* by a craftsman. But in fact when he bought it, it had come off the assembly line of a shop that specialized in making and selling fakes."

"That really is awesome. So even though it's Egyptian and two thousand years old, it's not worth anything?"

"A thousand dollars." Donald shrugged.

Evie leaned away from it. "I won't knock it over," she promised fervently.

"Zone Jameson found it in a shop in Rome. He bought it for a song." Donald smiled as if amused. "Smart man. He knew how to turn a profit."

"You know him?" Evie was surprised. Somehow from what Donald had said, she thought he knew the wife but not the husband. "Right, I guess you met him because you're both in antiquities."

"That's right. He gave it to me."

A pretty nice present! It hovered on the tip of her tongue, but she stopped herself. Donald was still smiling, but the amusement had shifted to something else, as if he had angled to get it and succeeded. "You don't like him?" she asked.

He looked startled. "Why do you say that?"

"The way you talk about him, like you don't *really* think he was smart."

"He helped me discover what I was truly good at."

"Oh." Donald made it sound as if that was a recent development. But how could it be? He was old. An adult. Adults knew what they were good at, and that was what they did for a living. "What is that?"

"I'm good at marketing antiquities."

She remembered the statues and the vase in the lighted

case. "Like the stuff in the case in the front room? Are those fakes, too?"

"Those are real."

"You're going to sell them? How much are they worth? *More* than a couple of thousand?"

"A lot more."

A lot more…was a lot of money. "I'll take a picture of them."

"With what?"

"They, um, gave me a phone." She fished the old Moto G7 out of her pocket and showed him. "It's refurbished. They give one to everybody when they're released so if, um…" *I've got it in case you turn out to be a perv, I can call for help.* Better skip that. "The photo? I'll take it? If that's okay?"

Donald looked as if he was contemplating something in the far distance. "All right. That might work." He returned to the present. "Now let's talk about your responsibilities."

The desk chair was adjustable in every direction, and Evie played with the levers while Donald gave her instructions.

Once he stopped and asked, "Shouldn't you take notes?"

She rattled off everything he'd told her about his annuities, SEPs, savings and checking accounts at different banks, the IDs and the passwords.

He examined her with a little too much intensity. "Aren't you too smart?"

"I learn very quickly," she agreed. More than one of her teachers had marveled at her memory.

"Scary smart," he said. Sometimes Donald had a funny way of looking at her, as if he was weighing what she said so he could respond without giving too much away. He was a private man, she guessed.

Photographs in matching silver frames lined one side of the desk. One was a couple in their wedding photo; the bride was beautiful, of course, draped in lace and silk, a woman with an elegant upsweep of dark hair and a gracious, excited smile.

The groom had a determined jaw, jutting out like a peninsula, an abundance of unruly black curly hair, big brown eyes with a fringe of dark lashes and a beaming smile. He wasn't handsome, but he was happy, a man who had achieved his dreams.

Another pair of photos showed a grinning toddler displaying four new white teeth next to a black-and-white of a cocky-looking sailor in a World War II uniform. "Are these people your family?"

Donald glanced down. "That's Michele Jameson and her family. She sold me the house. Remember? I told you."

"Yes, but why would she leave her pictures?"

"With her husband gone, possibly forever, she wanted to leave her memories behind."

Evie studied the photos, looked up at Donald White and didn't ask, *What woman would do that?*

But what other explanation could there be? None she could think of…

ALONE WITH ONLY OPTIMISM FOR A FRIEND

THAT NIGHT, EVELYN PUSHED autodial for JDC—Regina had preprogrammed her phone—and called San Jose. She couldn't wait to tell Regina that she'd landed on her feet.

Only she didn't get Regina.

"Regina resigned. I'm Walt. You've been reassigned to me."

Evelyn couldn't believe it. As soon as she flew out, Regina disappeared? "Where did she go?"

"Somewhere she got paid better, that's where. Not JDC." Walt sounded impatient. "Tell me how it's going. Regina left a note that she was worried about you and your new employer."

"Yes. It's okay." Evie got right back to the subject of Regina. "No, really. Where could she have gone?"

"I don't know." He paced out the words like she was ridiculous. "We weren't friends."

"Oh. But—" Evie would do some research herself. Surely she could track Regina down.

As if he could hear her plans, Walt said, "Look, kid, Regina's moved on with no forwarding address. Take the hint."

He hurt her feelings. Not because he was being mean, but because she feared it was true. When she got in trouble, even her mother and her sister had moved. They'd sent letters for a while, but when Evie didn't respond...

And why should she? They'd abandoned her!

The letters stopped.

Okay, maybe she had really screwed up. When her mother had visited her in jail, she'd said in no uncertain terms, *When you can make me proud, come home.* And, *You're throwing away all your opportunities with both hands. Stop. Think. Live!* And there had been that slap.

So Evie had dealt with worse stuff than Regina's disappearance. She didn't need support from anybody.

But she did. Being alone with no one to love or to love her—that was too hard. She *was* going to make her mama proud, and she *was* going to go home.

"Now, about this guy?" Walt asked.

"I know Regina was worried, but he's, like, this old man, my father's age. He assigned me a really nice bedroom. The door has a lock. He works at a computer in a little room off the entry. He wants me to go into town for him, get him groceries, go to the bank, that stuff."

"You're driving his car?"

"Yes." Walt sounded so alarmed, Evie didn't mention it was a Jag.

"Jesus. Be careful."

"I am. He said I was a good driver!"

"Yeah, so's my teenage daughter, and she cost my insurance thirteen thousand. So you think he's not a pervert or a serial killer?"

"I think he's weird. He's almost..." Evie hesitated, remembering the kids in JDC who were disturbing in their laser focus.

"Almost what?" Impatience tinged his voice. "Do you think you're okay or not? I can get local police to check on you if you think I need to."

"No!" God, no. "I'm okay. He's good. I'm safe."

Walt was clearly relieved. "All that work you did has paid off. You're lucky. It doesn't always work out."

Evelyn could almost hear him crossing Evelyn Jones off the list of people he needed to follow up on.

"Remember to check in with Rockin law enforcement. You have that information?"

"Yes, but I don't need to. Mr. White said he'd call them."

"It doesn't work that way, Evelyn." Walt sounded exasperated. "You have to take your ID and check in in person."

Evie groaned. She didn't look forward to that meeting.

"They're supposed to assign you a parole officer... I mean, if it's a real police department up there in the wilds of Alaska. Who knows about that? If there's ever a problem with the employer, tell the chief of police. In a week or so, check in with me."

"When?"

"You know. In a week or so."

"I will." Evelyn hung up and looked out the window. It was so dark, with forest all around and an early-winter sunset that blocked any light from sun or stars or moon.

Not important. Her mother and sister were close, so close. She had Googled their place; they lived in a narrow, small two-story house with a fence and a tiny yard. When Donald sent her into town to do whatever it was he wanted her to do, she would drive by, and maybe she'd see them and she'd stop and...

No. She had to keep focused on her goal. She wanted to

hand her mother her first paycheck, see her face, know she'd earned her way back into the family fold.

Next week she'd get her first paycheck.

She could wait that long.

EXACTLY AS I PLANNED

THAT FIRST MORNING IN Donald White's house, Evie woke without any clear idea of what she should do after she showered and dressed.

Her stomach made the decision for her.

Last night, after Donald had explained the basics of her job, he told her since it was Sunday, she would start work in the morning. When she asked what time, he had suggested nine o'clock. He said she should fix herself something to eat and entertain herself however she wished. He returned to his den.

Dinner had been meager, a can of soup and some crackers, eaten alone at the kitchen table, and now she was starving. She moved the chair out from under the doorknob—she trusted Donald, sure, but she wasn't stupid—unlocked her door and went downstairs.

The house had been built in the fifties and was up-to-date, but the kitchen retained that chrome and linoleum decor. Evie opened the refrigerator; it was even more barren than she remembered. She was hanging there, staring, wondering what

Donald White had been eating and, more important, what she was going to eat, when the door at the opposite end of the kitchen opened and Donald stepped through.

Behind him, she saw nothing but an empty space of stark illumination. He turned off the light switch on the wall, shut the door behind him, saw her and frowned. Really frowned. His expression was such a departure from yesterday's geniality, starvation seemed like a good idea.

"That's the basement," he said. "You don't want to go down there. It's dark and slimy. The washer and dryer are down there, but you don't want to use them. Take your clothes to the laundry in town. You can take mine, too. I'll foot the bill."

"Okay. But I do know how to use a washer. Before JDC releases you, you have to take a course on stuff like basic cooking, cleaning, taking care of yourself. If you want me to wash—"

"I don't want you in the basement. There's no handrail on the stairs, and if you fall I'll be liable."

She wanted to say she would be careful and not fall, and if she did, she wouldn't sue, but maybe he meant he didn't want her to waste his time while she recovered. Still, he had said he'd pay her health insurance—

As if he'd read her mind, he said, "When you get to your desk, fill out the insurance forms there. I need to send them to the company right away."

Relieved, she said, "I will!" Then, "Paper forms? I didn't even know anyone used paper forms anymore."

He waved that away. "Can't argue with insurance companies."

"Right." What did she know?

"After that, you're going to move money from the savings to the checking account to keep the household automatic bill payments current. Come and get me when you're ready. You know where I'll be." He headed toward the corridor, swiveled and asked, "What are you still doing here?"

"I need to eat."

He stared as if the idea of eating was foreign to him.

"Breakfast," she added helpfully.

"Oh." His gaze shifted between her and the door at the end of the kitchen. He left, but he didn't seem to like her being in here by herself.

Didn't he eat? Skinny as he was, she guessed not. She returned to the refrigerator, opened it and surveyed the contents again. Then got another can of soup out of the pantry and stuck a bowl of it in the microwave.

Last night, she'd looked for Donald White on social media. She found a dozen plus Donald Whites, but for this particular guy, there'd been a big fat zip. On the other hand…he was both wealthy and busy, so that made sense he wouldn't post his business online for everyone to know.

Still, she was curious—and not suspicious, just sensible—so she looked up the rest of the stuff.

Everything was right. The Jamesons had owned this house (the deed hadn't yet been transferred, but Evie figured that took time). Michele Jameson was a doctor. Zone Jameson was an antiquities expert, which was why he got into trouble. He'd been called to Magara, to a mountain excavation to verify a tablet believed to be Biblical in origin, and he and his team were kidnapped by terrorists and held for ransom. What Donald White had said to the trooper was true.

So it all made sense. The wife had been so distraught by her husband's kidnapping, she'd sold Donald the house, taken their son and gone to live with her parents where she could raise the money for her husband's ransom. Once Evie had confirmed that, she could sleep in peace—and she had.

After breakfast, she cleaned up, then followed the corridor to his office, which, now that she'd seen hers, seemed cramped and dark, and found him in the same spot, slumped on the love seat working furiously on his laptop.

"Mr. White… Donald."

He'd been focusing so hard, she'd startled him.

"Are you ready?" He closed the computer, turned off the tablet and locked them in the drawer of the end table.

Evie pointed at an upright stone monument, roughly one foot by three feet, etched with worn unreadable letters and illustrated with a battle scene, set against the wall. "That wasn't in here yesterday, was it?"

"I moved it from the dining room."

"What is it?"

"It's a stele."

Evie realized she had a lot to learn from Donald White.

He continued, "A stele is a column that's used to set out laws, commemorate battles or mark a grave. In this case, it's Mesopotamian and commemorates a battle."

She leaned down to inspect it. "He's standing on bodies."

"He's the king, he won the battle. He was a god, and victory over lesser beings should be exalted."

"He's dead, isn't he?"

"Thousands of years ago."

"Then he wasn't a god."

Silence answered her. She got an uncomfortable sensation between her shoulder blades. When she glanced at Donald, he was observing her coldly. "I'm sorry!" she apologized involuntarily. "I didn't mean to offend you."

"You didn't. I'm simply surprised that you would dismiss a man who accomplished so much when you…" He walked out.

She stood breathing hard, working to get over her humiliation. Everyone knew she was a big-time screw-up, but she *had* changed.

She would prove it to Donald White.

She would prove it to her mother.

Most important, she would prove it to herself.

She followed him to her office.

Donald pointed her into the desk chair, then unlocked and opened one of the drawers.

Evie's heart stopped.

He pulled out a battered notebook. "The passwords and account numbers are here." He used a tab to get to the right page.

She couldn't see. She couldn't hear. She wasn't thinking of the framed photographs, or how cool her new office was, or whether her sister would remember her or her mother reject her. For inside the drawer in the front right corner was a tall stack of hundred dollar bills banded with a mustard colored strap.

Donald was talking.

Evie's ears were ringing. She had never seen that much cash in her life. She couldn't tear her gaze away.

Donald snapped his fingers in front of her eyes. "Evelyn?"

She jumped, looked up at him. "What?"

"I'll tell you what to do with the cash in a minute." He slid the drawer shut. "First, let me walk you through the transfers."

"Right." With the cash out of sight, she could focus. She needed to *focus*.

He finished describing the online banking, showed her the insurance forms—they looked incredibly simple—then opened the drawer and picked up one of the stacks of cash. "Today's workload shouldn't take long, should it?"

"A couple of hours. Unless there's something else?" She

was back to doubting his intentions. He didn't need a private bookkeeper for this amount of work. What did he really want?

"I'll pass on more responsibility to you as you prove yourself."

She relaxed. "I'll be ready."

"Whether you're finished or not, quit at noon. Count out one thousand dollars. You'll need that to buy groceries and any office supplies you require. Take the car. Go to Rockin American Bank. Talk to one of the officers." He opened another drawer, got out a computer tablet and handed it to her. He rattled off its password, and when she had unlocked it, he said, "First thing on the list. Deposit the nine hundred dollars into that account."

She scanned the information on the screen. "Wait. It's going into an account with my name on it!"

"I've done the preliminaries to open an account for you. At the bank, you'll have to provide ID and sign a signature card. Is that a problem?"

"No." She wasn't sure. "Not at all."

"When the time comes, we'll have you transfer the whole amount into the fund to ransom Zone Jameson."

"You're going to pay Zone Jameson's ransom?" In a single moment, Evie went from doubt to veneration. "That is so nice of you!"

"It's the least I can do." Donald pressed his hand on Evie's shoulder, and in a voice so reassuring she relaxed and believed him, he said, "Trust me, it's going to work out exactly as I planned."

"I don't understand why my name's on the account, but I'm sure you know what you're doing. Except…" She looked up at him.

"You want to say something?"

"I'm not…experienced or anything, but it seems dangerous to keep your passwords in a notebook in a locked desk drawer. What if someone breaks in? The computer's right here, and it would be pretty easy to figure everything out."

"I'm older and set in my ways, so when you see a problem you should always advise me."

She couldn't help it. She beamed.

"Do you think the tablet's safer?" he asked.

"At least a little." The way he spoke to her made her feel important. "If there was the proper authentication and a backup on an off-site location."

"Why don't you start moving the passwords onto the tablet? It's yours, by the way, to use as you wish."

"I appreciate the thought." She was flabbergasted. She had a used phone the JDC had given her, but she hadn't handled new electronics since her father had moved out. "But in this instance, it would be better if this tablet was dedicated only to the account passwords and backups."

"I see it differently," he said. "If the tablet contains your personal email and texts, and your photos, apps and games, you'll take extra good care of it."

"I suppose, but—"

"Look, if you're in town and I need something about the accounts, you've got to be able to respond."

"Yes. I see." She still held the tablet in loose fingers, half-outstretched toward him.

He closed her hand around it and pushed it toward her. "After you're done at the bank, take the extra hundred and get yourself something for lunch. Better go to the grocery store and buy yourself something for dinner, too. No need to buy too much—you'll be going to the bank every day to make that deposit."

"Couldn't we deposit all the cash at once?"

"No!"

His vehemence made her jump.

"No." He took a breath, and his voice calmed. "This is an offshore account. The US government monitors deposits being placed in foreign accounts—to limit those trying to avoid paying taxes—and the banks are required to report any suspicious activity."

"Like what?"

"Large amounts. We're doing it this way to avoid attention." His voice got deeper and very earnest. "To rescue Zone Jameson."

The front doorbell rang.

"I'm expecting a delivery," he said. "Get it."

She opened the door in time to see the truck disappearing down the curved driveway. She picked up the box and brought it to him in his den, setting it on a table.

He used a razor knife from his pocket to slice the tape, then shoved the box back at her. "Open it. It's for you."

She froze. It was clothing. She could tell by the size and weight of the box. He shouldn't be buying her clothing.

As if he'd lost interest, he went back to work.

She opened the box and peeked in. A coat. A heavy coat with a fur-lined hood. And gloves that looked warm. She pulled back the lid.

"I hope it fits." He was scanning the screen of his laptop, paying no attention to her and her reaction. "I need you to make those deposits, do my mailings, run all my errands. I can't have you freezing in the first week. Oh, and don't forget to fill out those insurance forms."

"Right. Thank you." She picked up the box. "Mr. White, I will work very hard, I promise."

"I don't doubt that. That's one of the reasons I hired you."

KEEPING YOUR FEET

IT TOOK FOUR TRIES for Evelyn to parallel park the Jaguar, and when she finally quit, it was more because the people in the diner window were watching and laughing than because she'd managed to align the wheels with the curb. She hoisted her backpack onto her shoulder and got out to face the whistling north wind. She slipped on the ice, steadied herself and used the car for support as she inched around from the driver's side to the sidewalk. The cold of the metal cut through her insulated gloves. When she took her first unassisted step toward the bank, she slipped again and realized—to heck with not knowing how to drive in snow. She didn't even know how to walk in this stuff!

Those people in the diner were still watching and grinning, and for one terrible moment she wondered if her mother and sister were inside, watching and pretending they didn't know her. Or if they would be in the bank and she'd come face-to-face with them. What would she do? What would she say?

Then one old guy stood up as if he was going to come out and shout instructions.

Arms outstretched, legs stiff, Evie slipped and slid until she accidentally stepped in the fresh snow. That gave her boots some traction.

The old guy stepped out of the diner. "Do you need help?" He sounded as if he meant the offer kindly.

She was still embarrassed. She shook her head and made it to the bank's frosty marble steps. She grasped the handrail.

"There you go," he called encouragingly.

The bank must use some kind of antifreeze, because although the wind plastered snow against the marble columns and flakes danced across the broad porch, the ice was slushy and chunky and she made it to the tall, bronze doors. She grasped the vertical pull and tugged.

The door barely budged.

Evelyn couldn't believe it. She couldn't park. She couldn't walk. Now she couldn't open a door? She tugged again, harder, then leaned her hand on the other door and pulled as hard as she could. The door creaked open a few inches, enough for the wind to sneak in. She let go to stop herself from following the door's rush. It slammed against the doorstop; when the bronze hit, it boomed like a cathedral bell. She righted herself, grabbed the inner door handle, braced her weight against the wind and pulled. Inch by inch, the door closed, shutting her into the quiet space between the cruel outdoors and the bank's inner sanctum.

Gasping, she faced the interior glass doors.

She pulled off her cap, pulled off her gloves, flexed her numb fingers.

According to the sign, the Rockin American Bank's president was Mr. Dan Terwilliger, a square-jawed man with a steady gaze and a black suit. The bank itself had celebrated its hundred and tenth birthday, and as she peered through the glass, the sheer splendor of the place took her breath away.

The lobby looked like the set of a Hollywood western, long and narrow, with old-fashioned cashier cages along the left side and offices along the right. Everything was marble, mahogany and gilt. At the end, like an emperor on his throne, sat a man in a black suit with a white shirt and red tie.

As the heat thawed Evie's nose, it began to drip. She dabbed it on her coat sleeve and felt utterly out of place. Her mother and sister were nowhere in sight, and she should have been relieved, was relieved. But she didn't belong here—a former juvenile delinquent in this magnificent building?

But it didn't matter. She was working for Mr. Donald White, and she had to make his deposit. She knew it was going to involve paperwork. She needed to speak with someone who was in charge. She guessed the guy in the suit was him.

People inside were beginning to stare, so she wiped her feet on the huge mat, pushed open the glass door and stepped into Rockin American Bank.

As she walked through the center aisle, dragging her feet on the scrolled carpet, a woman came out of an office to her right and intercepted her. "Hello." She smiled and extended her hand. "I'm Stacey Collins, one of the bank officers. Can I help you?"

An officer? Should Evelyn salute? "I'm, um, Evelyn Jones." Great, she sounded like she wasn't sure of her own name. "I'd like to make a transaction." She dabbed at her nose again. Why wouldn't it stop dripping?

"I can tell by your reaction to the bank that you're new in town. It is impressive, isn't it? The relic of a bygone age when the Nome gold rush brought prosperity to Alaska. Of course—" Stacey leaned close and lowered her voice "—I've thought the only thing that separates it from Gringotts Bank in *Harry Potter* is the goblins."

Evie snorted loudly, moistly, and covered her nose and mouth with her hand. "Sorry," she mumbled.

Stacey said, "Come on," and led Evie into her office. She picked up a box of tissues from her desk and offered it.

Gratefully, Evie took one and wiped her nose.

"Better take a couple more," Stacey advised. "When I come in from the cold, my nose always runs."

Evie nodded and pulled a couple more.

Note to self: carry tissues.

"Have a seat." Stacey gestured to the chair in front of the desk, then walked around to sit at her desk. "What can we at Rockin American Bank do for you?"

Mindful of Mr. White's instructions to make these transactions about her, Evelyn said, "I'd like to transfer nine hundred dollars to an offshore account."

Stacey stared at her, eyes so wide they looked dry and painful. Then she blinked. "Of course. Is the offshore account set up?"

"Yes, I've got all the information." Evie pulled her backpack off her shoulder, dug around and found the computer tablet. She'd decorated the cover with flower stickers she'd found in her office. She thought it looked nice.

"The money will come from another account?"

"No." Evie dug again and found the envelope of money. She pulled it out and showed Stacey. "I have cash."

Stacey did that thing with her eyes again.

Evie wondered if she should be worried. "I know it's weird for someone my age to have a lot of cash, but it's okay. Really."

Stacey blinked. She asked, "Where are you from?"

"California. San Jose."

"California? Rockin must be a change for you. Are you an...intern?"

"An intern?" Evelyn didn't know what that meant.

"With a law firm or one of the local artists?"

Was she an intern? "No, I'm employed."

"I know most of the businesses in town. Who's your employer?"

"Mr. Donald White. You must know him. He set up an account for me."

Stacey turned to her monitor and typed. "Here it is, Evelyn Angelina Jones, a savings account. But it was set up online using an email with your name. There's no mention of your employer. Donald White, you said?"

"Yes. That's him. He's new in town."

"Like you." Stacey inserted a five-by-seven card into the printer behind her. She typed on her keyboard. The printer rattled.

"Yes, but he's important. He's somebody. He owns a big house, and he's, like, responsible and caring." When Stacey looked doubtful, Evie added, "He gave me a chance!"

"Good of him. I don't know who he is, but it's important to, um...offer a helping hand to those in...need?" Stacey put the card and a pen in front of Evie. "I'll need to see your ID."

Evie rummaged in her backpack, pulled out her California driver's license and handed it over. "That was me. I just got out of high school." It was the truth, mostly. She had graduated with a GED. "And trade school, and he needed a bookkeeper."

Stacey looked at Evie's photo, then into her face, then at the photo again. "He brought you from California to keep his books?"

"He did. I guess there's not very many people here to hire?"

"That's true." Stacey seemed to relax a little. She scanned

Evie's ID and handed it back. "Keep it close. You'll need to show that for the wire transfer."

Evie slipped the license into her pocket, signed the card, handed it back and realized she was talking only about herself. She knew better. *Don't tell too much. Make the conversation about the other guy.* She blurted, "Who are you? Where are you from? Why are you here?"

As if the barrage of questions was an assault, Stacey leaned back. "As you know, I'm Stacey Collins. I was born here. My mother was…" Stacey fluttered her fingers as if describing her mother in a not-flattering but diplomatic way. "I never fit in, but a few people here believed in me. They helped me. I got into UC Berkeley and got a business degree, and I came back here because I knew Rockin needed me. It's a small stage, yes, but for me, it's important. Right?"

"Yes." They had a lot in common. Like Evie, someone had given Stacey a chance. "It's great that you came back to your hometown to pay it back."

"You get it. I knew here I could make a difference."

"That's important."

"It is. Someday I'm going to do more than work at the bank." Stacey stood. "But right now, I'm not working. I'm enjoying a chat with you. Let's get your transaction set up."

Evie gathered her tablet and her envelope, pulled her backpack over her shoulder and followed Stacey into the lobby.

Stacey gestured her over to one of the tellers whose name plate said she was Norma Hathaway. "Norma will take care of you."

Evie approached the window.

Norma looked almost as old as the mahogany counter.

Stacey followed.

"What can I do for you, dear?" Norma's voice creaked a little.

Evie repeated Donald White's directive.

Norma did the same eye thing as Stacey.

Stacey said, "She's got cash."

Evie pushed the envelope and her license across the counter.

Like Stacey, Norma scrutinized the license and Evie's face. Taking the envelope, she counted out the bills. "There is nine hundred dollar bills here. The transaction will cost thirty dollars."

"Oh. I didn't know that." Evie thought about the hundred-dollar-bill in her wallet. She thought about the burger and fries she'd intended to devour, the groceries she'd intended to buy. Then she thought of Zone Jameson and his wife and son, and figured with seventy dollars she could get lots of groceries. She retrieved the last bill and handed it over. "Take the thirty out of that."

"Excuse me, with this much cash I have to make sure the bills are genuine." Norma walked away.

"Sure." Evie was starting to relax, so she added, "But they are." Because Donald was a good guy. He'd given her a job, and a new coat, and he hadn't laid a paw on her.

Norma returned with the cash and more of that wide-eyed discomfort. "Thank you for your patience. Do you have the account information?"

Evie pushed it toward Norma. "I suppose you're wondering where I got that kind of cash."

"It's not that I'm wondering." Norma went to work on her computer. "Only that it's so unusual to meet a young person with this kind of disposable income."

"It's not mine. It's my boss's. Mr. Donald White is really well-off."

"Do I know him?" Norma asked Stacey.

"The name didn't ring a bell with me," Stacey answered.

"You can't know everybody in town. Do you?" Evie asked.

"She's from California," Stacey explained to Norma.

"Ah." Norma chuckled; it sounded like creaky door hinges. "I do. I've been a teller here for forty years, ever since my first husband died. There's three banks in town, two grocery stores, four convenience stores, restaurants, maybe a dozen…?" Norma looked inquiringly at Stacey.

Stacey counted on her fingers. "With drive-ins and pizza places, I think more like two dozen. And bars. Bar food can be pretty good."

"People come and go, but people stick around, too. So yes, I know almost everybody." Norma smiled a smug, self-congratulatory smile.

"Whoa." Evie had never imagined living in a place that was so…confined. "Do you ever meet someone you don't know?"

"Of course. This close to Denali, we get tourists passing through. Not as many as we'd like—Talkeetna calls itself the gateway to Denali, it's closer to Anchorage, and the ranger station is there. But still, we're close to hiking, snowmobiling, dogsledding, bus tours, helicopter tours…" Norma counted out seventy dollars and passed it and the receipt to Evie.

"This is a bruising place." Evie started to put the receipt in her bag.

Norma stopped her with a hand on her arm. "Check. Always check. I might have made a mistake."

Evie felt young, inexperienced, foolish. She checked the cash and the receipt. "Everything looks good. Thank you." She gazed into Norma's eyes. "I'll be back tomorrow with the same amount, pretty much. Mr. White is putting money away to help Mrs. Jameson ransom her husband from the rebel nationalists in Magara. Isn't that nice? He's a really great guy."

"He sounds like a great guy," Stacey agreed.

Norma and Stacey watched Evelyn walk out of the bank.

Norma turned to Stacey. "At what point do we report this to the feds as suspicious activity?"

"She seems genuine, so I guess...not yet?"

INSIDE THE LAW

ON TUESDAY, EVIE WENT to the bank to make the next transfer. There Stacey told her about the lot behind the bank with nose-in parking.

Evie was wildly grateful. She didn't have to parallel park!

She walked from there to the Rockin City Hall/police station/municipal jail to register as a juvenile delinquent parolee. Because she needed to play by the rules. Also she figured on Tuesday the police station would be relatively quiet and no one would see her. She failed to account for the fact that the previous day had been the fifteenth of the month, payday. Jail cells were full of various folks who'd indulged too much, fought too much or loved unwisely.

The police station was one huge room divided between the waiting area and the secure area. In between stood a scarred wood countertop and bulletproof glass wall, accessible by a single door that released only to security fobs waved under the electronic eye by the law enforcement officers. The old building smelled like mildew and sweat. It sounded like arguments, crying and thinning patience. The atmosphere reminded her of San Jose JDC, and her skin crawled at the memory.

She almost backed out. Donald White had said she didn't need to come and check in. But Walt, the California JD officer, said she had to do this, and she knew her mother would want her to stay inside the law, so she got in the longest line—because it would take more time to get to the counter—and waited.

As the line shuffled forward, Evie kept glancing through the bulletproof glass and seeing cops, desks, TVs blaring on the walls. Most of the TVs showed rolling reports on traffic stops and various arrests, but one was showing the week's wrap-up of *Days of Our Lives*.

There was another, shorter line, a lot shorter than this one, and Evie couldn't figure out why, so she watched.

Behind the glass stood a middle-aged female officer, short, skinny, tanned, wrinkled, smoking a cigarette. She didn't speak, she blared. "Back again, are you? What's it been, what? Two months since you beat your wife? Or two months since she turned you in? I suppose she's coming to pick you up. A weak woman and a guy with heavy fists. You're made for each other. Pay the fine at that window.

"Smokin' weed before a band concert? You think that's going to improve your performance? Your band teacher isn't any too happy that his whole percussion section wasn't available for the concert. I'd hate to be you when you go back to class. There's your parents over there. They'll pay your fine at that window.

"Drunk and disorderly? That must have been quite the divorce party you gals enjoyed. How's it feel to have a record? Bet your kids will be proud, especially when they get teased in school. Pay over at that window."

"Who is she?" Evie muttered to the person behind her.

A huge guy—with bulging biceps, shaved head, tats on his neck—muttered back, "That's Chief of Police Gretchen George. Wretchen Gretchen we call her."

Caught by surprise, Evie snorted, put her hand over her mouth and nose, glanced up and met Wretchen Gretchen's eyes.

Uh-oh.

The guy behind her was still muttering. "She doesn't have to work that window. She does it because she loves to see people in trouble and add to their misery. Be careful of her. She likes young women, if you know what I mean, even if they don't like her. *Especially* if they don't like her. Abusive old hag."

"Thanks for the heads-up." Evie kept her voice soft. She slumped her shoulders and looked at the floor. Acting abject and beaten didn't always work to divert attention, but standing straight and proud made the mean cops want to beat respect into her.

She got to the front, talked to the officer behind the window, presented her papers, played the abject, shamed adolescent.

He didn't assign her a parole officer, just told her to check in next Tuesday, and she got the hell out of City Hall.

She'd come out okay.

Wretchen Gretchen hadn't really noticed her.

DON'T TELL THEM

BY THURSDAY, EVIE KNEW for sure Donald White was behaving...oddly. He still wasn't eating more than a bite or two, sometimes with a sip of caffeinated water. But for hours and hours, he remained glued to his computer, his green eyes reflecting the glow like an alien from outer space.

"Mr. White, I'm going to the bank now. Is there anything you need?" Evie waited, hoping he would chide her for calling him Mr. White and ask her to bring home something he'd like to eat.

He never lifted his gaze from his computer. "Go to the bank. Make the transfer. We have to save Zone Jameson. Buy whatever you want to eat. I'm not hungry."

She went to the bank where she knew people. She parked in the lot behind the bank, the same spot every day. She went into the bank, grateful to be where people liked her, or at least were used to her showing up every day with her fistful of cash and her deposit slip.

The bank was quiet. But then, it usually was.

Stacey Collins stood in the door of her office, wide-eyed and frowning.

From the window of her teller's booth, Norma urgently gestured Evie to come to her.

Evie walked that direction and didn't notice the scrawny, uniformed figure standing over by the ever-present coffeepot—until Police Chief Gretchen George spoke. "There's our young juvenile delinquent from California."

Evie tripped on the rug.

That voice. That smoke-rough, nasal voice, that mocking shout out.

No. No! Don't tell them what I did.

Norma said, "Evelyn Jones, come this way, and we'll take care of your transaction."

"She has a transaction? A girl like her?" Chief George lit a cigarette.

Stacey Collins rushed at her. "You can't do that in here."

"What are you going to do about it, honey? You with your mother and your background?"

Stacey plucked the cigarette out of Chief George's fingers and looked around as if unsure where to go.

The bank president, Mr. Terwilliger, rose from his desk and offered his trash can.

Stacey headed that way.

"That is so cute." Chief George poured herself a cup of the bank's coffee. "They're so in love. Too bad about his wife."

Everyone in the bank turned into statues created of horror and embarrassment.

Chief George looked around. "What? Like you didn't know Terwilliger was married and Collins is in love with him?"

Stacey, who had been so nice to Evie, stood shaking with embarrassment.

Mr. Terwilliger stared at Stacey as if he'd heard something new.

The tellers were frozen in place. All except Norma, who was ever more frantically gesturing to Evie to come and make her deposit.

But Evie couldn't leave the situation the way it was, everyone embarrassed for Stacey Collins. So she said, "Wretchen Gretchen."

Chief George whipped around to face her. "What?"

"Wretchen Gretchen. That's what they call you, isn't it?"

A gasp rose toward the vaulted ceiling, a gasp that came from everywhere.

"No, no, no." Stacey hurried toward Evie. "You can't say that."

Wretchen Gretchen stalked toward Evie, all tough chief of police/lots of handcuffs/big handgun. "Kid, I can't believe you had the nerve to say that."

"I know." Evie cast off her slumped-shouldered, bowed-head demeanor. "Who am I to call you out? You might tell everybody that I am a juvenile delinquent. Wait. It's too late. You already did that. Your bad. You have nothing else you can use to embarrass me."

Chief George, all five foot two of her, got right in Evie's face. "I could embarrass you by arresting you for—"

"For what? Making a deposit in the Rockin American Bank?"

No sound. No breath. Only Evie and Wretchen Gretchen eye to eye, staring each other down.

Chief George broke first. "Kid, you're going to be sorry you ever came to Rockin." She stomped out of the bank.

The whole building exhaled a sigh.

Norma called, "Come here, child, before you get into more trouble." In a lower tone, she said, "That was good of you. Stacey didn't deserve that humiliation. But now I fear for your safety."

"I'll be okay." She met Norma's eyes. "I'm not doing anything wrong."

DON'T ASK ME

ON SATURDAY MORNING, EVIE came down prepared to go to her desk, and Donald said, "It's the weekend. The bank's only open this morning, so make your deposit, then take the day off. Go for a drive. Explore Rockin. Go do whatever eighteen-year-olds do. Don't get in trouble, I need you."

His words warmed her, as did the stern glance he sent her. He cared about her. It had been a long time since anyone cared.

"Call if you need me. I'll come back, no problem." She didn't think he'd call. After the first couple of days, he didn't have enough projects to keep her busy, while he appeared to be working feverishly on his computer. When she had asked if she could help, he said no, he was making sales, and glanced at the locked cabinet where the ancient-looking stuff sat behind glass doors.

When she'd first arrived, there had been more objects in there, but he'd slowly been moving pieces into boxes and sending them with her to the post office or leaving them on the porch for shipping services to pick up.

When she exclaimed about a pretty seventeenth-century enamel box, he told her to take it to her room to enjoy. She kept it on her nightstand. Last thing before she turned off her light, she looked at it, touched its smooth surface, enjoyed the brightly decorated female figures and the handsome brown dog that cavorted between them. In a weird way, it comforted her to know that with her appreciation, she kept those people and that dog alive.

Now she got her coat and keys. He'd grown noticeably thinner since she'd arrived, so she asked, "Do you want me to get you anything? You need to eat!"

He shot her a killing glance.

She stepped back.

His expression smoothed. "Thank you for worrying about me. Of course, you're right. Bring me a sandwich and some soup."

"Any preferences? Chicken noodle? Butternut squash? Roast beef? Tuna salad?"

"I don't care." He returned his gaze to his monitor.

Fine. She'd done her duty. She picked up the stack of bills, placed them in the zippered inner pocket of her new mini-backpack and skipped out the door into the garage. She pushed the button to open the garage door, and as it rose, she paused and stared out.

For the first time since she'd arrived at the house, the sun was shining. Feebly and low on the horizon, but it was shining through the trees, lifting her spirits, making her feel warm (an illusion), happy and, for the first time in a long time, young.

She started the Jag, backed out and realized she'd forgotten to set the security system. She debated with herself; should she get out into the whistling wind, run into the garage, type in the numbers, run out, leap back into the car and close the garage before the minute's delay was up? All week, every day, she'd been faithfully making sure Donald White's house and possessions were safe from intruders.

But this place was out in the boonies. She'd seen that one woman on the first day and, except for the occasional delivery driver, no one since. The doors were always locked… Donald White was a big guy and could take care of himself…

Oh, well. She'd been conscientious so far. She couldn't stop now. Payday was next week! She couldn't jeopardize that moment of pride when she showed Mama her paycheck.

Evie set the security system to Stay, then drove as fast as she could into Rockin, taking care to slow to the legal speed as she passed the city limits.

The town felt different today. At first she thought the weekend had changed the pace, but only Stacey and Norma were working the bank.

Stacey said, "I wasn't supposed to work, but the other teller called in 'sick.'" She used air quotes. "I can't believe I have to be inside today. I hope it's still light when I get everything squared away and close it down."

Evie realized the sun had made all the difference. "It'll be," she said reassuringly.

"Maybe. If a storm doesn't come in."

"The bank's not busy." Evie glanced around the lobby, empty except for the three of them. "That'll help, won't it?"

"Fingers crossed. What are you up to today?"

"I was going to see if I could find out the best spot for gamers, but maybe not. I may grab lunch and eat in the park instead."

As Norma handled the transaction, Stacey said, "It's cold, but yes. Worth freezing for a little light."

"Then groceries. Mr. White doesn't want me to get too

much at a time, but tomorrow I won't come into town because the bank's closed, so I'd better figure it out or go hungry."

Stacey's voice was cautious. "Your mysterious Mr. White sounds like a tyrant."

"He's nice. Thoughtful. He works hard."

"What's he do?"

"Sells stuff."

"What kind of stuff?"

A warning bell clanged in Evie's mind. She shouldn't give out too much information about the reclusive Donald White. "I don't ask his business."

"I thought you were his bookkeeper."

"I am, but not for that."

Stacey shot a glance at Norma. "Huh."

"Here's your receipt." Norma handed it to her, watched approvingly as Evie made sure it was correct and waved her off. "Have a nice day!"

Later Evie remembered the odd little questioning, but at the time, all she thought was *Time off! Lunch! Sunshine!*

She was so happy. Carefree, like the typical teenager she hadn't been…ever. Determined to do her chores first, she went to the grocery store, and as she pushed her cart around, she thought about what to do afterward.

She *could* go find gamers. But no, the boys were notoriously unwelcoming, and today was too nice to deal with that stupid gender divide.

She could drive around or go to the park. Even if she walked along the river facing that flesh-ripping wind, the sense of freedom would free her soul from the years and the chains of disappointment and heartache.

She got milk out of the cooler on the back wall, glanced at

the woman walking toward her down the aisle, and a shock of recognition fried her nerves.

Mama. Oh, God. Mama.

PRETEND TO BE NORMAL

EVIE BACKED UP AS fast as she could, through the swinging doors and into the grocery store's back room. She ducked down, crouched beside her cart, frozen with horror.

Mama.

Had she seen Evie?

Evie was pretty sure not. Mama had been walking slowly, looking at the yogurt, sour cream, butter. Whatever.

"Miss?"

Evie looked up and squeaked.

A tall, broad guy stood there, wiping his hands on a blood-smeared apron.

She recognized him. The butcher.

"Miss, if you're looking for the restroom, it's over there." He pointed between the stacks of boxes and the wall.

"Thanks." She didn't move.

He stared as if she was being weird. "Did you drop something?"

Because she was squatting, hugging her knees. "No." Keeping a death grip on the cart, she slowly rose.

"Are you sick?" He was a nice man, concerned.

But she couldn't pretend to be normal. Not now. *My mother is out there.*

With the newness and the bustle of the last week, she'd almost forgotten why she'd come to Rockin. Because her mother and sister lived here. It was a small town; of course she was bound to run into one of them. Both of them, eventually. For the first few days, every time she left the house, she'd thought about them. What would she do if she saw them? What would she say? Would they rush to hug her? Would she act all mature, or be the big, lonely kid she felt like inside?

Now she knew. She was hiding.

She swallowed. "Thank you." For what, she didn't know. She pushed her cart in the direction of the restroom, walked past it to the entrance to the butcher's back room and peeked out the smudged window.

She didn't see her mother. Cautiously, she pushed the doors open and looked around, first one way, then the other. She didn't see Mama. Relief ripped at her, and disappointment.

Was Mama gone?

No! Evie didn't want her to be gone. She abandoned the hindrance of her cart and walked briskly along the end aisle, scanning up and down.

There Mama was, talking to someone in the bakery. Evie could see her profile. She was beautiful: carefully made-up, neatly dressed, as curvaceous as a swimsuit model, blonde, fit. Evie's mother.

Mama smiled at the baker, who smiled back in a daze of appreciation. She headed toward the front of the store.

Evie circled around, saw her get in the checkout line. Head down, coat wrapped tightly around her, Evie hurried out to the Jag. She watched the store, saw her mother come out and put her groceries in the trunk of a Honda Civic. Mama pulled out onto the street.

Evie followed her. After a couple of turns, she knew where her mother was going. Home. Home to the neat little bungalow where she lived with Marya.

Mama pulled into the driveway.

Evie parked across the street.

As Mama approached, the automatic garage door opened. She honked as she passed the bay window; someone flung open the side door, a young woman…

Evie's sister. Marya. She was so tall, so mature, almost seventeen. Now Evie remembered—seventeen *tomorrow*. That's why Mama had spoken to the baker; Mama always made a big deal about birthdays.

Evie watched them exchange a kiss, unload the groceries, laughing and talking. They shut the garage, went inside… and closed the door.

Evie had never suffered a broken heart. Not over a guy.

But right now, her heart hurt.

Inevitably, she wondered what would happen if she walked up and knocked on the door. Would they let her in? Or would Mama block the entrance, demand an explanation, tell her to go away? Worse, Evie had changed. She was taller, thinner, her hair was long, she wore no makeup. It had been four years. Would they recognize her?

At the thought, Evie shriveled into her seat.

She had to remember her goal. Get her first paycheck. She would have something to show her mother, proof that she had turned a page in her life.

She should leave, but she stayed until the clouds covered the sun, then until sunset, then she watched the lights come on inside her family's home. She stayed until she noticed an old gentleman in the house next door peeking out his window. He might call the police. Worse, he might call her mother, who would march out and demand what Evie was doing parked there and—

Evie started the Jag and drove away. She was shivering; while she was sitting there, the car had grown cold, and not even the seat heater could warm her.

Back at the Jameson house, she used the remote to open the garage door, parked inside, collected her backpack and Donald's dinner, realized she'd forgotten to disarm the security system. The alarm went off with a violent shriek. She stabbed in the code, took a long breath and realized she'd forgotten to buy anything for herself. But she couldn't work up a give-a-damn, and she went inside.

Donald was still on his computer, tapping furiously on the keyboard, apparently uninterested in the alarm.

She paused in the doorway. "I've got your dinner."

He didn't look up. "Put it in the kitchen."

She did and went into her office to drop off the tablet and the bank receipt.

Something had changed...

He'd added another antique to the shelves behind her desk, one she'd admired in the locked cabinet. She supposed he was being kind, but right now, she didn't care. In fact, she didn't like the way he moved things around, sold them as if he cared nothing for them. Had he bought the house only to gut it?

Her gaze drifted over the photos on the desk: the happily married couple, the baby, the little family. She thought of the wall upstairs in the bedroom she occupied, all the framed snapshots haphazardly arranged to form a montage of family memories.

Those damned photographs.

She had known before that her bedroom was big, the bathroom luxurious, but now she realized she was sleeping in the master bedroom. Why? Why was she working in the big office while Donald worked in a windowless den? Why was she sleeping in the master bedroom while he slept somewhere downstairs? Or on his love seat?

Something was not right.

She hadn't explored the house. Before it had seemed intrusive, rude to Donald White.

But he didn't act as if he appreciated this beautiful home at all; it was a place for him to work, nothing more.

Earlier, she had thought of it as the Jameson home.

Now she climbed the stairs. Standing in the dark upstairs corridor, she flipped on the light. The master bedroom—her room—was the first door on the left. She started opening the other doors. A bathroom, a spare bedroom, another spare bedroom and…a nursery. Painted blue with a mural on one wall of a red car, blurred by its speed. A wooden toy box, a bed with railings, an open closet and a closed dresser. On the bed, a worn, much-loved teddy bear rested against the pillows.

THIS ISN'T RIGHT

THE BEAR WAS STARING at Evie with his one plastic eye.

She wandered across the rug, scrutinizing the framed photos on the wall. She stepped on a stray Lego, twisted her ankle, exclaimed in pain and annoyance.

The teddy bear still stared.

In the tiny bathroom, toys surrounded the tub: a selection of floating toys and a bag of stick-on men and women with various superhero uniforms. A little boy had played here in the tub, creating stories until the water wrinkled his toes.

Where was he now? Living with his grandparents?

She wandered back into the bedroom and tried not to look at the bear.

But the bear insisted.

His dark fur looked as if it had been the object of a teething child's affection, with one ear that had been stitched repeatedly. She leaned closer. He—for the bear was a boy—smelled a little like night terrors, potty training and fervent childish love.

Evie could not believe the child had left him here.

Maybe his mother had forgotten to pack him. Maybe the child had found another creature stuffed with affection. That had to be the case. Any other explanation was unacceptable. Donald White wouldn't lie.

He wouldn't.

But the teddy bear had summoned her to his side, and she had obeyed.

This isn't right.

She heard him in her head.

You know it isn't right.

She spoke out loud. "I know no such thing."

It was funny in a horrible way. She'd lived through four years of juvenile detention, and she hadn't cracked…until now. Now a stuffed bear was talking in her head.

She plucked the bear off the bed, tucked him under her arm and left the little boy's room…to meet a smiling Donald walking briskly toward her.

She jumped dramatically. She exuded guilt. She hid the bear behind her.

Donald's gaze noted her expression: frightened, defiant, worried, afraid.

Adrenaline blew through her, preparing her for flight or fight. Because Donald had never come up to the second floor, not that she knew of. And she was vulnerable.

His gaze flicked to Timothy's room behind her.

Could she run back there and lock the door?

Probably not in time.

His gaze noted the teddy bear peeking from behind her back.

Could Evie run past him to the stairs?

Impossible.

She had no chance, not if he knew anything about street fighting, but she would have to try to take him down.

"I'm done with my project." His voice was as warm and persuasive as it had ever been.

But of what was he trying to persuade her?

"I've been thinking, why should we worry about the US government investigating our contributions to the offshore fund to rescue Zone? He needs that money now. Let's go online, put ten thousand into the account, and damn the consequences!" Donald's green eyes were bright, as if they still reflected the computer screen's glow.

"If it's that easy, why haven't we been using online banking to add to the overseas account instead of me going into town?"

"Because I wanted you to establish your identity. That's important for someone like you who's doing business."

That made sense, she guessed. Yet he had turned scary, like he was on meth. Or blow. "If you make that big deposit, what kind of trouble will you get into?" *You. Because there is no we.*

"A fine, I suppose," he answered.

She was trapped in this house with him, and what was she to do? She wasn't from the area. She was a juvenile delinquent. If she went to law enforcement, well, Chief George had a case of the ass now and wouldn't care when Evie reported the rich guy she worked for had glowing eyes, wasn't eating and seemed obsessed with mailing packages to post office boxes in New York, LA and New Orleans.

"Won't the IRS get involved?" she asked.

"I have to think of that poor man, languishing in a dank prison in a foreign land, starving, tortured, waiting for his ransom to be paid." Donald didn't sound concerned. He sounded lively.

That made her regard him with even more suspicion. "Do

we know that his wife hasn't already succeeded in freeing him?"

"He's not back." Donald yawned, stretched and rubbed his eyes. "I'm exhausted."

Let's go to bed...together. Evie could almost hear him; all of her self-preservation instincts heightened. She tensed, ready to run.

He turned and headed for the stairs.

His disinterest gave her a twinge of guilt. Maybe she was being irrational. Maybe her suspicions, vague as they were, were unfounded.

"In the morning, I'll get online and make the deposit," she called.

"First thing! Make sure you do! I'm headed down to get some sleep." He waved and kept walking.

She went into the master bedroom. Her bedroom. She locked the door behind her.

On the wall there was a snapshot of a grinning two-year-old in the tub, holding the soaking wet bear out of the water. Carefully she removed the photo from its frame and turned it over. She read *Timothy and Tuddy* written in sprawling handwriting. "Come on, Tuddy," she whispered, and she carried him to her bed.

Until further notice, he would sleep with her.

SINKING AND SINKING

THAT NIGHT, EVIE DREAMED.

Of Donald White walking with glowing eyes toward her room, past her room, down the corridor until he disappeared into the smoky dark. She heard a child crying, fretful and unhappy, then a shriek…and silence.

She dreamed of sinking into a slow-flowing river. She couldn't move her legs or arms. Sinking and sinking. She realized someone had pulled the covers over her head. She couldn't breathe. She fought until she reached the surface and sat up in bed.

No covers over her head. She'd gone to sleep only a few minutes before, the sheet tucked harmlessly under her arms.

She got out of bed, went to the door, unlocked it and tiptoed to the top of the stairs.

From below, she could hear a thunderous snoring.

Donald White had collapsed at last.

Her disturbance was nothing more than a nightmare.

But it felt so real.

IF YOU DON'T DO IT, WHO WILL?

IN THE MORNING, EVIE ROSE, starving. Last night's upset had spoiled her appetite, but now, in the light of day, Tuddy looked like merely a teddy bear, and she knew there had to be a good explanation for all the stuff the Jamesons had left behind.

The father had been kidnapped by rebel nationalists.

The wife had sold the house and gone to live with her parents; probably now Timothy was crying for his Tuddy, and Michele would contact Donald and ask if she could clear out her belongings. He would let her because he was a good guy—look what he'd done for Evelyn!—and he didn't want that stuff anyway.

It all sounded good until she came downstairs and checked for Donald in the den.

Donald wasn't there. He wasn't in the kitchen or anywhere downstairs. He wasn't outside. He wasn't upstairs. Maybe he was in the basement doing his wash…

The basement.

She shivered.

Evie went to her bedroom, picked up Tuddy and hugged him to her chest. "Where else could he be?" she whispered to him and carried him with her as she looked in the garage.

The brown SUV was missing.

That didn't mean anything except that Donald had left, gone to town for a decent meal, or a smoothie, or to shop. Which he had not done the entire time she'd been here—what? A week?

She went back inside, to her office, and logged onto her computer. Nothing had changed. It looked the same as it had last night.

Her worry deepened.

No reason. It just…

Something isn't right.

"I'm hungry," she told Tuddy. Because no matter how scared she was, she needed to eat. After she ate, she would think more clearly. She could figure out what to do.

Maybe Donald White would return, and all this fuss would be for nothing.

In the kitchen, on the table, she propped the bear against the napkin holder and poured cereal into a bowl. She started for the refrigerator, turned to the bear and said, "Donald White isn't a bad guy."

Unless he was the worst guy she'd ever crossed paths with, and that was saying something.

"He hasn't done anything wrong. Not that I know of."

The bear watched her, that one black eye shining with silent challenge.

"I don't want to go in the basement."

Why not?

"He told me not to."

Why not?

"Because the stairs are steep, there's no railing, the concrete is hard, he's afraid I'll fall." She paused. "It's dark down there."

What are you afraid of?

"I'm afraid of the dark."

This isn't right. You know it's not.

"I don't have to find out what's wrong."

If you don't do it, who will?

She paced, wrapped her arms around her waist and bent her head. The silence in the house was profound, broken only by her breathing. She didn't want to find out Donald White was one of those guys like Ramous, pulling a gun and shooting into a house without knowing or caring who was inside. Even when he knew that he'd killed a child, a nine-year-old girl, he hadn't shown any remorse. Ramous was broken, separated from his feelings by a vacuum of humanity. If Donald White was like that…

"Okay!" She snatched Tuddy from the table and tucked him under her arm. "Come on. I'm not worried what I'll find."

She opened the cellar door.

The basement light was switched on, a bare lightbulb hanging from the ceiling, waiting for her to descend.

She tucked Tuddy in place to stop the door from closing. "Wait for me," she whispered and descended the stairs. A crack of sunlight from somewhere above seemed to provide Evie with a layer of protection from the smothering dark in the far corner.

Donald wasn't lying about the railing. There was none. If she fell, she would plunge to the concrete below. That knowledge heartened her. He'd told the truth about that. He'd been concerned about her.

This isn't right. You know it's not.

The gray concrete stretched out from the bottom of

the stairs. At the back wall, a shroud of plastic encased…
something…that leaked fluids and oozed toward the drain
in the middle of the floor. Something smelled rancid, as if
the chest freezer in the corner had been left open and all the
meat inside had rotted.

Evie didn't need Tuddy to tell her this wasn't right. She
knew. She *knew*.

She paced toward the bundle, moving lightly, making no
sound, as if a footfall would wake whatever rested beneath.

As she approached, the odor grew stronger.

She stopped three feet away.

She couldn't do this. She couldn't stand it.

This isn't right. You know it's not.

She did know. She swallowed terror and saliva, watched
her own hand reaching for the white plastic, saw her fingers
tremble, steady, grasp the corner and pull it back to reveal—

Faces. Two faces. A woman and a child. Swollen. Eyes
sunken. Staring. Those fluids…

She wanted to scream. She gagged with the need to scream.
She wanted to vomit. But she had nothing in her stomach.
She wanted to…

To get out of here.

To call the cops.

To save herself from Donald White, from a man who could
do this to Michele and Timothy.

Before she could move, Timothy opened his eyes. He
looked at her. Just looked at her. In Tuddy's voice, he said,
This isn't right.

Whirling, she ran, skidded on the slick concrete, recovered, bounded up the stairs, pushed the door open and in
one swoop, rescued Tuddy from his position as doorstop.
She paused. Should she race for the porch or into the house?

Where was Donald White?

The porch. She needed to be outside. As she ran, she whipped out her phone, called 9-1-1, yanked the door open—and screamed.

A woman grabbed her around the waist, tackled her, brought her down. "Where are you going?"

A cop. The chief of police. The cops had got here already.

"Thank God, you came. Bodies. There are bodies. In the basement. He killed them. Donald White killed them. They're dead. That little boy and his mother. It's so awful." She clutched at Chief George's arms and looked into her eyes. The ground was cold and hard beneath her back. "You have to find him. Stop him. Before he does it again."

"Sure."

Cold and cops were streaming around them, rushing into the house, talking to each other, into their phones, into their radios. The noise slapped at Evie, distracting her, making her babble louder. "He killed them. It's awful. I can see them—" In her mind, she could see them. Michele. And Timothy. She could hear Timothy saying, *This isn't right.*

It wasn't Tuddy she'd heard in her mind.

It was Timothy.

"Oh, God." Evie was bereft. What horror had taken possession of her life?

"Feeling sorry?" Chief George smirked. Facing the death of an innocent woman and her child, she smirked.

"What? What? Sorry? No, I…" The meaning clicked in. "You think *I* did it? You think I murdered them? No. How could you? No!"

PART THREE

ZONE

HOW LONG?

THE GUARD TOLD ZONE JAMESON his wife and son were dead, murdered by one of the female dogs who thrived in his godforsaken country. Michele and Timmy were dead, as everyone in America would soon die.

Zone had been held in a cold, dark cell for days, weeks, months...he didn't know how long. He only knew no matter how much he wanted to resist, his body demanded he eat.

So when the guard brought the food, Zone snatched up the metal plate and shoved the food in his mouth with his fingers, and when he had licked the plate he said, "Fuck you. Why would I believe you? My wife and son are alive."

The guard laughed, a great, booming laugh. "See the pictures?" He shoved a computer tablet in Zone's face.

One glimpse.

One view.

One sight of Michele's still, white face, of Timmy's blind, staring eyes.

Zone couldn't... He couldn't believe...

His wife, heat and body and come-hither smiles and the memory of her love that kept him alive through his imprisonment.

His son. Teething, drooling, a sturdy body toddling toward him, arms flung up, wanting hugs and kisses. His innocent little boy attacked. Murdered.

Both of them murdered.

The guard laughed again.

Zone, emaciated, broken, half-mad from loneliness and terror, rose to his feet.

He made the guard scream.

When the others rushed in, Zone had the guard on the cell floor, beating his brains out on the rough stone. The guards kicked him, grabbed him, stood him up and thrashed him with rods and sticks and...

He didn't wake up for a week. Maybe longer. A passage of time marked by light and dark and him not being able to respond even in his mind. When he came to consciousness, all was pain. His jaw burned, his ribs stabbed at him, his hip was broken. He rested on a mattress on a floor. Still a cell, still in the mountains, sure, but no longer in the depths of a dungeon. Here, light leaked through a window, and the man who watched him had shrewd cold eyes.

The man explained that he was Adham, leader of the rebel nationalists fighting to free Magara from the northern oppressors...

Zone faded during the tirade and came back when he heard "All the other American prisoners have been released. You were not. You were unconscious. That would be bad publicity."

"What else?" Zone knew there had to be more to it than that. The rebels were fighting a constant, desperate battle against a superior force. They didn't want an extra mouth to feed.

"We need you. We use the artifacts dug from the ground to pay for our weapons, our technology. I have read your credentials."

Might as well be hung for a sheep as a lamb. With insult in his voice, Zone asked, "You can read?"

Adham smiled unpleasantly. "I graduated from École Polytechnique. Yes. I can read." In French he added, "And in more languages than you, American."

He could be lying. But if he was, good job. The mere weight of his claim convinced Zone of its truth.

"To sell our artifacts for the proper amount," Adham said, "they need to be authenticated, and you—you are the man to do it."

Adham was correct. Zone was the man to do it. When he picked up an authentic artifact, he could feel the buzz of history. He felt the bustle of the workshop where it had been created, the intense concentration of the artist, the hope of beauty and the intent of genius. He dated the material more accurately than anyone alive. "If I refuse?"

"The world believes you're dead, and I, Adham, will make sure that is the truth."

Zone turned his face to the wall. "I don't care. Kill me. I have no reason to wish for life."

Adham took Zone's broken jaw—the pain made Zone see double—and yanked his face toward the window's light. He leaned close. "You are not so shattered as you would like to believe. You want vengeance on the woman who murdered your wife and son. You want to bathe your hands in her blood."

Zone stared into those pale blue, killer eyes, smelled the

sour breath, wished to hell that the desire for revenge hadn't stirred in him. "Let me see her."

"Who?"

"The woman who killed my wife and son. Let me see her picture. Prove to me she exists."

Adham shrugged, let go of Zone's chin, pulled his phone from his pocket—the rebel nationalists kept on top of the newest technology—did a search and handed it to Zone. "There."

In a news story from Rockin, Alaska, the bold headline read *California Juvenile Allegedly Kills Local Doctor and Son*. In sub-caps: *Doctor's Husband Held by Terrorists*. The photo showed a pretty, tearful teenager in handcuffs being escorted by the police into the local jail.

Evelyn Jones, the caption read.

Zone zoomed in on Evelyn Jones. He memorized the features, an odd mixture of Asian and Northern European. He read the story, memorized the words, went onto the next story about the start of the trial, read her protestations of innocence—and he hated her. Evelyn Jones was alive, making up stories about a man who had brought her to the house, who claimed he owned the property, a man who no one could discover through any record—and Zone's wife and son were dead, rotting in the ground.

Zone was rotting, too, in this prison, and he wanted out. He wanted to find this murdering whore, confront her, demand an explanation.

No. No. He wanted to see Evelyn Jones die.

He was angry about Michele. Yes, he was.

But what kind of person killed a small, helpless boy?

He looked up into Adham's eyes. "How long?"

"How long what?"

"How long do I play your game until you let me go?"

Adham's eyes shifted to the side. "A year."

Fucking liar. Zone's lips cracked as they formed the words. But he didn't say it out loud. Because if he was to get vengeance, he had to survive.

THE WAY IS OPEN

ADHAM BROUGHT ANTIQUITIES TO be verified.

Sometimes he brought in fakes to see if Zone knew what he was doing.

Zone always tossed those aside with contempt.

Sometimes Zone picked up a piece of the ancient world and felt the age, the depth, the worship of days past…and because he hated his captors and their cause, he lied. He told them the pieces were minor, worth little, and pretended that he cared nothing about their eventual destination. It wasn't true, but it saved those pieces from being placed with a collector in a home with sophisticated security; he knew at least those pieces could be rescued.

He began to plot how he would rescue himself. He imagined grabbing his guards' guns. He thought he would knock them out, grab their keys and release himself from his cell. The fight he imagined was always a terrible battle…and how would he win? His broken hip had not healed well. He walked with a limp.

If he was going to survive to destroy Evelyn Jones, he had to play it smart.

One day: shouting, shooting.

Everyone disappeared. Adham, the guards... No one came with his meals. No one paced the prison corridors. He was alone, trapped in a cell, dying of hunger, of thirst. Minutes turned into hours. Hours turned into days. He knew the rebels who had imprisoned him were now all dead. He was dying, too...

In his head, he heard Adham. *You have to live, or they die unavenged. What feeble kind of man would allow that murderous woman to survive when she had destroyed everything he loved?*

Zone staggered over to the door of his cell. He shouted and begged. He beat his fists on the wood—and the door creaked open.

He stared at the widening gap.

The door wasn't locked.

He pushed it open, looked up and down the corridor.

He heard no sound.

No one was in sight.

He was free.

The guard had forgotten to lock it.

Fuck it all to hell. Zone could have been out days ago.

With his shoulder, he pushed the door open all the way, shuffled into the corridor, looked up and down.

He heard no sound.

No one was in sight.

He was free.

He staggered on his feet. He walked to the left, the direction from which his guard always came, and found an overturned desk surrounded by a flurry of papers.

No one was in the caves. No one except him.

He walked farther, found the primitive kitchen with fire

pits filled with cold ash and half-cooked meals. Half-cooked was good enough for him; he took the serving spoon and ate whatever slop was in the pots, and when he'd satisfied the worst of his hunger, he knelt and lit a fire. He cooked flat breads on the heating stones. Careless, perhaps, and audacious, considering the constant state of war up here, but he had to get to the capital and the American Embassy, and to do that, he needed food, clothes and ammunition.

Within two hours, he had filled his pack, dressed himself in rebel clothing, gathered discarded firearms and for the first time in fourteen months, he headed outside.

The mountains were high. Winter was coming.

A week later, he limped into the American Embassy.

PART FOUR

EVIE

THE FACTS

EVIE PLEADED INNOCENT, BUT...

But a neighbor had called in a report. She'd seen Evie driving the road in Michele's Jaguar.

No one had seen Michele and Timmy for two weeks.

No one in Rockin or in the neighborhood had ever laid eyes on Donald White.

All packages had been sent in her name.

She had an expensive enamel box in her bedroom and a new tablet with all the Jameson passwords and codes.

According to all evidence, Donald White did not exist.

When Evie insisted he did, that he had owned the house, she was told the title was held by Zone and Michele Jameson.

When she said he had lived in that house, she was told the home's security video showed no evidence of him.

The state trooper who had stopped her and Donald White would have been an unassailable witness to his existence, but her surname, Johnson, was one of the most common in Alaska, and Evie didn't know her first name. If only she'd been given a warning ticket... But Donald White had cajoled Officer Johnson, and Evie had been given a reprieve, and she had been *grateful*.

According to the forensics specialist, the decomposition of the bodies started the morning after Evie arrived.

She remembered Donald coming out of the basement, but no one listened when she said he must have murdered them and placed the bodies in the chest freezer and removed them when she arrived from California. No one listened when she said he must have wiped down the house to eliminate his fingerprints and cleaned away any evidence of DNA.

No one listened because...

Because Evie had a record. She'd been involved in a drive-by shooting that resulted in a child's death. Which should have cleared her—her caseworkers knew she'd come to Alaska for a job with Donald White.

But the guy who had handled her case had quit. Regina before him had quit. The records had been misfiled or accidentally deleted. No one cared enough to find either of the officials or to locate the records because...

Evie had called out the chief of police for what she was: petty, nasty and vengeful. She'd made Wretchen Gretchen look bad, and Wretchen Gretchen *wanted* to convict her.

Most damning, as Norma and Stacey reluctantly verified, every day Evie had transferred money into an offshore account—an account in her own name.

She hadn't understood that that account would be evidence of motive.

To law enforcement and to the public who watched the trial in avid horror, Evie had murdered a woman and a child for her own cold-blooded profit.

She was the only suspect in a sensational case.

On May 13, in a Rockin, Alaska, courtroom, Evelyn Jones

was convicted of the first degree murders of Michele and Timothy Jameson.

She received ninety-nine years, the maximum, and was sentenced to serve her time at an Alaska State Correctional Facility.

ON THE WAY

ON A COOL SPRING DAY, the bus that would take Evie to the state correctional facility parked in the alley behind the Rockin jail.

As Evie shuffled out, shackles restricting her movements, rain fell on her head, the smell of garbage from the dumpster made her feel sick, and she looked around the alley, hoping to see a familiar, loving face.

There was only a reporter calling her name and snapping photos, and strangers, cold and staring, wanting a last glimpse of the Jameson baby killer.

During the long weeks of her incarceration and trial, her mother and sister had never come. All those hours alone in the cell, haunted by the death she'd witnessed, by Timmy's eyes opening and his voice saying, *This isn't right.*

Down in the basement of the Jameson home, she'd had a mental breakdown. She must have; it was the only explanation for her vision of Timmy. She wanted to tell her mother about it, be comforted and reassured, told that she was not evil or crazy or cruel.

And she knew it was stupid, but she kept thinking Donald White had never paid her, so she never got to show Mama her paycheck—and her good intentions.

But neither Mama nor Marya were there.

Evie's orange prison jumpsuit hung on her skinny frame. Shackles encircled her wrists and ankles; iron cuffs connected by chains to the thick leather belt around her waist. The gear weighed her down; the first potent taste of incarceration.

She lifted her foot to take a step onto the bus.

The short length of chain caught her ankle.

She fell up the stairs, bruised her arm and her ribs.

Wretchen Gretchen laughed.

So did the female guard and both female inmates already aboard.

The driver said, "Hurry up! I've got a schedule. I've got to get home for my kid's birthday party."

"Don't tell her about your kid," the guard said. "She'll want to murder him."

"Oh!" The driver turned to stare at Evie. "Is she the one?"

One of the inmates said, "Baby killer."

They all knew her. They all hated her with their eyes.

It had been the same in the jail. The other prisoners from across the borough were drug addicts, thieves, prostitutes. They despised Evie because they believed she had killed Michele and Timmy. They wouldn't let her sleep. The ones who did the laundry peed on her clothes. Her food always tasted funny and made her sick. Evie should have been used to the animosity.

But how did someone grow indifferent to hatred?

The guard pushed Evie past the cage that protected her and the driver from the criminals they transported. About halfway down the aisle, she shoved Evie into a seat nowhere near the other inmates. Using a master key she kept in her waist pack, she locked Evie's shackles to the metal chair leg. "I'm Barb Husvich," she said. "If Alaska had the death penalty, I'd be honored to flip the switch for your electrocution."

She walked back to the front, shut the cage door and locked it.

As the bus pulled out, Evie watched, but no sign of Mama or—

Wait! There's Marya!

Evie lunged toward the window, wanted to wave at her sister, to let her know she'd been seen.

The chains on her ankles yanked her back.

She shouted, she struggled, over and over she called Marya's name.

Marya waved and threw kisses, although there was no way she could see Evie through the dark tint and the confining wires on the window.

Then she was gone, the bus passed through Rockin's streets on the way out of town, and Evie was with people who edged away from her as if she was insane.

"Are you going to start frothing at the mouth, too?" one of the convicts asked.

Barb was standing at the front, holding her cell phone pointed at Evie. "Keep it up, sister, and you'll be the star of my social-media pages."

She was filming Evie's misery.

The bus turned on the bypass that led to Highway 3 and soon left Rockin behind.

Evie was on her way to prison.

BURIED ALIVE

EVIE STARED OUT THE window at a world she would never see again.

As the trial had unfolded and evidence had been produced, Evie had been forced to realize how thoroughly Donald White had conned her.

She realized, too, she had lived with a man who had murdered a woman and a child, plotted his own disappearance and calculated Evie's apparent guilt down to the last detail—without a shred of remorse. She remembered those times when she'd said the wrong thing, and he'd moved close, and she thought now if she'd been smarter about him, he would have killed her, too.

Death would have been better than the courtroom, the jail, Wretchen Gretchen with her sneering face and her wandering hands...

God. Wretchen Gretchen was nothing but a nasty perv, threatening Evie, groping Evie, making lewd suggestions, until Evie had swung her braid and nailed her in the face.

Wretchen Gretchen punched her in the gut—she didn't want anyone to witness bruises on Evie's face—and after that allowed some privileged folks access to the jail to view Evie in her cell.

Evie curled in the corner of her bed, head turned toward the wall, like a lark trapped in a cage. She didn't sleep, she barely ate. She had no appetite, and the food was tainted.

When Wretchen Gretchen noticed, she said, "Listen, kid, if you think you're going to take away my hour of glory with your suicide, you're stupid. I'll have a tube shoved down your throat. In fact, I'll gladly do it myself."

Evie still had enough spark to say, "Make the food eatable or be damned."

The food improved, and Evie consumed enough to survive.

Now the bus driver slammed on the brakes hard enough to make Evie thump forward and then back and Barb fall against the windshield and soundly curse him.

"The river's over the bridge," he said. "It's this damn warm spring weather and the rain melting the snow."

Barb struggled to her feet. "What are we going to do? Take the long way around?"

"I told you, I have to get home for my kid's…" He glanced back at Evie in loathing. He made a decision, ground the gears and made a U-turn in the road. "I know a shortcut."

He turned onto a narrow road and drove into the mountains.

The motion, the twists and turns, the shadows flashing light and dark…

"I'm going to be sick," Evie said softly, then louder, "Barb, I'm going to throw up."

"Don't call me Barb. You call me ma'am!"

"Ma'am, I'm going to throw up." Evie swallowed, and swallowed again. She'd always been this way, carsick on windy roads, but it had been so long since it last occurred, she thought, hoped, it wouldn't happen again.

"Oh, you want me to unlock you from your seat? You, a baby killer? A crazy person who tries to break her chains and escape out the window?" Barb mocked her mercilessly.

"I wasn't trying to escape, I was trying—"

One of the inmates gave a jeering laugh.

Evie repeated, "I'm telling you, I'm going to throw up."

Another inmate said, "She doesn't look good. Maybe you should put her in the lav."

Barb said, "She might as well get used to not getting her own way. It's going to be an ugly surprise when she—"

Evie leaned over and tossed her cookies right there in the aisle. Only she didn't have many cookies to toss, so mostly she made retching sounds that made the other inmates gag and Barb curse louder.

Barb retrieved the master key from her waist pack, unlocked the gate that separated the inmates from her and the driver, and stalked down the aisle. She freed Evie's shackles from the metal chair, then unlocked her wrists from the leather restraint belt at her waist. Throwing a wad of tissue at her, she yelled, "Clean it up!"

Evie threw up again.

"You little bitch." Barb dragged her to her feet and shoved her into the lavatory at the back of the bus and locked the door behind her.

As the bus swayed and swerved, Evie crouched over the toilet, gagging, holding on to the rim, in a narrow windowless room.

The convicts and Barb could hear Evie's misery, and they snickered.

Evie thought she was going to die in confinement, spasming in misery, tasting sickness. Then—

Then the bus rolled as if it had been hit by a wave. Rolled and rolled.

The women outside the lavatory screamed.

Evie was thrown around that tiny compartment. Her face hit the toilet and her bones…broke.

She put out her arms to protect her head.

One arm broke.

Her ribs cracked.

She churned like a rock in a tumbler. She could hear the bus snap and crumple, on and on, as if the whole frame was being wadded up by a giant's hand.

When the wild movement stopped, the bus was pitched forward, hood down, headlights and front bumper scraping along.

The women's screaming grew fainter. The ceiling was collapsing. The side of the bus bulged in. The compartment was closing.

Evie's heart pounded. Sweat and blood and vomit drenched her. She held her broken arm close against her side. Her other hand shook as she struggled to open the door.

What had happened?

What was happening?

Finally the pressure broke the lock, but the door was caught at the top and the bottom. She could see through the crack… into a rising sea of mud.

The bus had been caught up in the soon-to-be famed Licking Mudslide.

ESCAPE TO LIFE

THE OTHER PRISONERS WERE no longer screaming.

That silence. Evie would never unhear that silence, nor forget the sight of the top of a head and two cuffed hands outstretched, reaching out of the mud, pleading for help.

As the mud carried the bus along, it was sinking.

But the opposite back corner of the bus was still free, and the blast of mud had peeled away the glass and wire of the window.

I have to get out.

She used her good arm to clear blood from her eyes, and saw movement.

Barb climbed the side of the bus, clutching at the benches and the metal window frames, staying ahead of the surging mud, all her focus on that open window.

Evie screamed, "Help me. Barb…ma'am…please! Pass the keys!"

Barb grinned like the savage she was, patted the pack at

her waist, said, "Sucks to be you," and went out the window, leaving Evie to drown in mud, pain and terror.

The pressure on the bus continued to buckle and twist the bathroom door and the door frame. Suddenly, Evie had an opening large enough for a half-starved female to squeeze through.

And she was out, into the remaining space of the bus, seeing the ooze rise in a threatening tide. She did as Barb had done, using the metal window frames and balancing on benches, crying from pain yet climbing toward that window.

Evie needed out before the mud rose to consume her. But what if she slipped, put her foot into the cold, thick stew, made contact with one of the other prisoners?

They were dead. She hoped to God they were dead.

The broken glass sliced her fingers. Her maimed arm could barely hold her weight.

The bus lurched and rolled. She lost her footing, found herself dangling above the mud, so injured she couldn't lift herself through to freedom.

The mud in the bus rose to touch her foot. In her mind, she could imagine the other prisoners, cold and dead, yet struggling to reach up and pull her down to join them.

Galvanized by terror, she shot through the window, squeezed herself out like a newborn out of the birth canal.

As she floundered away from the bus, the mud sucked it down. It disappeared from sight, and she was alone in a landscape as bleak and cold as the surface of the moon.

For miles around her, the mud still flowed, a heavy black liquid that carried white spruce like driftwood on ocean waves. She looked around and up at the mountains.

The peak above her...was gone. The entire top of the mountain had given way, taking with it tons of glistening wet mud, ancient boulders, trees as old as time.

The road had disappeared. No one was in sight. Nothing was alive. Not even a bird took wing. All that was left of the world was creeping, wet, black earth that longed to swallow her and take her to a premature grave.

Evie had to move.

She took the path of least resistance. She walked downhill.

Every breath was agony. Her arm, her face, her ribs…

Yet she couldn't stop. With every step, she sank into the mud to her knees, hoisted herself up, took another step and sank.

Iron cuffs circled her ankles.

The chains connecting them to the leather restraint belt restricted every movement.

Iron cuffs circled her wrists.

She staggered. She fell.

She reached out. Her hands sank into the muck, which stopped short of the iron cuffs. As she struggled up, she glanced over her shoulder and up the slope.

Massive spruces rolled down sideways, slid down with roots and crowns extended. Each tree sought to catch her, carry her, bury her—and she could not run.

The mud was Alaska-spring-ground cold, and as she struggled, she was both freezing and sweating. At the same time, the chill numbed her pain and kept her moving through this weird, mad, desolate wonderland.

When Evie found Barb, the guard was facedown in the ooze. She'd been captured by Evie's nightmare, brought down by the trunk of a massive spruce as the slick mud carried it toward the valley. Barb's feet had tangled in the roots, pulled out from underneath her. She had struggled. Clearly, she had struggled, but inevitably the tree had won, then had come to a temporary halt below her body.

Barb was dead, already cold.

Evie was halfway dead, too…but Barb held the key to her chains.

Evie couldn't give up. Not now.

She pulled the waist pack off Barb's body.

With fingers that trembled with excitement, fear and hypothermia, she tried the locks that held the cuffs on her wrists.

They opened at once.

If Evie could have moved, she would have danced.

This triumph was a sign of hope, the first in many long months.

Cautiously, she sat on the log on the uphill side. It felt steady, and she could lean down and reach her ankles.

The locks were so caked in mud, she couldn't get the key into either hole.

Barb had a bottle of water in her pack, and even though Evie longed for a drink, she used the water to rinse out the locks. After many futile, panicked tries, she freed her ankles.

But no matter what she did, she couldn't get the key to unlock the belt at her waist.

For a few minutes, she'd had a vision of freedom. Of at least dying free. But that damned leather restraint… She ran out of water trying to clean and open it.

Finally, in desperation, she stripped.

She was thin, so thin that when the prison jumpsuit was gone, she was able to push the thick leather over her skinny hips and off.

She rolled Barb over, removed her clothes and her identification. She dressed herself and hid the jumpsuit and the chains under Barb's body…and shoved her deeper into the mud. Evie used a broken branch to bury Barb and felt no regret for the heartless woman who had left her to die.

She didn't know how much farther she staggered. Not far,

she suspected, but she didn't really remember much more of her journey.

She could barely see or breathe for the swelling in her face. She could only gasp for air, and soon she was walking blind.

Then her throat began to close.

She didn't hear the helicopter flying low, desperately searching for survivors. She only knew that, when the paramedics tried to put her in the basket to lift her out of there, she fought them.

Even as they spoke kindly to her, gave her drugs, sedated her, one thought wholly possessed her.

She had not survived *this* to go to prison.

Somehow, she would escape.

NEW FACE

THEY TRANSPORTED EVIE TO the medical center in Anchorage. The physicians performed surgeries and more surgeries on her arm and face. Months of hospitalization followed, and months in the convalescent wing.

Barb's family visited, taking their moment of fame from Barb's tragedy. They didn't realize Evie was not their daughter, sister, cousin. No one figured out that Evie wasn't Barb… except the plastic surgeon who worked on her face. He told Evie it wasn't possible for him to recreate the bone structure to approximate her former appearance.

She understood what he was saying.

She asked what he wanted for her silence. She thought blackmail or rape.

Instead he said, "Sometimes God gives a second chance. It's up to you to be worthy."

He was a good man, and he reminded Evie that good people existed.

He was also one fabulous plastic surgeon.

The next spring, when it was time to take off the bandages, to remove the last of the stitches, Dr. VanHooser came to her alone, and while he worked, he told her Barb's family had called a news conference. They wanted her to speak about her ordeal. Barb's mother had written a book about Barb, and they wanted the publicity for book sales.

The hospital was invested in the press conference, too.

He said there was a lot of public interest in the miracle survivors of the Licking Mudslide, specifically in Evie because her recovery had been so laborious. Cameras and reporters were lining up in the conference area.

Then Dr. VanHooser showed her her new face. Evie could barely stand to look in the mirror, but when she did... Her face was still swollen and bruised, but she didn't look like Evie, and she definitely didn't look like Barb.

She didn't know who she was, but she knew she couldn't go to a press conference.

Dr. VanHooser handed her a prepacked backpack and a wallet with money and told her to go to Hawley Foggo at the Midnight Sun Fishing Camp for a job. He said if she was willing to work for cheap, Hawley wasn't too fussy about things like social security numbers or background checks.

That was the truth.

She got a job.

No one ever found the wreckage of the bus or Barb's body. No one knew Evie was alive.

She was lucky.

Except she didn't immediately go to Midnight Sun.

First, she went home...to her mother.

CLEARING THE FOG

EVIE STOOD, SHOULDERS HUNCHED under the burden of her backpack, in the line to get on the bus. She kept her head down, her dyed brown hair hanging over her face, her ticket clutched tightly in her hand.

The ticket had put a dent in the cash Dr. VanHooser had given her. The guy who had sold her the ticket had determinedly not looked at her. He insisted he could send the e-ticket to her phone, then acted weird when she said she didn't have a phone. After making a fuss about his broken printer, he'd finally handed over a paper ticket.

The line to get on the bus was full of scary people, strange, silent people who watched her out of the corners of their eyes.

Did they recognize her? Would they hurt her?

The driver took her ticket and said, "I don't want no trouble on my bus."

"No, sir." She scampered up the stairs, down the aisle and slid into the first window seat. She looked out at the street, watched the rest of the line shuffle onto the bus, avoided all eye contact—and jumped when a lady plopped down beside her and loudly asked, "What happened to your face?"

Evie looked at her with wide eyes. "What?"

"Your face? It's warped."

Evie assessed the woman and decided something wasn't quite right. She was in her midtwenties, blonde, sunburned, facial skin peeling. She smelled like garbage. She was loud. She lacked social skills.

And everybody on the bus was straining to hear Evie's answer.

"I, um…" She didn't want to remind them of the woman who had survived the landslide, the one who was supposed to have a press conference and was a no-show. She didn't want to be associated with the accident ever again; someone would figure it out. So what should she say?

"Did he hit you?" the woman blared.

"What?" Evie should have thought this through.

"The guy you live with. Did he beat you up?"

Dazzled by the excuse, so believable, so likely, Evie blared back, "Yes. Yes, he did. That's why I'm all, um—"

"You look rough, and one ear is smaller than the other." This woman might be peculiar, but she was observant. "You running away?"

"Yeah?"

"Where you getting off?"

"Rockin."

"Oh, Rockin." The woman pronounced it like the adjective. Or maybe she was giving approval. "You got somewhere to stay?"

"I think so." If her mother would take her in.

"Good. They're kind of snotty there." The woman offered her hand, and when Evie didn't stick hers out fast enough, she grabbed it and forcibly shook. "I'm Weezy. Louise, but don't call me that. I hate that name."

"Sure. I'm, um, Evie."

"Petie? Petunia, am I right? Petie's better."

"Petie is good." Really good.

"This bus will stop at every podunk town and take forever to get to Fairbanks. I can't remember why I'm going there. But it's the seat of the Fairbanks North Star Borough!" While Weezy talked, the passengers settled in, the driver shut the door and the bus left Anchorage headed north, following the same route Evie had driven with Donald White.

Curiously, she remembered very little of that time; lifting that tarp in the basement had caused a mental break, or the trial and the miscarriage of justice had broken her, or the mudslide and her escape from the bus had bent her mind, but the details of those days in the Jameson house had grown foggy. If she didn't do something, she'd forget it all. "I've got to remember what he looks like!" she said aloud, interrupting Weezy's monologue.

Weezy stopped talking. "The guy who hit you?"

"The guy who destroyed me."

"I can draw." Weezy reached into her backpack and pulled out a drawing pad. She thrust it into Evie's hands. "Look!"

Evie flipped open to the first page. "Wow." Weezy wasn't bragging. It was the truth. This wasn't drawing; it was art. "How did you learn to do this?"

"I always knew." Weezy watched Evie flip through the pages. "My mother was good at art. I mean, really good. When she was in the institution, she was better than the art teacher. The teacher didn't like that."

The lady across the aisle said, "You're Louise Larson! I have one of your pieces. You called it *Winter Dark*."

"Oh. That was a bad time. I was angry." Weezy squinted

as if she could see into the past. Her voice got soft. "A bad time. I'm better now."

"My husband was upset because I spent a hundred dollars on it. Now it's worth a thousand, and he's upset because I won't sell it." The lady leaned across the aisle and put her hand on Weezy's. "I could never part with it. It makes me see...differently."

"I'm glad you like it." Weezy's voice modulated, and for a moment, Evie saw the flash of a woman sure of her gift. "Hold on to it for a few years. When I die, it'll be worth ten thousand. Hold on to it long enough, and you'll get six figures."

The lady across the aisle sat with wide eyes. "But I don't want to sell it."

"You'll have to. The insurance alone will cost you a fortune," Weezy told her.

Evie began to understand. "You're a famous artist."

"I could be. If I didn't have the episodes. Sometimes I see the world and it's all...it looks like your face. It's wrong." Weezy shook as if in pain, then reached into her bag, pulled out a pack of charcoal pencils, precisely sharpened. She took the sketch pad away from Evie and opened it to a clean page. "Okay, Petie, tell me what he looks like, this killer of yours."

"I didn't say he was a killer!" *Please don't recognize me. Please don't recognize me.* She didn't want to be the center of attention, but everyone on the bus was still listening.

"Start with his eyes. You'll always remember his eyes. Caucasian?"

"Yes."

"Wide? Narrow?"

"Wide. Wide-spread. Innocent."

Weezy nodded and sketched eyes in the middle of the page.

"Nice lashes," Evie said.

Weezy feathered in the lashes. "Brows?"

"Nicely shaped. Really perfect."

"You think he had them waxed?"

"Maybe. Yes. I wouldn't be surprised. He liked being handsome."

"Don't tell me he was handsome." Weezy used one dirty finger to turn Evie's head toward the window. "Look out there, picture him and tell me the shape of his jaw."

Weezy talked Evie through the drawing, asking what seemed like random questions, repeating some questions, making sounds of disgust when Evie wavered on her answers. Evie could hear her scribbling, erasing, and while she longed to look, Weezy insisted she talk about his nose, whether his nostrils moved when he breathed or if the bridge of his nose was strong enough to hold up glasses.

The bus stopped at one small town after another, dropping people off, picking people up. Evie got hungry and thirsty, but Weezy wouldn't let her get off to get anything; Weezy was obsessed.

Finally when it was dark outside, Weezy said, "That's about the best I can do," and thrust the sketchbook into Evie's hands.

In the dim overhead night-light, Evie stared. Weezy had somehow captured more than just the resemblance of Donald White; she had captured his personality, his profound disregard for anyone but himself. "That's him," she said softly.

"I've seen him before."

Evie looked from the drawing to Weezy. "Him? Or someone like him?"

"Him." Weezy pulled an aerosol out of her bag, lightly sprayed the charcoal and waited while it dried. "I met him in the psychiatric institute. What did you say his name was?"

"I didn't." Because she hadn't wanted to associate herself with the trial. But she trusted Weezy. "Donald White."

"That wasn't it. But the last name was a color, and the first initial was the same..." Weezy squinted into the past. "Davey. That was it. Davey."

"Why was he in the institute?"

"He killed his older brother. Davey was a kid, early teens. The mother insisted he had to be guilty. She made the cops investigate, and yep. Davey admitted to it, said the brother kept him from being the favorite. He was surprised when no one thought that was a good reason for murder. They put him away. I'll say this for him, he learned the ropes in a hurry."

Evie watched in amazement as Weezy tore the drawing from her pad, tucked it into a large envelope with a thin piece of cardboard and handed it to Evie. When it came to art and seeing beneath the surface, she was the master.

Weezy continued, "Davey convinced his psychiatrist that she had cured him, and the warden that he was in love with him. Davey got everything he wanted—and he got out. I hadn't seen him again before today." Weezy looked sharply at Evie. "Beating you up like that doesn't seem like his bit."

"He didn't do it personally. It happened because of him."

"Sure. He's good at setting events in motion. Events that benefit him." Weezy tapped the envelope in Evie's hand. "Treat it with care. Charcoal's notoriously fragile. Good luck with the hunt."

"What hunt?"

"Better get off now."

Evie realized that while she'd been focused on Weezy and the sketch, the bus had arrived in Rockin.

She thanked Weezy with a fervent squeeze of her hand, got off and started walking.

MOTHERS AND SISTERS

IT WAS EARLY MORNING when Evie got to her mother's house. It looked the same as last winter; a narrow, two-story, white bungalow with dark green trim and a white picket fence. Spring bulbs poked their heads out of the flower beds. She lingered on the sidewalk, held by a fear unlike any other she had faced in her ordeal.

When she realized the identity of the stranger on her doorstep, would she even let Evie in? More important, was she even home?

Someone was, because someone passed by the living room window, then by a side window toward the back of the house.

Evie walked up the driveway toward the garage, opened the gate, shut it behind her and walked to the side door. She stood, fist raised, wanting to knock.

The door jerked open.

They were face-to-face.

Her mother.

And Evie.

Both were startled.

Evie should explain who she was. Because how could anyone recognize her with her changed features?

But Ioana's face crumpled. "My baby." Without needing a word or a second glance, Ioana knew her. She pulled Evie into her embrace. "My Evie. You're alive. You're alive."

Evie cried. Even with her broken, rearranged face, her mother knew her.

The moment lasted ten seconds.

Ioana caught her breath, muttered, "We can't do this here. Old Mr. Gagnon sees everything," and yanked Evie inside. She shut the door and locked it, closed the blinds, came back and hugged Evie again, held her and rocked her. "How is this miracle possible?"

"Mama, it's such a long story, and I'm so hungry."

That was all it took. Ioana whipped into action, and in ten minutes Evie was eating last night's *chaladnik*, her mother's cold beet soup with rye bread, and a glass of milk.

Ioana took a container of *kalduny*, her own beef-and-potato dumplings, out of the freezer and put water on the stove to boil. "Feeling better? You must tell me how you came alive. What did they do to your beautiful face?" When her mother was excited, as she was now, her Belarusian accent strengthened.

Evie thought she'd never heard anything so good.

"Your hair. Such a tangle. Wait. I will brush it." Ioana rushed out of the room and returned immediately with a natural-bristle brush. The water came to a boil, so she dropped the brush, gathered the dumplings and tossed them in. "They'll be ready in a few minutes. Can you wait that long?"

"I can't. Do you know how long it's been since I've had your dumplings?"

Ioana gave a sob. "Five years. Now, tell me, Evie, what

happened. How did you come to be in Rockin that winter? How do you come to be at my table now?"

Evie put down her spoon and started talking.

Before she was done, Ioana had called her real estate office, coughed delicately and taken the day off.

Evie was impressed. Her mother had an ironclad work ethic. In all her life, Ioana had never faked a sick day.

Evie and Ioana finished the soup, the bread, the dumplings with sour cream, and her mother had fried *syrniki*, a cheese pastry, and served it with strawberry *varenye*. More than once, they interrupted their feast and Evie's story to embrace, cry and exchange protestations of love.

Evie was happily stuffed and happily convinced that at last her mother understood her.

But when the morning had passed and the afternoon began, Ioana glanced at the clock and said, "You need to go. Marya will be home soon."

Evie felt the same way she'd felt all those years ago when her mother had slapped her: shocked, shaken and forced to face a dark reality. "But, Mama...no one knows I'm alive. I could stay here..."

"No. No. You said you have a job at a fishing camp in western Alaska. You must go to it."

"Mama, no one has found the wreckage of the bus or Barb's body. No one knows I'm alive. We can tell people I'm your cousin from Belarus. I've been lucky!"

"Shh! Don't brag about your good luck. It can turn in an instant—and you cannot stay here."

"Why? Why?" The cry came from Evie's heart. "Why do you love Marya better than me?"

"Love her better than you? I don't—" Mama took a long breath. "Do you know what happened to her after you were arrested for the Jameson murders? What they said to her in school? How they treated her? She came home bruised, beaten up. I went to the principal's office and demanded they protect her. They said she started the fights. She stopped talking to me."

"I didn't kill them!"

"I know that. That doesn't protect Marya. We have to protect Marya."

"*We?* What about *me?*"

Mama stood, fetched the brush, gathered Evie's hair in her hands and gently pulled the brush through the ends. "In Belarus, when my father was alive, we were a family. Him, my mother, my three sisters."

Mama had never talked about her life in Belarus. Evie knew if she was speaking now, she should listen...even if she didn't want to. "I didn't know you had a big family."

"My father was a teacher. An educator. He taught English. He stood up for justice and punished the wrong child. The child of an official." Mama worked the brush up Evie's hair, untangling as she went. "They came for him in the night, and he was gone forever. My mother...she went to seek him. She never returned. My older sister went on the streets to feed us. One night she didn't come back. We were starving. My second sister went to the authorities, and they took us into custody. Into an orphanage. My second sister—"

Almost at once, Evie realized she was going to lose this combat. Because this story showed her what her mother had survived in the past and how she viewed the future. Gently she asked, "What was your sister's name, Mama?"

"She was Ana-Maria." Mama plucked a tissue from the decorative box on the counter, swiped at her nose and returned to brushing Evie's hair. "One of the men who ran the orphanage took a liking to her, and she disappeared. I didn't know what happened to her, either. It was me and my youngest sister. She was Mihaela. A sweet girl, only five when we entered the orphanage."

Mama sounded even sadder than she had before, so sad Evie wanted to cover her ears. She didn't want to hear this.

"Mihaela was a delicate child. The winters were hard for her. The summers were too brief. She cried for Mama and Papa. She coughed. God, how she coughed." Ioana's accent thickened. "No medication was allocated for an orphanage. I cared for her, bringing her food and water, stealing milk for her, blankets. I fought when they came to get the blankets back, told them the blankets were infected. I showed them the sore that had opened on her hip."

"Mama!" Evie reached for Ioana's hand.

But her mother pulled away. "No. If you do that, I can't speak."

Evie felt the sorrow that gripped her mother by the throat.

Ioana continued, "The sore oozed and spread. Mihaela no longer cried. She suffered in agony and in silence. I held her in my arms, gave her my body heat, my rations. She was ten when at last she died. I was thirteen."

Evie pulled Ioana's chair around. "Sit down, Mama."

Ioana didn't sit so much as collapse. "I don't know what they did with her body. I had nowhere to mourn and no one to mourn with. The official who had taken my sister came to me and beckoned—and I coughed."

Astonished, Evie stammered, "Wh-what?"

Ioana smiled faintly. "No one has ever called me a fool, my darling daughter. I knew if they thought Mihaela's disease was contagious, they would shun me. I made myself small, wrapped myself in shawls and blankets like an old woman, crept about and coughed and limped. But I couldn't fool them forever. Those men, those corrupt ones—they were used to having everything they wanted. If one of them saw me without my disguise—"

"One did."

"He tried to rape me. I stabbed him. He shouted for help. With a thrust to the heart, I killed him. Then I was on the run, living on the streets, protecting myself with my knives and my wits…until I found my second sister."

"Was she…okay?"

Mama was breathing hard now. "Ana-Maria had syphilis, although her lover didn't yet know it. She said I wanted a rich American husband. She helped me take a picture. She said to wear little makeup. The men who bought wives wanted someone fresh and innocent. She helped me write up the advertisement and sift through the applicants."

"How many were there?"

"Not a hundred. Eighty or ninety. Most of them wouldn't offer marriage, and that was my first demand. They wanted proof of my virginity, and they wanted to be the ones who proved it."

"God." Evie turned her face away.

"No, through it all, I grew strong." Mama clenched her fist to her chest. "I met with the five best, assessed them, agreed to undergo a doctor's examination. When they were satisfied I was virgo intacta, I interviewed them and chose your father. He wanted passion, he wanted love. I had none to give, but I persuaded him he could teach me. We married. He brought me to the US on a cruise ship, and before I landed in New York, I was pregnant with you."

"How old were you?"

"Sixteen."

"Mama!" For the first time, Evie realized her father was more than a shallow man, a vow-breaker, indifferent to the duties of a father. He was also weak, selfish, a child molester.

Like Wretchen Gretchen, but somehow the law made it okay for him. "That's horrible."

Ioana smiled. "No. It was the best time. I showed him intense passion, and he had hopes of a son. He was disappointed you were a girl, but he promised he would raise you as his heir." Ioana's expression shifted from satisfaction to fury. "When he discarded you, I wanted to kill him. But I knew that killing him would stain you children. You'd be left alone, the offspring of an immigrant murderer and an Asian American. So I left him unharmed."

"No wonder you never complained when he didn't take us when he was supposed to or pay his child support."

"I wanted to keep all custody. Of course, I think it would have been better for you if I'd killed him. But so, so much worse for your sister."

"Yes. So much worse for her."

Ioana sighed in exasperation. "You think it's still about you? No. No! You're strong. You will survive. You're like me. You and me, we have to protect our young." Her face grew lonely, and her eyes looked into the past. "Or they will die, and the future dies with them."

"If you were sixteen when I was born, and I'm eighteen now—"

"Nineteen!"

Evie jolted a little as she realized it was true; while she was in the hospital, her birthday had come and gone. "You're now only thirty-five. You could marry again."

"Not as long as I have a daughter under my roof. I would never risk my child for a man."

Evie's mother had shared her story, and Evie now knew why Ioana would see her out the door, and why Evie would never contact her. Ioana was right; Evie had already disappeared off the face of the earth. Marya was alive, and she deserved her chance to thrive.

"All right." Evie rose from the chair. "I'll go."

"I've saved money for Marya's graduation party. It's yours." Ioana went to a kitchen drawer, pulled out the place mats and from the bottom dug out a pile of twenties. As she handed it to Evie, she said, "Eight hundred and eighty dollars. I wanted her to have a big party, but you know her—she'll be happy no matter what, as long as she's with her friends."

"Mama…"

Ioana caught Evie's cheeks between her hands. "You go. You find your way. You can do this. But never come back. If you do, someone in town will recognize you. That man whose wife you killed—"

"I didn't kill her!"

Ioana gazed into Evie's eyes. "I know. I never wanted to think—"

"Did the neighbors spray paint your windows again?"

"What?"

"In California, you said the neighbors spray-painted your windows *GO BACK WHERE YOU CAME FROM.*"

"No. No, they didn't do that." But Ioana didn't look at her.

"When I was in JDC, you said, 'When you can make me proud, come home.' Mama, I got that job because I was trying to make you proud. I wanted so badly to come home." It was a cry from the heart.

"I am glad you came home." Ioana's voice choked, then cleared. "The neighbors were kind. I did have to change jobs."

"I'm sorry." Evie hadn't thought she could feel worse.

"I do not blame you. But people in Rockin knew the Jamesons, and they sincerely mourned them."

Evie hadn't thought of that; how many friends and patients

Michele must have had, how many rejoiced at Timmy's birth and cried in horror at his death.

Ioana continued, "The husband, Jameson, he came back. He had been held hostage for more than a year. He was maddened with rage. He came for me, wanted to kill me for raising a monster. Your sister... Marya thrust herself between him and me. I feared for her."

"She's brave."

"She's like me. Like you. She's the best of us."

Evie wanted so much to hate her sister. But she remembered the loving child, and she heard the pride in her mother's voice, and she couldn't. "I'm glad she saved you. What happened to him? Was he arrested?"

Ioana snorted. "Him? A hero returning to a dark future? Not at all. I heard he went south into the lower forty-eight. Wait here. I have something more for you." She went upstairs and returned to thrust a gift bag decorated with sparkly teddy bears at her.

Evie heard a whisper. *It's not right...*

Ioana smiled at Evie. "One of the police officers gave it to us. He said it was yours."

Clumsy with terror, Evie pulled the stuffed animal out of the bag.

Timmy's teddy bear, its black eye still glossy with knowledge and reproach.

"Mama, please, I don't want this. He talks to me."

Evie thought her mother wouldn't comprehend. But Ioana stared at Evie, then at the bear. "He talks to you?"

"About the murder. He tells me the truth. He tells me what happened to Timmy. He tells me to seek justice." Evie thrust the bear at her mother. "You keep it!"

Ioana held her hands up, firmly refusing it. "My grandmother heard voices, knew things no one else knew. She died because she spoke the truth for the dead. You must be careful to never tell."

"I don't want this!" Again Evie thrust the bear at her mother.

"It's not one you can reject." Ioana took the bear, slid it in Evie's backpack and helped her put the straps on her shoulders. Taking Evie's arm, Ioana led her toward the door. "You know where you're going?"

"Yes." To the fishing camp, where she would become Petie.

"Go with God, and when the voice speaks, you listen. There's only truth in that voice."

"I will not listen," Evie vowed.

SISTERS TO FRIENDS

Midnight Sun Fishing Camp
Katchabiggie Lodge
Two years ago

EIGHT YEARS INTO PETIE'S EXILE, in the dead of winter, she stood in the kitchen prepping her lunch when she heard the lodge's phone ring.

She ignored it. Sometimes it was a fisherman planning next summer's outing. More often it was a spam call. Some days the spammers were so constant, she shut off the ringer. After four months alone, silence was easier than the constant intrusion of a mechanical voice.

Anxious to get back to her search for a lost twelfth-century illuminated Bible, she mixed her leftover Kraft Mac and Cheese with cooked broccoli and placed it in the microwave.

Behind the check-in desk in the great hall, the answering machine clicked on. She heard a woman's voice, no doubt warning her unless she called back immediately, her computer security would be breached, her car would be towed or, most amusing in her case, the police would come to arrest her. Looking out at January's dim almost-daylight where the howling wind blew snow into drifts and left the frozen ground slick and bare… Petie doubted it. No sane cop would come out in this weather, not even to capture a convicted and escaped murderer.

She grinned. That was the real definition of cold comfort.

She ate lunch and headed back to the computer in Hawley's office. Seated in front of his massive monitor, she virtually crawled through obscure records in Latin. In her eight winters here, she'd watched movies, read books and gained a working knowledge of Mandarin, Belarusian, Spanish, French, Quemadese and a *little* Latin. But not enough, and the online translator always screwed up with Latin. So she was grateful when she got to Early Modern English, to a monastery looted in Henry VIII's reign. That monastery and the land surrounding it had been granted to one of Henry's nobles; the Bible had been a point of pride until the family lost their fortune in the early twentieth century. A businessman had bought the Bible for a whopping sum, and finally it had passed to one little old lady…from whom the Bible had been stolen.

The little old lady, Miss Merchant, was Petie's client, and she was fierce in her fury at the loss. She'd contacted Petie, given her a list of possible thieves, and before the meager afternoon sun had set, Petie had established the culprit and the buyer, and when and where the deal would take place.

Petie leaned back in her chair, pleased with herself.

The phone rang again.

"I don't care if you're coming to repossess my car," she said toward the answering machine. She wrote Miss Merchant an email and sent it off, describing what the next steps should be to rescue said Bible and gave instructions on how and where to deposit her finder's fee. She hoped Miss Merchant was good for it. Not all little old ladies were honest.

She stood and stretched. She might as well listen to the phone messages, and when she'd weeded out the spam, she could return the calls from those enthusiastic fishermen. Sometimes she even knew them from previous years, and that gave her a sense of being connected to the real world. A false sense, she supposed.

She punched the blinking button on the phone. Seven calls over the last day and a half. She put pen to paper and waited.

Spam call.

Delete.

Spam call.

Delete.

Spam call.

Delete.

Spam call.

Dele— Wait. A woman's voice, but not a robot. And almost…familiar.

"Hello. Hi. This call is for, um, my sister. I think she goes by the name of Petie."

The pen and paper fell from Petie's hands, and she stood still, breathless, broken at hearing Marya's voice after so many years.

"I think she works there at the fishing camp. All the time, if I'm reading it right. Not that she's on the website. No official photos. But I read reviews, found her name mentioned lots of times. Then I went looking at people's family vacation pictures, and there she was. Most people wouldn't recognize her, but I—" An audible swallow, as if Marya was trying to keep from crying.

Petie answered the recording, "You did, because you're my sister."

"Our mother… After we were informed that Evie had been killed, I was afraid for Mama's life. Because she said she hadn't told Evie that she loved her." Marya cleared her throat. "Mama turned the room where she kept Evie's belongings into a shrine, and every night she sobbed herself to sleep. Then all of a sudden, she stopped mourning, and when I asked why, Mama said, *Your sister is alive in my heart.* I checked, and Evie's belongings were gone. That teddy bear was gone! Mama wouldn't have given her stuff away. I knew then Evie was alive. I knew!"

Marya's enthusiasm warmed Evie's heart, and she smiled at the answering machine. "You always were the smartest kid."

"I started investigating what could have happened, how she could have lived through that terrible landslide, where she could have gone… It took years, but I found the name of the doctor who treated her in the hospital. He'd gone on a two-year medical mission to West Africa, and he was killed there."

"Oh. I'm sorry to hear that." The world needed more people like Dr. VanHooser.

"I despaired, but his daughter told me her dad sent desperate cases to Midnight Sun Fishing Camp for work, and… Never mind. The details aren't important. The thing is, we haven't talked for so many years. My name is Marya."

"I know," Petie answered. "I know you. I've been watching you." She read the *Rockin Herald* and the *Rockin Business Journal*, anything that would help her keep track of her mother and sister.

"Tell Evie Mama's fine. I'm fine. I just… I wanted Evie… Petie…to know… I want to talk to her. I'm in California."

"I know that, too," Petie whispered. Marya was at UC Berkeley, in law school.

"Please. Evie, if you're listening, please call me. I love you. I miss you." Marya gave her phone number. "Okay. That's all. Goodbye." There was a long pause before she hung up the phone.

Petie found she had her hand pressed to her chest over her heart. "My God," she whispered. "My God." She didn't know if she was praying or talking to herself or…

The next recording started. "Hi, Petie, you pretty young thing. This is Skeeter Brown from Texas. How about giving me a call about a fishing trip in August when here it's hotter than the hinges of hell and up there it's practically a Texas winter?"

She smiled involuntarily, grabbed for her forgotten pen and paper and jotted down his number.

Two more spam calls, and she was done. She called Skeeter and got him and his daughter scheduled, promised there would be at least one bear sighting and every day would be clear weather, and when she was done, she felt calm enough to think about what to do next.

Marya had tracked Petie down. All the photos Petie had seen of Marya, growing up, graduating from high school, from college, going to graduate school… She was pretty, she was bright, she was fiercely dedicated to righting wrongs, she never seemed to be afraid of anything.

Petie envied her that. Sometimes as the hours and days and months and years rolled on, it seemed Petie constantly lived on the edge of fear, terrified of what would happen if she didn't find Donald White, what she would be forced to do when she did and if she would find the courage needed to end his reign of terror.

She glanced at the clocks lined up on the wall. Each gave the time of a major city in the world: New York, Quemada, London, Paris, Istanbul, Beijing, Sydney, Hong Kong, Honolulu, Los Angeles…

It was five-thirty in the evening in LA, so the same time in Berkeley. Petie could call Marya now. She could.

But maybe Marya was busy. Maybe she was studying. It

was Saturday; maybe she was getting ready to go out. She probably had a significant other...

If Petie didn't call Marya now, she'd think about it all night. She'd be afraid to call her in the morning. Hawley would tell her if she didn't call, she didn't have a hair on her ass.

Petie didn't know what that meant, but it wasn't a compliment, so she picked up the phone and dialed.

Marya picked up on the first ring. "Evie! You called!"

PART FIVE

WRONG ALIBI

9

Midnight Sun Fishing Camp
Inside Jeen Lee's cabin
Late that same night

"**NOW, I'M PETIE. I** live full-time at the camp. During the summer, I'm the camp director. During the winter, I find things. Stolen objects, mostly, and antiquities. Sometimes I work online with a department of the US government, the MFAA—Monuments, Fine Arts and Archives—to halt the flow of the contraband. They don't care who I am, only that I find what they're seeking. I still have no real identity, but I've made myself someone I'm proud to be." Petie looked at Jeen Lee, then at Matella and Tziamara.

Jeen viewed her with what looked like substantial respect and, for the first time, a sense of comradery.

The young women watched her warily, as if they saw a menace visible only to them.

Petie glanced up at the clock.

It was almost midnight.

She put her hand to her throat. "Please, could I have water?"

Tziamara got a bottle of water out of the room's tiny refrigerator and gave it to Matella.

At arm's length, Matella offered it and mumbled something in a dialect Petie didn't recognize.

"What did she say?" Petie asked.

Tziamara answered, "That you are a walking corpse."

"That's enough, both of you." Jeen frowned. "Miss Petie is a survivor. The blessed saints watch over her. Should anyone try to harm her, it would go ill for them. Go now."

Matella and Tziamara exited to the second bedroom, and as they left, Matella gave Tziamara a hard push that slammed her into the door frame.

"Shut the door behind you!" Jeen called.

"I am *not* a walking corpse." Furthermore, Petie didn't like that image, not when Michele and Timmy wandered in her nightmares.

"Forgive them. In their youth, they were abused. They are not educated. In Quemada, I've employed a tutor for them, but superstitions die hard." Jeen Lee walked to the dream catcher Hawley had hung in the window of every cabin and touched it lightly. "We all know that, don't we?"

"It's true." Petie thought of Timmy's teddy bear and how often she'd been tempted to get rid of it and how she always stopped short of the trash. The bear was nothing but a bear, she assured herself, yet to throw away a murdered child's beloved stuffed animal seemed to her to solicit damnation.

She looked out the window. The sun had dropped close to the horizon. "I should go. I've been talking all day." More than once, she had faltered; in the telling of her discovery of Michele and Timmy, when recounting her harrowing escape from the mudslide, when recalling the moment of connection with her long-lost sister.

Through it all, Matella and Tziamara had been there, cutting, buffing, polishing, moisturizing…listening. They had viewed her with caution. It was as she feared; when she told her story, attitudes toward her would change.

Now weariness dragged at Petie, and she swayed when she stood.

"Speaking the naked truth is exhausting. I'll walk you back to your cabin." As Petie reached for the door, Jeen warned, "Be careful of your nails."

Petie pulled her hand back. Tziamara had cut her nails to a workable length and applied clear polish filled with subtle flecks of pearl. "How long do I have to be careful?"

"Beauty can be delicate." Jeen opened the door and gestured Petie through. "I'm a practitioner of tai chi. Starting tomorrow, I'll lead my people in classes. Join us. It will bring balance to your life and ease your mental turmoil."

Petie wanted to deny she had any mental turmoil, but somehow she couldn't convince herself of that.

Since the last time she spoke to her mother, nine years ago, Petie had *never* given anyone even the slightest hint of the truth. Hawley didn't want to know. She trusted no one else. Yet during this painful retelling of the past, Petie had begun to like Jeen Lee. The woman might be a killer, but she was intelligent, insightful and, in her own way, honorable.

As they strolled the gravel walks toward the staff housing and Petie's private cabin, they heard music and laughter from the lodge.

Jeen listened and smiled. "Today's encounter with the bear has given my people reason to celebrate life."

"It seems so long ago!"

"Since then, you've relived your whole life."

"It feels that way."

"The story is amazing. At the same time, you are and were an intelligent woman, yet you didn't have an inkling about

Donald White, his past deeds and his intentions." Jeen truly sounded troubled. "How is that possible?"

It was a question Petie had pondered, too, so she answered promptly, "His voice."

"His voice?"

"It seemed as if he was a voice talent. He used his voice like a violin, soothing, warming, relaxing. It was deep and kind, and he built trust with cunning words. Looking back, I believe that's how, when Zone Jameson was gone, he convinced Michele to let him stay. Even in those brief moments when I would begin to doubt, he could speak and I knew all was well."

"The smallest words and gestures can build a tower of trust, and a single wrong move can bring it crashing down," Jeen said sadly. "I know that."

Remembering Jeen Lee's son, Petie said, "I suppose you do." Petie pushed a handful of hair back. As Tziamara had promised, it would be an easy style to manage, but to have the strands loose, the ends touching her shoulders—this would take getting used to.

"Your sister—she hasn't come to visit you?"

"We video-call. Every Wednesday night and sometimes just because." Petie smiled fondly.

Impatiently, Jeen Lee asked, "Why doesn't she come to the camp?"

Petie was precisely as sharp. "I asked her not to. I don't want her to have to lie to Mama and—"

"You're afraid someone's watching!"

"Of course I'm afraid someone's watching!" Petie climbed the steps to her door, grimaced at her nails and retrieved her key card out of her shirt pocket. "You didn't even know I was alive, and you found me. What about someone who actually suspects Evelyn Jones is alive and searches? They're going to track me. I'll go back to prison. Donald White will be free forever—and as my mother feared, my sister would be at risk. At risk of being an accomplice to her felon sister and, worse, at risk if Donald White realized the girl who knows all the ugly truths about him still lives." She opened the door and walked in.

Jeen followed her into the compact yet well-appointed cabin. "Why would he care? He set you up to rot in prison."

"It's been ten years. If I was caught, it would refocus attention on the case. It would be a media circus, and I'd make such a fuss, insist so loudly I was innocent... One good investigative reporter would find the shoddy police work and the truth would come out."

"You've had the time to consider every eventuality."

"I've had time to make all my plans."

They smiled at each other.

"One more thing." Taking Petie's arm, Jeen pushed her in front of the mirror. "Look what Matella and Tziamara have done."

Petie had never seen that woman before. Her black hair shone. Her skin had the appearance of the finest polished moonstone. Her brows had been waxed, and whatever oddities remained from the landslide and the plastic surgeries had been eased away by the skillful application of cover-up and bronzers and brighteners.

She turned to Jeen Lee and spread her arms in surprise.

Jeen nodded. "You can go forth now. You have a new look. I can get you a new identity. You could work for me. You could work for anyone. You have a mind unlike any other, sharpened by isolation. You have gifts, Evelyn Jones. You can live in Quemada. You can have a life."

Petie looked at her fingers, at the prints that identified her to law enforcement. "And never come back."

"Not unless you can track your Donald White, turn him over to the authorities and prove his guilt."

"I haven't pinpointed him yet." Petie lowered her head. "So many times, I've been so close."

"You might never find him. Someone could discover who and what he is. He could cheat the wrong person. He could die a peaceful death. Or he could be killed for his misdeeds. You might never know."

"I could never be redeemed." For the first time, the hopelessness of her aims weighed on Petie. "I could live here forever and never, never have justice."

"That's right." Jeen put her hand on Petie's hand. "Come with me. Work for me. Or let me find you something. You speak my language. You speak Mandarin. You speak Spanish. I don't know how many other languages you speak."

"Belarusian."

"Belarusian," Jeen repeated. "You could find things online—Asian artifacts, South American artifacts, Middle Eastern... You could rescue them, restore them to their rightful owners or place them in museums. You could be successful, rich, revered."

Petie felt as if she was being assaulted by new thoughts, new possibilities. Her throat tightened. Her breath caught.

She had to relax. She had to breathe.

When she managed to gain control, she spoke in a wispy voice. "I can't. I can't leave."

"You won't. That's different." Jeen Lee watched Petie struggle. "I found no trace of your mother's family in Belarus, but if you come to Quemada, you can go on to visit your family in China. Your grandmother would welcome your visit."

"Honest?"

"I have been in contact with her. I would not lie."

"I know you. I know! But I never thought..." Petie wavered between disbelief and excitement. "She adored my father, and I thought he had let her think the worst of me. Which was—" she faltered "—easily done."

"He did. And that time is past. But with his divorces and the worthy children he has discarded, she is disillusioned."

"My grandmother. Really." Petie remembered the tall, strong old woman who had conversed with her in the local dialect and insisted Petie stumble along and learn. After so many years alone, to have family in China... "That makes me happy."

"If this interests you, I wouldn't wait too long. Your grandmother is elderly."

"She must be. I should consider that." Petie wiped her hands across her eyes and looked at her fingers. Black smeared them: eyeliner and mascara. She looked at herself in the mirror. The perfect image had been smudged, yet still she was not herself. Still she looked polished and urbane, not like the Petie who worked at the Midnight Sun Fishing Camp but like a businesswoman at the end of the day. "No. I can't go."

Jeen stepped up behind her, met her eyes in the mirror. "You're agoraphobic."

"I'm not!" The thought had never crossed Petie's mind. She *wasn't* irrationally afraid of being in public. She was with people all the time...in the summer. She wasn't afraid of the constant barrage of words and humanity associated with cities, with civilization, with places where the air hurt to breathe and smog blocked the stars.

Jeen's shrewd eyes saw too clearly. "You're afraid and forever condemned to live in a fishing camp in Alaska."

Petie gestured at her cabin. "It is luxurious."

"A luxurious prison!"

"When I find Donald White, I will come out of hiding, I will prove his crimes and I will be released."

"If Donald White appears, will you be able to walk out of this place to hunt him down? Or will you hunker down, your head hung low and watch your dream of revenge pass you by?"

Petie would leave here when the moment was right. She would leave without a second thought. She wouldn't cling to the years of loneliness because she was afraid to go elsewhere...would she? "I hate you."

"No, you don't. You hate yourself."

"I'm not going with you."

"My business card is on the table. If you find the courage to leave, call me. I'll help you. I owe you my help whether you want it or not. While I am alive, you will never be alone."

Petie reached out her hand.

Jeen met her halfway. They shook. Jeen turned to go—and stopped. She stared at the ragged stuffed bear that sat propped up on a shelf of well-used paperbacks and gestured with an upraised palm. "Is that the infamous Tuddy?"

"That's him."

"I would have thought you'd hide him out of sight."

"I tried him in the closet for a while. I felt mean. It's not his fault his little boy was killed." Now Petie felt foolish, too.

Jeen picked up Tuddy, squeezed his stomach, looked into his one eye. "Does he still talk to you?"

"No." Evie was firm. "I'm older, and all the imagination has been knocked out of me."

Jeen carefully put the bear in place. "In my culture, it's not imagination that triggers the voice. It is the person who can hear the truths that beg to be spoken."

"I am not that person."

Jeen inclined her head. "As you say. You gave me my son. I

do owe you a debt which I seek to repay. Are you at all close to finding Donald White?"

Soon... The whisper sank into Petie's mind.

She didn't look at the bear. She didn't really hear any words in her head. "I don't know, Jeen."

"Soon, I expect," Jeen said.

Petie took a long, slow, soothing breath and assured herself that neither one of them had heard any whisper of premonition.

"Remember what I told you," Jeen said. She walked to the door and out into the nighttime sunlight.

For the first time in days, Petie was alone, drained by the recitation of events, the memories of horror, the loss of her youth. During all the years, she had clutched the pieces of her soul tightly and watched as she changed from a young woman fired with hope to a female made mature first by loneliness and disappointment, then by finding strength in her studies, in her ambitions, in herself.

Remember, Jeen Lee had said.

Remember what? Everyone wanted Petie to remember something.

Jeen Lee wanted her to remember she could call on her when she wished to leave.

Tuddy wanted her to remember Michele and Timmy.

Her mother wanted her to remember what she owed the family.

All Petie could remember was the years alone, without affection, without kindness, learning to depend only on herself. If she decided to leave, where would she go? If she remembered Michele and Timmy, what would she do for them? If she remembered what she owed her family...would she pay the debt or would she consider it already paid?

She was not the defiant girl she'd once been, so angry at

her father and at life that she had willfully ruined her life. Nor was she the foolish young woman, trusting in the appearance of wealth. Nor was she the lonely person, haunted by ghosts and dreaming of suicide.

She was mature. She was educated. She was attractive. And for the first time in her life, she would accept her ability to hear Tuddy and trust the time for Timmy's justice would come *soon*.

10

WHEN THE EMBASSY OFFICIALS saw Zone, with his long, black beard and his dark, angry eyes, they thought he was a rebel. But his fingerprints proved he was Zone Jameson, American citizen.

He went to a hospital, then to the US and another hospital. They worked on him, operated on his shattered jaw, wired it shut, rebroke his hip, set it correctly, fixed a few other physical problems...then he was free to go home.

He visited his parents first, who looked at him with wretched eyes and spoke platitudes about the deaths of his wife and child.

He visited Michele's parents, who looked at him with accusing eyes and said plainly they blamed him for the deaths of their daughter and grandson. If he had stayed home...

He agreed with them. Damn it. If he had stayed with Michele and Timmy, ignored the call to go to Magara, they would be alive today.

In a morass of guilt and pain, he went high into Washington's Olympic Mountains. He took possession of a forest-service lookout and, using all his survival skills, he lived. He hid his face with his giant, black beard because, God help him, he wanted no person, no tree, no Native American earth god to recognize him, the man who had killed his family. So he survived, alone, in misery.

He took jobs authenticating stolen artifacts for the MFAA. Zone knew firsthand about terrorists who used artifacts to finance their campaigns, and in each success in restoring an artifact to its rightful country, he took a grim pride.

He looked every night at the stars and wished he could somehow avenge his wife and son...but the woman who had killed them was dead.

She had died in the Alaskan mudslide, and he was alone and would never have a chance to retaliate.

He believed that until the day of the phone text.

11

THE FIRST TEXT CAME in on a Saturday evening.

She's alive.

Zone figured it was part of the barrage of spam that hit him periodically. Never mind that he was in an isolated lookout in Washington's mountains. The spammers found him anyway, offering sex with virgins, a chance to claim his royal-family fortune or a cure for toe fungus. No reason for him to notice the *She's alive* text.

The next text caught his attention.

She never died.

Who never died? Was someone stalking him, tormenting him about Michele and Timmy? If there was one thing the internet had taught him, it was how cruel people could be to a man who'd left his family to be murdered. He deserved it, but still. He blocked the number.

They came after him from a different contact.

She changed her face.

A photo of a young woman appeared on his screen. The background behind her was a forest and stream. She had black hair in a long braid, a firm, unsmiling mouth and a face that was oddly asymmetrical.

He blocked that number, too, and immediately deleted the photo.

What the fuck kind of asshole targeted and tormented a man who had lost his family?

The kind who targeted and robbed the elderly, who stole from the desperate, who perpetrated evil in all its guises. Zone supposed he should have expected something like this sooner, but while the murders were still fresh in everyone's minds. Not now. Not a decade later.

In the middle of the night, he got up and dug the photo out of the phone's "recently deleted" file. The woman looked like someone he knew. But who? Someone who was alive who should be dead. Someone who—

No. That was not Evelyn Jones.

No. The face was different.

The hair was the same, long, black and straight, restrained in a braid, but—

But she died in the landslide. They hadn't recovered her body, and the only person who survived was the guard...who after all the surgeries had disappeared.

If he were a suspicious type of man...

He enlarged the photo, studied every aspect of that face. That face that was not hers. Evelyn Jones had looked Chinese, a little, and Eastern European, a little more. She had been the quintessential American mix of human beings, if human beings were heartless bitches who murdered women and children.

And he knew they were. He'd been there, seen the worst of human nature, wished that he could forget and knew he never could. My God, the horrors of Magara in which he'd been imprisoned were nothing to the horrors of knowing an eighteen-year-old girl had heartlessly murdered his wife and child.

This wasn't an eighteen-year-old.

No, she looked like a twenty-eight-year old. A twenty-eight-year old who'd had facial surgery that had transformed her into an unremarkable woman of indeterminate ancestry.

Except for that hair…

He wasn't going to rest until he knew.

He unblocked the number and texted, **How possible?**

The answer came back immediately. Whoever was on the other end had been waiting.

Guard killed.

Fingerprints?

A match to EJ.

Zone said aloud, "You bastard. You'd better be lying. If she's still alive—"

Where is she?

Midnight Sun Fishing Camp, Alaska. Her name is Petie.

Zone sat in the dark, breathing hard, trying to think, to get beyond his incredulous rage to some sense. He was being played. Even if it was her, he was being played. Why? Who was this? What did they have in the game?

Apparently he didn't answer fast enough, for another text popped up.

No SS#. I can turn her in. Take down the camp. Matching fingerprints.

NO LEAVE HER TO ME YOU LEAVE HER TO ME

It was the text equivalent of screaming. He was screaming.
A long pause. Was his correspondent done?
Zone forced himself to calm, to behave like a civilized man who could handle this in a civilized manner.

Leave her to me. You didn't find me to tell me you were going to turn her in for social security fraud. You came to me for vengeance. I'll investigate further. I don't know you. I don't trust you. I'm not hurting some poor woman on the advice of an anonymous tipster. But if what you say is true—you leave her to me.

He started to block the number again, then paused.
No. The phone would stay right here. When he left to find Evelyn Jones, he would get a burn phone. This ghoulish bastard would not be able to track him.
He would do what had to be done alone.

12

PETIE DID WHAT SHE had trained herself to do: put the turmoil in her mind away and live for the now. She plunged into the work that accompanied the height of the fishing season. Her nail polish chipped. The illusion of sophistication vanished. The sun was up twenty hours a day; she labored every one of those hours. When sleep forced itself on her, inevitably she would wake in her bed and stare into the semidarkness, review the past, her mistakes, her exile and Jeen Lee's offer to help her escape the camp, become a different person and go on with life.

She should. Petie knew she should.

But she was afraid. If she moved on, went to Quemada, got a job that utilized her language skills, abandoned the search for antiquities stolen and lost to the world and instead lived a life of work, vacation, relationships… If she focused on the future, not the past, eventually Donald White would fade from her memory, and he'd never be caught, at least not by her.

What of her vow to see him pay for his crimes?

Her gaze shifted to Tuddy.

What of the justice owed to Michele and Timmy?

The bear stared, that shiny plastic eye solemn.

"Fine," she said. "If I'm making all the decisions, we're here until it's time to go. We'll know when that is, won't we?"

Soon...

The word slipped into her mind and sent a shiver down her spine.

She hadn't heard it because no one had said it.

Sitting up in her bed in her room, she picked up the phone Hawley had given her and clicked through her bookmarks.

She checked on her sister in California. The day before, Marya had gone to the Santa Cruz boardwalk and posted pictures. Petie grinned at the snapshot of her screaming on the roller coaster.

She tried to resist, but she gave in to temptation and logged onto the *Rockin Herald*, motto: *Be Part of It.*

After she'd first arrived at Midnight Sun Fishing Camp, for a long time she combed the pages looking for glimpses of her mother, who was active in local charities, and her sister, who won scholarships and graduated as her high school's valedictorian. But the other news, the politics, the editorials complaining about everything—the schools, Mother's Day, tourists, no tourists, the neighbor's dog—was relentlessly ugly, and for her own sanity, she'd had to give up reading the *Rockin Herald*.

After all, simply because her mother lived there didn't mean it was home.

But that also meant Petie didn't have a home, just like she didn't have a real name, so she kept her subscription paid for the times, like now, when she brought up the online paper and read every story.

It had been more than a year since she'd bothered, and she

was surprised to find the stories more upbeat. There'd been an increase in population (commenters lamented the loss of their small community). They'd built a new grade school and a new library (commenters said the old ones were good enough for their grandparents and should be good enough today). The worst crime she could find was six-year-old twins who broke windows at a construction site and were now working off the cost of the damage under the supervision of their parents (commenters suggested more severe punishment).

Petie made a conscious decision to stop reading the comments.

Hey, look! A new chief of police had come to town. Chief Rodolphe Dumas, from Louisiana of all places.

His official portrait showed a solemn, clean-shaven, middle-aged man staring straight at the camera. The candid photos proved him to be rotund and of short stature, smiling while attending a parade, looking grim when called to the scene of a crime.

She could find no mention of former Chief "Wretchen Gretchen" George. Maybe someone had killed the corrupt old bat. Petie could only hope.

She got into the society section and found a CrossFit fundraiser for breast-cancer education with photos and videos of women of all ages lifting weights, rowing and doing pull-ups, squats and push-ups in pink T-shirts and tights.

Then Petie saw a video that stopped her in her tracks.

Her mother, Ioana, all five foot three of her, squatting with a barbell loaded with one hundred and ten pounds, standing and lifting it over her head. She did it twice, then dropped it, but my God. She was forty-four!

Petie beamed with pride.

She clicked on the gallery of photographs taken at that

evening's breast-cancer education ball at the Rockin Hotel ballroom.

What hotel? There hadn't been a nice hotel in Rockin.

The first picture caught her attention. Rockin city councilwoman Stacey Collins, looking attractive and more mature than when Petie had known her, shaking hands with the mayor, who was congratulating her on her generous donation to the cause. The caption speculated on the rivalry between them; word around town claimed Stacey was preparing to challenge him for the office of mayor.

"Go, Stacey." Petie scanned the other photos, group shots mostly, until she found a photo of…her mother.

Ioana looked glamorous and shapely in a formfitting, shoulder-baring gown that showed off her muscled arms and back. She was holding the arm of her escort and radiantly smiling at him. Petie didn't recognize him. But then, she didn't recognize many people in Rockin. Not unless they'd been in the bank at the time she'd been making her ill-fated deposits. In fact…

She did a quick search for Norma, the elderly bank teller. She'd died, age seventy, soon after Petie left town. At the time, she'd seemed so kind and so sharp, Petie had wished her a long life.

Petie went back to the society page and the picture of her mother. She made the photo larger and gloated. Mama looked so good. And she was dating!

Petie examined the guy in the larger format. He looked about the same age as Mama, very thin, and he wore his suit with distinction. His dark hair had been cut by an expert hand, his eyebrows were perfect arches and a cool expression in his eyes made Petie think of—

She gasped, tossed the phone aside and ran to the computer on the desk. She brought it to life, flipped to the *Her-*

ald, clicked on the society section, missed because her fingers were trembling so hard, tried again and got the right page. She zoomed in on the photo of her mother and zoomed again on that man's face.

He didn't *really* look like Donald White. The face was different, younger somehow.

But she was hardly one to say that an appearance always stayed the same. This face was a little stretched, a little wide-eyed, a little full-lipped: all the hallmarks of plastic surgery, filler and Botox.

But the look in his eyes: absolutely pleasant, aware of the people and events around him and uninterested in anything but himself.

She tried to dissuade herself.

It couldn't be Donald White. He wouldn't return to Rockin. That would be madness.

His name. His name. What was it?

She searched the article, the captions.

She found him.

No, he wasn't Donald White.

His name was Derrick Green.

First name starts with a D. Last name is a color.

That was her man.

13

PETIE WALKED INTO HAWLEY'S office to find the giant man staring at his computer screen with a discontented expression.

Automatically she said, "What's wrong?" Because she fixed everything for Hawley, whatever it was. But not this time, she reminded herself, and before he could speak, she said, "Hawley, I'm leaving."

Without looking up from his screen, he asked, "Leaving what?"

"The camp. I'm leaving the camp."

Without moving his head, he shifted his gaze to her. "What?" He looked as he always did, immaculate in his suit and tie, but his voice was like fingernails on a blackboard, glass across skin. She hadn't heard him use such a tone since... since she didn't remember when.

No, wait. Since that spring he returned, after her second winter. It was as if he hadn't expected her to survive. When he returned from that winter in the South Pacific and saw her alive and his resort unharmed by the bitter winter, there had been a shift in his attitude. He changed from an indifferent employer into the boss who cared for and protected his employees.

But he didn't look caring now. He exuded a chill like that first cold of an Alaska winter.

Yes, she supposed she should have thought this through. He'd come to expect her to be here, day and night, winter and summer. "I understand you're shocked that I would want to leave the camp. I've been here ten years, and in all those years, I've never left. I'm a fixture."

"What the hell are you talking about?"

"Leaving."

"Why?"

This was Hawley. She could tell him the truth. "The man who murdered two people and set me up is back in Rockin."

"Why should you care? You've been here ten years. You have no connection to that situation."

"He's—" she wanted to say *dating*, but she couldn't choke out that word "—become close to my mother."

"I repeat, what the hell are you talking about?"

She didn't think she could be shocked. But she was. After ten years of silence, of keeping her history to herself, she had opened herself up to Hawley—and he didn't care? For years, he had been the one person she considered a friend. Not that he'd ever bothered to check up on her in the winter or lift the burdens from her in the summer, but somehow, she had always imagined if she told him about her past, he would react sympathetically.

Okay. Her little dream of Hawley's friendship had been crushed. She'd faced worse betrayals. She should have handled Hawley, taken into account his vast laziness. "It's no big deal. You're here. You know how to do everything. But you won't have to. Taylor is competent, the staff is the best we've ever had."

"You're not going."

"You're being weird. Do you think you can keep me against my will?"

"Yes."

Incredulous. She was incredulous. "How?"

"What are you going to do, *walk* to this place, wherever it is?" He was sarcastic.

"Rockin. It's on the east end of Denali on Highway 3."

He gestured like, *There you are.*

"No, I can't walk there. But I can walk to the airport."

"I call in the planes."

"I've already called in my plane."

"Right. Jeen Lee." His teeth clacked together. "What are you going to do for money? Is she going to fund this suicide expedition?"

"I have money." As an afterthought, "It's not a suicide expedition."

"You have money—and I'm the gatekeeper."

She was suddenly, finally, blindingly livid. "Are you threatening to steal my investments?" Her voice rose. "The investments I made from the meager goddamn salary you pay me? What is wrong with you, Hawley? Employees come, and they go. You don't care. They're Alaska natives or immigrants or people with social problems or ex-cons or escaped cons. Some don't have social security numbers. Like *me.* As they walk out the door, you wish them well, wave them off with a smile. What is it about *me?*"

He stopped breathing. She would swear he did. Sweat beaded his forehead. Beneath his tan, his color faded, leaving him an odd brown-green. She was still angry, but she was concerned, too. "Are you having a heart attack?" He could be. In fact, it was a miracle he hadn't had one before.

He caught his breath. His color returned. He pulled his handkerchief from his suit pocket and dabbed his forehead. "If I had a heart attack, that would be inconvenient for you, wouldn't it? All your money becoming part of my estate."

"We have a signed agreement."

"Which is not notarized. My sister isn't at all openhanded."

Of course, he was right. If anything happened to him, her money was gone. Perhaps she should be ashamed, but Petie's concern about his health faded.

He opened the desk drawer where he kept the cash. He counted out twenties and hundreds, twenty-five hundred dollars, and held it out.

She wasn't sure she felt safe getting close enough to take it. He shook it at her.

She closed her fingers around one end of the stack, careful not to touch him. "I could get the capital from Jeen Lee, you know."

"I know. That's why I'm giving it to you. I'll check you into a Rockin hotel."

"I haven't slept, so I'll have to stay in Anchorage tonight."

"Aren't you afraid this guy will whack your mother tonight?"

"A little. Yes. But my mother always takes work so responsibly. She would never go out on a date on a weeknight. I mean, I don't think she would." Petie closed her eyes to give them a rest. "I don't know. She never dated before." She opened them again. "Do you think I should drive to Rockin tonight?"

"You'd run right off the road." He went online, moved unhurriedly as if their swift, brutal argument had never happened. He tapped and tapped, used his fingerprint to authenticate his credit card and announced, "I sent you the confirmations. Tonight you've got a hotel room in Anchorage and starting Friday, you're booked in the Rockin Hotel, in the Bono Room. If you know who that is." Again he gestured his, *There you are.*

Irritated, Petie said, "Of course I know who Bono is."

"In Rockin, you get breakfast and a wine tasting with afternoon appetizers. It's yours until you're done with your foolishness. My treat. When will you return?"

Weird conversation. Very weird. "When he's caught. Or dead."

"You'll be free. You won't have to return at all."

"Not if you intend to steal my investments." The bright, hot anger had subsided, but she still didn't understand what had just happened. She didn't understand his attitude.

"How long until Jeen Lee's jet arrives?"

"A few hours."

His gaze swept her from top to toe. "You're looking a little rough around the edges. Get what clothes you need from the gift shop."

"Jeen Lee is handling all that. She's sending one of her attendants."

"Right. Jenny. Your new best friend."

He was being really edgy, acting as if Petie had betrayed him. But he'd been on Jeen's side in every conversation and every dispute. What the hell? "Look, she offered to help me leave before. Get a new identity, give me a job, teach me how to…to navigate out in the world. I didn't go."

"Go now." He waved an impatient hand and returned his gaze to the computer screen. "I hope you survive, Petie. I really do. If you do, your money is yours."

"Okay, Hawley." She found herself shifting her weight

from foot to foot. Should she hug him? Shake his hand? "Goodbye."

He didn't answer.

So no hug, no handshake, mostly a *Don't let the door bang you in the ass on the way out.*

She performed a military about-face and left.

As the door shut behind her, Hawley looked up, around his office, ran his hand over his face as if bewildered. Pulling out his phone, he texted Taylor and told her to come to the office: it was time to talk about a promotion.

He returned his gaze to his computer screen, where a slide-show of Petie in all her years at the camp and in all her guises slid and shifted, faded and popped.

14

PETIE WATCHED JEEN LEE'S SMALL, sleek plane buzz the airstrip, making sure the way was clear of wildlife, then set down smoothly. When it came to a stop, the pilot lowered the stairs, and Petie boarded, clutching her small backpack loaded with the barest necessities—and Tuddy.

Jeen had said she was not to worry about clothes. So she didn't.

But it was only fair that she brought Tuddy so at last he could witness justice.

The plane's interior had been constructed for comfort, with rich leathers, a conference table and one luxurious thronelike seat that sat conspicuously alone. Matella greeted Petie with a gesture that placed her there. As Matella knelt to buckle her in, she said, "This is Miss Lee's chair. She wishes you to be comfortable."

"This is very kind of Miss Lee to so generously help me."

"As she has helped me. I know I am in debt forever, and

thankful always." Matella stayed kneeling at Petie's feet. "I wish to practice English. Okay?"

Petie wished Matella would get up. "As you wish."

"Miss Petie is also a most generous individual." Matella loosened the top on a bottle of sparkling water, handed it to Petie and disappeared toward the back of the plane. Petie heard the click of Matella's seat belt, and a blur of Quemadese as she spoke via internal phone to the pilot. Within seconds, the plane taxied and was off the ground, headed to Anchorage.

Petie watched out the window as the plane ascended. She craned her neck and caught a glimpse of Midnight Sun Fishing Camp before the complex was swallowed by forest and clouds, and she left ten years of her life behind.

She clutched the water bottle so hard her knuckles ached. She was afraid.

Midnight Sun Fishing Camp had been a prison of sorts. Not like juvenile detention, where she was never alone, always hearing arguments among the inmates, lights on all the time, a constant barrage of noise, smells and humanity.

But winter had accustomed Petie to isolation, dark, great stretches of time spent alone. Now she was going out into the world that had treated her so cruelly, back to the very place of murder, fear and injustice.

The plane leveled off. The bell dinged. Behind her, Petie heard Matella's seat belt snap open. In a moment, Matella arrived with a cart laden with moisturizers, makeup and nail polish. She picked up Petie's hands and clucked in horror at the chipped polish. She turned Petie's face to the window and sorrowfully shook her head. "Miss did not continue the beauty regime we prepared for her."

"I had to work."

Matella tossed a black cape around Petie's shoulders. "I cut hair first. You have been to Anchorage before?"

"Once, ten years ago, and merely passing through. It's the same this time. I'm headed to a little town called Rockin."

"Is beautiful there?" Matella's comb and shears moved swiftly to bring Petie's hair back to its well-groomed state.

"I guess." Petie didn't remember the beauty, only the horror. "It's close to Mount Denali. There's a lot for tourists to do, and—"

A bell dinged.

Matella opened the armrest, brought out the monitor tucked inside and arranged it on a viewing arm. "Miss Lee wishes to speak with you."

She touched buttons, and the screen lit up to show Jeen Lee in her office, at her desk, head turned, speaking in precise French to someone out of camera range.

Matella cleared her throat. "Miss Lee? As requested, I have Miss Petie for you."

Jeen waved away the person in her office and, when the door shut, spoke to Petie. "It is good to see you, my friend."

At the sight of Jeen's perfectly made-up, calmly competent face, the worried knot in the base of Petie's stomach loosened. "You, also, my friend."

Jeen frowned. "You look tired. Have you been working too hard?"

"Last night was sleepless," Petie acknowledged. "Jeen, I'm grateful for your help in this matter."

"I told you. I am forever in your debt."

"That's not why I searched for your son."

"Which makes me all the more appreciative." Jeen's gaze roamed the cabin of the plane. "I see Matella has taken your grooming in hand."

Matella nodded at the monitor's camera.

Jeen's expression became serious. "I've sent identification for you. You are now an online accountant, Petie Jeenli."

Petie laughed at the surname. "I like it!"

Jeen remained serious. "More important, in moments of stress, you'll remember it."

Matella opened a drawer and handed Petie a small leather wallet. Inside she found an international driver's license, a passport, insurance cards and credit cards. There was also a substantial sum of cash.

"I have cash," Petie told Jeen Lee. "Hawley insisted on funding me."

Jeen's expression underwent a subtle change, one Petie couldn't read. "Interesting. Please take the bills, anyway. If anything goes badly, cash is a good thing to have."

Petie tucked the bills back into the wallet.

"Matella. Straighten the fringe on Miss Petie's forehead!" Jeen frowned as she examined Petie's cut. "The line emphasizes the awkwardness of her face and draws attention away from any similarity to pretty young Evelyn Jones."

Matella picked up the scissors and clipped at Petie's bangs while Petie sat with closed eyes and tried not to inhale any itchy bits of hair. Matella dusted Petie's face with a soft shaving brush and stepped back so Jeen could see.

"Much better," Jeen said to Matella, and to Petie, "I imagine Hawley was not happy with your defection."

"No."

"When Matella tried to book you into the Rockin Hotel, you already had a room. He did that?"

"Yes. In the Bono Room. And tonight he booked me into a hotel in Anchorage." Petie found she didn't want to discuss Hawley and his strange behavior. She showed her the wallet. "Thank you. You thought of everything."

"There's a folder with your cover story printed out. Read and discard."

"Right." That made sense. Whatever her cover story was, she'd better know it by heart.

"Before you disembark in Anchorage, Matella will prepare you—cosmetics, nails, clothes. At the airport, there's a car reserved in your new name. Matella has luggage packed for you with clothing that creates a different persona than the rustic Petie or the youthful Evie."

Like a model, Matella gestured gracefully at the large Louis Vuitton wheeled bag and matching backpack.

Jeen continued, "Matella has a handgun for you."

From the drawer in her makeup cart, Matella produced the small black case which opened to reveal a pistol and ammunition.

"It's a striker-fired Ruger LC9s, light, compact enough to carry in a purse—"

"Which you have provided," Petie said with some humor.

"Of course. Also a Louis Vuitton." Jeen patiently reminded her, "Part of your new image, Petie. You're now a woman of the world."

"I'll try to remember."

"The Ruger has a smooth, crisp trigger pull and a block-pin safety lever. Try the safety, please."

Petie examined it; it wasn't loaded. Nevertheless, before she clicked the lever, she pointed it at the floor. "Easy release," she said.

Jeen produced an identical pistol from underneath her suit jacket. "I keep mine with me at all times. It's powerful enough to bring down any attacker."

Petie put the weapon back in the case and shut it with a decisive click.

"I understand," Jeen said. "You don't like to shoot. That is not a reason to allow yourself to be killed."

"Or to allow my mother to be killed."

"While I respect your mother, it is not she who concerns me. You are my friend. I wish you to live. When Matella dresses you, you'll find the side holster I chose is quite comfortable." Jeen leaned back in her office chair and steepled her fingertips. "You have found your Donald White at last."

"He's not my Donald White," Petie said fiercely.

Jeen continued, "And in the most unlikely place possible, and with the most unlikely person. I am surprised that after so many years, he returned to the scene of his successful robbery, and even more surprised he zeroed in on your mother. I don't believe in coincidence, Petie Jeenli."

Put like that— "Are you saying by being Evelyn Jones, his pawn, I put my mother at risk?"

"Not necessarily. I suspect he must know she is your mother, but no matter from what angle I examine the situation, I cannot discern his motives. Specifically, why date your mother? Does he gain some twisted enjoyment in her ignorance of his deeds?" Jeen seemed troubled by her inability to follow his reasoning.

In Petie's rush to leave the camp, she hadn't thought of this angle. "I don't know. That doesn't seem like him."

"Regardless, I must ask—what are your plans? When you arrive in Rockin, when you find this man who wreaks cruel havoc everywhere he goes—what do you intend to do?"

"I'll speak to my mother, get her well away from him, then look for the scheme that's brought him to Rockin. He isn't there on vacation. Once I have a reason to give to the police that will satisfy them, he can be arrested, fingerprinted… and they'll know they caught a serial killer." From the look of him, Petie thought Chief Dumas would find that exactly to his taste.

"Would that end satisfy your need for revenge?" Jeen asked.

Petie started to answer right away, a hot, snappish answer—but no. Jeen had a point. Besides the safety of her mother, what was Petie seeking? "I don't know whether I want *revenge* anymore. At the time, what this guy did to Michele and Timmy was so horrifying that eighteen-year-old Evie wanted him caught and stopped before he killed again. I was so desperate for that grisly chief of police to find him. Instead she was happy to have me in her jail to abuse sexually. When I physically put a stop to that—I'd been in the system before, and she wasn't the first who had tried—she promised she would put me in prison forever."

"Your kindness in the bank, drawing attention away from Stacey Collins and her unrequited love, could not have been more ill-timed."

"I know. But Stacey had been nice to me, and I hate that kind of bullying."

"You are so American." Petie couldn't tell if Jeen was condemning her or praising her.

Probably best not to know.

"My desire for revenge came at the trial, when I realized how methodically Donald White had set me up."

"No one likes to play the fool." At least that was universal. "What's changed to make you wish for more, or less, than revenge?"

"At first, when I tracked him, I'd locate him because the people who welcomed him into their accommodations discovered he'd stolen their treasures. Of course, they then reported him to law enforcement. Several times, he was almost caught. By the time I'd learn all this, he'd be long gone. Perhaps—no, probably—he recalled his success in Rockin, realized it was easier to escape if no one remained alive to report his thefts. For him, murder is common sense."

Jeen hummed a little. "That is, in its way, more disturbing than a fiery desire to kill."

"Yes. In his case, it's not madness. It's a choice. Every move he makes is his own choice." Petie made the logical connection. "I'm back to my original desire. I want him stopped before he kills again. I want justice with a capital *J*."

As they landed at Anchorage International Airport, Matella put the finishing touches on Petie's makeup. "You will remember everything I taught you and apply your cosmetics to enhance?"

"I promise I will." Petie stood and slipped the black leather jacket on over her button-up red silk shirt. Her black slacks fit perfectly, as did her black platform sandals. Everything about her spoke of subtle wealth—and she thought she could get used to that. As she gathered the bags and prepared to descend the stairs to the tarmac, she said, "You asked so many questions about Alaska. Will you disembark and spend some time in Anchorage?"

Matella looked down at her toes. "I work for Miss Lee. She wishes me to return immediately and did not give me a passport."

Petie felt bad for asking. "Oh. Well. If you can only visit one place in Alaska, Midnight Sun Fishing Camp has better scenery."

"Yes, miss."

"Thank you so much for all you've done. Give my best to your sister."

"My sister?"

"Tziamara."

"Tziamara is not my sister." Matella seemed offended.

"I thought she was. The two of you share a similar look and similar backgrounds. You seem alike."

"Not so much, miss." Matella reached into Petie's old backpack, the one she had brought onto the plane. "Miss, I placed your goods into the Louis Vuitton backpack Miss Lee sent. But do you wish this?" She raised the tattered, one-eyed brown bear.

Petie's breath caught. She had almost left Tuddy behind. Not on purpose, but wasn't that what she wanted? To be rid of the psychic talking bear through no cause of her own?

"I throw away?" Matella gestured at the trash bag hanging on her cart.

"No. No, I'd better take him." They would finish this journey together.

Matella tucked the bear into the bag on Petie's shoulder.

Impulsively, Petie gave Matella a hug and made her way carefully down the stairs and toward the hotel shuttle services.

One night in Anchorage, and tomorrow morning she'd pick up her vehicle and be on her way to Rockin.

"Don't worry, Tuddy," she murmured. "Justice is at last in sight."

15

ON THURSDAY, ZONE JAMESON arrived at Midnight Sun Fishing Camp in a battered truck driven by a gray-haired woman who had picked him up on the side of the road. When he told Meriwa where he was going, she shook her head. "Bad timing."

Whatever that meant.

Meriwa pulled up to the front of the lodge in time for Zone to see a harried-looking woman loading her bags into a Land Rover. An equally harried-looking and desperately young camp employee sat in the driver's seat, nagging her. "Hurry up, Taylor. I've got to get back before Hawley starts screaming again."

Taylor snarled at the kid, climbed in, and they roared off.

Zone looked at Meriwa.

Meriwa said, "Told you."

He tried to pay her, but she shoved a crumpled piece of paper at him. "Here's my number. Pay me on the way back."

He wanted to think the lodge would give him a ride,

but he hadn't planned for the pilot having to buzz the land-
ing strip looking for moose or bears before setting down or
for him being unable to rent a vehicle to get to the camp.
In Washington, he lived primitive, yes. But after nearly ten
years away, no amount of knowledge could have prepared
him for the sheer size and scope and, well, *wildness* of the
Alaska wilderness.

He thanked Meriwa, tucked the slip of paper in his raincoat pocket and climbed the steps to stand on the wraparound
porch. On the plane to Alaska, he'd researched the camp. If
the online reviews were to be believed, the place was bucolic,
teaming with wildlife, the ideal place to fish, drink, meet old
friends and make new ones. Apparently, the food and drink
were exemplary, the service prompt and a guest's every wish
granted before he even expressed it.

Right now, as far as anyone was concerned, he could be a
guest. A drop-in, but still a guest.

So where was everybody?

"Where the hell did you come from?" A tall, fat man
dressed in a dark suit and starched and crumpled white shirt
lumbered around the corner of the porch. He looked hot,
tired and irritated, and the lopsided ends of his red power tie
hung from his open-necked collar.

Zone recognized him from his photos.

Hawley Foggo. The owner of the camp.

Zone replied, "Washington." Then because everyone
thought *DC*, he added, "State."

"You don't have a reservation."

"No."

"You simply dropped in and expected we could accommodate you?" Hawley oozed sarcasm.

Zone began to think he might have stepped into a situation that conflicted with his idea of a simple mission. "I'm looking for Petie."

Hawley took a step back. He looked Zone over: his broken-in hiking boots, jeans, rain gear. His gaze lingered on Zone's face, his rough-cut black hair, black-rimmed glasses, long, black beard that hung to his chest. "Petie. Really. Why?"

"She and I have business."

Hawley advanced; it was like an earthquake rolling irrepressibly across the earth. Hawley grabbed Zone's beard and tugged like a disbeliever testing Santa Claus.

Reflexively, Zone swung a fist at Hawley's face. Zone never saw him move, but he found himself in a headlock, crunched between Hawley's arm and ribs and uncomfortably close to his pit—and the big man smelled as if he'd been working hard.

Hawley demanded, "What business?"

Zone found himself staring at the boards of the porch and at Hawley's enormous shoes. He thought he could stomp on those shoes. He also thought Hawley could crack his neck. "Not saying."

Hawley's arm tightened.

Zone could slam his elbow into Hawley's ribs. But Hawley's ribs were nowhere close to the surface of Hawley's body. Hawley was enormous, upholstered in a protective layer of flesh, and any damned fool could see he held the upper hand.

Zone was not a damned fool. "Let me go, and we'll talk."

To his surprise, Hawley did let him go. "Come on." He turned and walked into the lodge.

Zone stared at Hawley's back. Zone could bring him down. He really could. It would take effort and would end in injury for them both.

As if Hawley heard him thinking, he called back, "Try anything, and you won't get any information."

"Right," Zone muttered and followed.

The Great Room was empty except for servers setting up the five o'clock appetizers and wine tasting. They peered at him curiously and at Hawley nervously and continued working.

Hawley walked behind the check-in desk, opened the massive wooden door and gestured Zone inside his office.

Zone went to the wet bar and removed the bottle of Patron Reposado tequila from the pocket of his raincoat. He poured two shot glasses full. He opened the minirefrigerator, found a plastic bag of lime wedges and filled two small bowls with kosher salt. He stacked everything on a small serving tray, brought it to the desk where Hawley had settled himself and slid one glass in front of Hawley.

Hawley viewed the pale gold liquor. "My favorite."

"I know." The information had been in one of the reviews for the camp, and Zone had thought he might need something to grease the wheel.

He placed the bag of lime wedges in the middle of the desk and one bowl of salt within reach of Hawley's hand. Zone collapsed into the chair with a groan. He'd been on the road for forty-eight hours, most of it spent hiking out of the Olympic Mountains, hitching a ride to the Seattle airport, discovering his delayed flight meant an overnight stay in Anchorage and scrambling to charter a different private plane to Midnight Sun because the first one had scheduled another job.

"I don't care," Hawley said.

"About what?"

"About your travel woes."

"Call Petie in, and you won't have to see my ugly face ever again." Zone stroked his beard. His jaws and chin still hurt from the jolt Hawley had given him.

Hawley toasted Zone and downed the tequila.

Zone toasted in return and sipped. It burned all the way down. "No salt?" he croaked.

"Bad for my blood pressure. What do you want with Petie?"

"Do you know who she is?"

"Why don't you tell me?"

"Petie is her alias. Her real name is Evelyn Jones."

"Evie. Petie." Hawley waggled his fingers. "Close enough."

That blithe dismissal gave Zone pause. This was not going to be easy. "Ten years ago, she was convicted of a gruesome double murder. She killed a young mother and child."

Hawley appeared unfazed. "You're a bounty hunter."

"No. I'm the husband and father."

Hawley's brows rose, giving Zone his first good look at those shrewd, dark eyes. "No shit."

"You'll call her in."

Hawley tapped his glass.

Zone filled it.

Hawley pointed to Zone's glass.

Zone sipped again—it still burned—and topped it off, also.

"How did you find out Petie works here?" Hawley opened his desk drawer, dug around and produced a bag of salted jalapeño peanuts, a bag of cheese horseradish chips and a giant bowl of trail mix. He tossed back the shot.

"I got a text." Zone was starving, so he munched on a handful of trail mix.

"From who?" Hawley opened the chips and lovingly spread them across his leather desk pad. With two fingers, he picked up a chip and ate it.

Zone started to talk, realized he'd eaten some kind of Japanese wasabi hotter-than-hell-oh-my-God-I-can't-breathe trail mix. He cast around for something innocuous to drink.

Hawley stared impassively at him and ate another chip.

Zone drank the tequila.

It didn't help.

He coughed and wheezed, ran to the wet bar and drank about a gallon of water one shot glass at a time. Then he blew his nose. When he could finally breathe, finally speak, he turned, expecting to see Hawley laughing at him.

Instead, Hawley was eating the wasabi trail mix and staring at Zone as if puzzled by his reaction.

That guy had an iron gut.

"From who?" Hawley repeated in a patient tone.

Zone had to think what they'd been talking about. The text telling him about Evelyn Jones. "Oh." He coughed to clear his throat and nose. "I don't know."

"You don't know?" Hawley's eyebrows rose.

"It was an anonymous text." Throat still scratchy.

"That's bullshit." Hawley didn't tap the glass this time, he just ran the lime around the rim and poured for them both.

Zone staggered over and sat down. He wasn't intoxicated… was he? He was still awash with water and exhausted and God…so broken. He was broken. Usually he knew. Usually he was aware. Usually he could ignore the pain of the past and avoid all the truths that ripped at his soul like razor blades.

Your fault. Your family. Your failure.

Here, in Alaska, now, in Alaska, he was too close to the tragedy.

Timmy dead. Michele dead. His fault. All his fault. "I know it's bullshit. Something's fishy about the anonymous thing. So I left my phone in Washington. Whoever it was… He doesn't know where I am or what I'm doing."

"He?"

"I don't know. Maybe she. But…" This shot went down a lot easier. Must be the water. And the lime he squeezed into his mouth. "I don't know."

"But he knows where she is. Was."

"Was?" This time, when Zone leaned forward, the liquor buzzed in his system. "Where is she now?"

Hawley shoved the bottle toward Zone and tapped his glass.

Zone took the bottle, poured two more shots. Realized he'd dribbled part of the tequila on the desk and poured again. Shoved one glass toward Hawley and took one glass for himself. "Petie's been working here for how long? Without a social security number?" He was at that point where he felt sharp, ready to fight the world for justice for his family. "If you've paid Petie a salary, the IRS is going to want their cut. If you haven't paid her at all—"

Hawley's small eyes narrowed to mere slits in his enormous face. "I can't decide if you're exorbitantly stupid or exorbitantly careless of your life. When you were flying in, did you look down? Did you see the wilderness, how it stretches in every direction? I own this land. I own the lakes, the river. My people do what I tell them to do. I could order your death, toss your body out for the wolves to eat and the coyotes to scavenge, and no one would ever find a single bone."

"I don't care about my life." Zone slammed down his glass and came to his feet. "I'm only living for vengeance."

"There's a lot of that going around." Hawley lifted his hand in a hypnotic gesture. "Look down at your boots."

Zone looked down. "What about 'em?"

"Now look up at the light." That same hypnotic gesture.

"Yeah, what…?" The single ceiling light separated into a thousand lights and spun in a circle.

Zone fell backward, knocked the chair over, landed flat on his back.

And stayed there.

16

HAWLEY SHOOK HIS HEAD. "Kids." He heaved himself to his feet, drank his shot and Zone's, came around and hefted the unconscious man over his shoulder. He opened the door and walked out into the Great Room and into a group of returning fishermen.

They gaped at him.

He rumbled a laugh. "The boy can't hold his tequila. Good fishing?"

A little laughter. General agreement.

"Let me get this guest up to a room to sleep it off. I'll be back in a minute to pour tequila for all of you." As he turned away, he gave Miska a look.

Miska followed him down the corridor. "There's no beds."

"He'll sleep in my room. It's not like I'll get to sleep anytime soon."

Miska opened the double doors that led to Hawley's suite and stepped back.

Hawley strode in, through the sitting area and over to the

low, massive California king. He dropped Zone on the comforter and surveyed him. "I want to see his face."

"Sure, boss." Miska stood at Hawley's right side. "You want me to shave him?"

"Yes. Cut off his beard. Shave his face." Hawley shot Miska a warning look. "Don't hurt him."

Miska looked offended. "Why would I do that?"

"Because I know what you did in your country." Hawley was as incisive as a surgeon's knife. "I know what your occupation was before you came here to work."

Miska took a step back.

Hawley viewed him with sour amusement. "A little late for caution, isn't it? Did you think I don't know the past of every one of my employees? That I would let someone work here who wasn't motivated to stay straight, learn fast and never betray me?"

"No, Mr. Foggo." In his country, Miska had played a dangerous game. If he had continued, inevitably he would have lost. He would have died. So he had made the decision to flee, to become someone else with a different vocation. Midnight Sun Fishing Camp had been a place where he could launch himself into a new life. Now he discovered Hawley Foggo had learned secrets Miska thought were buried deep. "I have great respect for your intelligence."

"Now you have a little more. Clean him up, then let him sleep. He's got one helluva trip ahead of him." Hawley rubbed his forehead. "I don't know, Miska. I don't know."

Miska hoisted Zone's body off the bed and over his shoulder. "Don't know what, sir?"

"I don't like the direction this is heading."

Miska headed for the bathroom.

Hawley uncorked the bottle beside his bed. He poured a shot glass full of tequila, picked it up and followed Miska.

"Petie leaves, then he comes looking for her? Something's happening. I hate to say it, but hell's a mile away and all the fences are down."

Miska dumped the unconscious Zone in the bathtub and dug Hawley's long scissors out of the bathroom drawer. "I don't know what that means, Mr. Foggo."

"It means we've got trouble. *She's* got trouble."

"I like Petie." Miska grabbed a handful of Zone's beard and chopped away at the length.

"Doesn't everybody?" Hawley spoke through his teeth, angry and sarcastic.

The sarcasm didn't make it through Miska's language filter. "No, sir. Sometimes guests don't like Miss Petie at all. Like the guy last month from Quemada. The one who came in with Jeen Lee. He hated Petie. She made him small."

The beard got more and more compact.

Hawley cast around in his mind, and the face popped up. "The one who left in the middle of a tantrum?"

"Yes. Him."

"Bradley. Bradley Copeland." Hawley looked at the unconscious Zone. That would explain who had sent the texts that brought Zone to the lodge intent on murder, or maybe just justice.

But Hawley was an acute judge of character, and he'd been observing Petie too closely for a damned long time. No matter what this guy thought, she had never killed anybody, most definitely not his wife and child.

So Hawley made a tough decision. Tough because it involved him getting over his ill humor. Tough because it would make his life more difficult. "Here it is, Miska. Someone's after Petie. They want to cut her off at the ankles."

"At the ankles?" English idioms seldom got through to Miska.

"Yeah." Hair from Zone's beard now covered his chest and fell into the tub. "Take off that mop of head hair, too," Hawley instructed.

Miska rolled Zone over and went to work. "Mr. Copeland wants to cut her off at the ankles?"

"Not literally. But yes, probably. Yet something else is going on." Which Hawley considered need-to-know, and Miska didn't need to know it all.

"Mr. Copeland is not what made Petie leave here." Miska was shrewd enough without Hawley's contribution. "Hand me the razor."

Hawley's shaver was fully charged. Good thing, because taking that mess off Zone's face and head would be a labor. "She left on a matter of her own, and someone's got to give her a fair chance to clean up the mess of her life."

"What can I do?"

Hawley told him.

17

ZONE WOKE AND WAS instantly off the bed and on his feet.

He didn't know where he was. In someone's bedroom.

He didn't know how he got here.

He only knew his heart pounded with the fear of a hunted beast. With the fear he'd felt in Magara. *Someone wants to feed me to the wolves.*

He was alone. The huge bed had been slept in, but only one pillow was rumpled. His mouth tasted like cheap cigar ash, and his head…

Fuck. He'd gone into a drinking contest with that giant Hawley Foggo. And he'd lost.

No shit. He never held his liquor well, sure as hell not straight tequila, and that guy outweighed him by a hundred pounds.

He closed his eyes and rubbed his hands over his forehead. His fingers didn't touch what they should touch.

His eyes sprang open.

He grabbed at his hair.

It was gone!

Then he grabbed at his beard.

He touched his bare and stubbled chin.

"What the fuck?" he shouted, and rushed to the mirror.

He'd been attacked by a barber! He'd been shaved, and his hair cut short and neatly trimmed. He looked like a goddamn businessman, not a woolly-mammoth mountain man. "Goddamn you, Hawley Foggo!"

"Good to see you up, sir." Some excessively normal-looking guy with a foreign accent waltzed through the door. He wore a black suit, white shirt and hiking boots, and he held a steaming tray of food. "I'm Miska. You'll want to eat before you see Hawley. He's easier to take on a full stomach."

Zone's anger evaporated in a rush of nausea. He leaned his hand on the bedpost. "You want me to throw up on you? Go ahead. Talk about food again."

"No problem, sir." Miska set the tray down on the chest of drawers. "We have hot coffee, black, and hot beet and cabbage soup. That will put you back on your feet."

"You've got to be kidding."

Miska walked toward him holding a soup spoon. "Old World hangover remedy. Works with vodka, whiskey, gin. Should work with tequila, too." He offered the spoon.

Zone grabbed his wrist. "Are you the one who cut my hair?"

He didn't know what happened, but all of a sudden he was on his back staring at the ceiling.

Was every person in this place a goddamn ninja?

Miska stood over him and straightened his cuffs. "Yes. On Mr. Foggo's request, I shaved you, too. You look better."

Zone rolled over onto his hands and knees. He thought hard about whether or not he could get the rest of the way to his feet and thought harder about whether standing up would be a smart move.

The fall had not improved his headache.

Miska put his hands under Zone's chest, picked him up and set him on his feet. "You've slept more than twelve hours. With food, you'll be fine."

Miska must be right, because Zone wasn't about to take him on. He staggered over to the chest of drawers.

The spoon appeared on the tray, conveyed by Miska's hand.

Zone took it and cautiously swallowed a little of the broth and waited for it to come up.

It didn't.

In fact, it tasted pretty good, replacing the ashes in his mouth with some decent flavors.

"Beef and bacon, potatoes, cabbage and leeks," Miska told him. "Bathroom's in there. Mr. Foggo had me secure you fresh clothes."

Zone lifted the mug of coffee and paused. "What? Clothes from someone he actually did kill, whose bones were a snack for the wolves?"

"The clothes came from the gift shop, so I think not. You'll want to shower, shit and shave, then Mr. Foggo will meet with you and give you the information you require."

Zone stopped eating and turned to Miska. "About the location of that bitch Evelyn Jones?"

Something about the way Miska stood made Zone remember how quickly Miska had smacked him to the floor. "It would be wise to remember Miss Petie is much beloved by the employees of Midnight Sun Fishing Camp."

"She killed my wife and child."

"Sir, I know a lot about such matters, and I promise you she did not."

"Hawley told you to say that."

"No."

"Whatever." Zone turned back to the soup, but after a few more bites, he decided that was enough. More than enough. Going into the bathroom, he locked the door, followed Miska's advice and prepared to meet Hawley one more time.

Hawley sent Zone Jameson out of his office with an updated schedule of Petie's destination, the name of her hotel, the room she occupied, a room in the same hotel reserved in Zone's name and a terse account of what Petie claimed had occurred in her past.

Obviously, Zone believed none of it and left with all his original intentions intact. Whatever they were.

Hawley knew he hadn't done his best by Petie. He knew she had problems he'd never imagined and could never solve. He had never asked her about them. Never. All these years.

But was that any reason to leave him?

Hawley rose and groaned at the effort. He walked to the bar, poured a tumbler of the Patron Reposado tequila the boy had brought him, returned to his desk and seated himself.

From the beginning, life had taught Hawley Foggo many brutal lessons. He paid life back by going his own way, never caring about people, only things. So when had he come to think of Petie as his? He had set himself up for heartbreak.

He lifted a glass to his monitor. "Good luck to you, Evelyn Jones." Leaning forward, he deleted the photo file labeled *Petie*.

18

THAT MORNING, THE HOTEL shuttle service drove Petie to the airport car-rental company, where she obtained the use of a gray Infiniti QX60 with all-wheel drive. Jeen Lee had wanted her to take a BMW M2. She said it would make the drive from Anchorage to Rockin enjoyable.

Petie had shuddered and politely refused.

Jeen argued a sporty car would lend her cachet.

Petie explained she wanted to blend in not stand out.

The truth was, the last fast car Petie had driven was Michele Jameson's Jaguar, and she didn't care if she never again drove a sports car. All she wanted to do was get from one place to the other as efficiently as possible without attracting a second glance, and the Infiniti SUV would perform that task admirably.

Anchorage had grown since Petie was there last. Construction was everywhere, the traffic sucked and the car's GPS sent her in circles, but at last she was on the highway to Rockin. She had to stop at Eklutna Village to use their facilities and converse politely with the resident friendly person who wanted to tell her the whole history of the village.

By the time she saw the sign welcoming her to Rockin and she slowed to the required thirty-five miles an hour, she was sick with anticipation and fear.

Her mother was nearby.

Donald White was somewhere in the vicinity.

Mama was in danger.

Should Petie have called Ioana?

She shuddered at the thought of conducting that conversation over the phone.

Should she drive to her mother's workplace?

Yes. Yes, she should.

She stopped, programmed in Frontier Real Estate and drove five blocks to the small office. She stopped in the parking lot, looked at the cars and realized it had been ten years and she didn't know what her mother drove.

Then she lucked out.

A blue Nissan Murano pulled up, and Ioana got out of the driver's side.

A couple got out of the back seat.

They were all smiling as they walked into the real estate office.

Petie laughed a little. Not only was her mother alive and well, it looked like she'd just made a sale. Mama... Seeing her, being so close, watching over her... Petie experienced the solid knowledge she'd made the right decision to come to Rockin. She could, she *would*, save her mother from harm.

Okay! Back to the hotel.

The population had grown, the city limits had expanded, and Petie passed a Walmart and a Red Apple Market.

Wow. Those were new.

To the left an old drive-in had been remodeled, and carhops brought out *The Best Burgers in Rockin.* Petie almost swerved in and parked. She hadn't had a real hamburger at a real drive-in for...more years than she wanted to count.

As she entered downtown, she slowed again to twenty-five, much to the disgust of the Ram pickup behind her. But he could tailgate as much as he wanted. She was not going to get picked up for speeding. She didn't care if Rockin did have a new chief of police, she planned to get in and out of town without a confrontation with law enforcement.

All along Main Street and the side streets, she observed people walking briskly, biking intently, strolling into small boutiques and art shops and coming out carrying packages. She knew the bustle would be different in winter; heads down, fighting the wind and the cold. But many of the old, sad buildings had been replaced with new restaurants, new medical and legal businesses and an expanded regional hospital.

In the ten years since she'd left in a prison van, Rockin had changed its face.

Unable to stop herself as she drove past, she glanced at the Rockin City Hall.

That hadn't been updated. It was the same, stolid lump of wind-scoured gray stone it had been before, and irresistibly the memory of sitting in a cell, shivering with fear and cold, made her lower the window.

She needed air.

The bank hadn't changed, either. Marble columns supported a roof where carved Greek gods posed beneath the peak, and stone stairs led to that impressive porch. One of those absurdly large bronze doors was propped open. Petie remembered how hard she had pulled at that door, how the winter wind had finally caught and slammed it back, how embarrassed her eighteen-year-old self had been. Her cheeks burned with remembered humiliation, and Petie missed the turn into her hotel.

Carefully she flipped on the blinker and went around the block.

The pickup roared past, the guy inside expressing his opinion with two loud engine pulses.

"You've got a small penis," she said aloud and turned into the portico of the Rockin Hotel.

The hotel covered the city block where the run-down grocery store had been located…the grocery store where she'd seen her mother and hidden in the butcher's back room.

This four-story building looked new and prosperous.

Elvis Presley came out of the revolving door and hurried to the SUV's driver's side.

No, really. Elvis, all in white with sideburns and spangles. She lowered the window.

"Are you checking in?" he sang. He did a pretty good Elvis impression.

"Yes?" She wasn't sure if she was supposed to sing back.

He tore off a ticket and handed it to her. He waved at the valet desk; Elvis Jr. zipped over and unloaded her wheeled bag onto a cart. When he tried to take her backpack, she held tight and shook her head. She tipped Elvis the valet—working in the hospitality business, she knew the importance of tipping—and followed Elvis Jr. and her luggage into the lobby.

The girl behind the check-in desk was made up to look like Adele, but to Petie's disappointment, she didn't sing.

Petie laid out the driver's license and brand-new credit card that identified her as Petie Jeenli.

"Your room isn't ready yet. It'll be about—" Adele checked the computer "—thirty minutes. We'll store your luggage. If you'd like to sit in the library, cookies, fruit and beverages are there for you to enjoy."

"Thank you, I'll do that." Petie wandered toward the library, feeling oddly out of place, as if the people in the lobby could see that she hadn't left Midnight Sun Fishing Camp for ten years. The air felt different, faintly abrasive, buzzing with a different vibe. She'd once lived in California, where it was busy, overpopulated, but here, now, she was weirdly aware of all the human beings, the ones she could see and the ones beyond these walls. Cars and trucks rumbled past the hotel, a disturbance she couldn't hear but could sense. The lobby, with its colorful rock-star cardboard cutouts and the autographed photos, offended her eyes. The music was, not surprisingly, rock. She liked rock, but really, this was all too much.

"Excuse me."

The touch on her arm made Petie jump and turn in a smooth, defensive stance.

The woman who stood there backed up, palms forward in the universal surrender gesture. "Sorry, I didn't mean to startle you. I was wondering if I could help. Are you looking for something?"

Her. Stacey Collins from the Rockin American Bank.

Petie had thought she was prepared to meet someone from her past, but she lost her breath.

Stacey Collins had borne witness against her. Reluctantly, but she had.

Worse, just now Petie had almost punched her.

No, worse—Stacey Collins could know her.

But Stacey was smiling, no recognition in her face. Petie's continued frozen horror made a mark, though, for Stacey asked, "Is there something wrong?"

Petie caught her breath, remembered why she was here, straightened and said, "I'm supposed to go to the hotel library until my room's ready. I was distracted by the, um, rocker memorabilia."

Stacey looked around. "Isn't this the *best*? People were fighting the idea of building the hotel, said it wouldn't do enough business and would fail, and we'd be stuck with a big, empty building in the middle of town. But I said we had to have vision. The number of visitors coming to Denali is increasing every year, and I knew if Rockin was bold, we could woo them, grab them, get in on the action."

Petie nodded because Stacey seemed to expect a response.

Stacey nodded back. "I was on the city council, and I helped push through the hotel. While I was on the council, I helped bring in Walmart. Having a major shopping center has brought prosperity, too."

Petie finally snapped to the situation. Stacey was running for mayor. She was soliciting Petie's vote. "I'm sorry, I don't live here. I merely came to, um, work. I'm an accountant. Online."

Stacey smiled. "I suspected you were a visitor. I know everyone who lives here."

Petie flashed back to her first visit to the bank. Norma had said that, too.

Stacey cocked her head. "Although you remind me of someone. Have we met?"

Petie lifted her chin, smiled in the way she knew emphasized her asymmetrical face. "I'm originally from California. Did you go to school there?"

"Yes. And I've visited since!" Stacey laughed at the tenuous bridge between them. She stuck out her hand. "I'm Stacey Collins."

They shook. *Yeah, I know.* "I'm Petie Jeenli."

"My fundraiser's about to start, and there's food and wine, and a bunch of women who love to talk and would gladly welcome you. Rather than go to the hotel library, why not come with me?"

"Women?"

"I'm going to run for mayor of Rockin, and I'm not nuts. If I'm going to be elected, it's the women who will do it."

"I suppose that's true." Petie swallowed. Her mother might be there, and Petie was torn between desperately wanting the reunion and dreading the moment her mother saw her. Would Ioana be happy? Furious? Torn, as she had been before, between relief and fright?

And when Petie told her about Donald White... She had imagined every possible scenario, and none of them turned out well. But it had to be done, and she'd planned to find Ioana as soon as she could put her luggage in her room and head out. "If you're sure I won't be an imposition, I'd love to come to your fundraiser."

Stacey linked arms with Petie and led her to the corridor behind the elevators. "Come on, then."

19

PETIE BROKE A SWEAT as they entered the ballroom.

At the far end, the stage was set up with a lectern. Along one side ran a long buffet with cold dishes—dips, cheeses, charcuterie and breads—and hot dishes—wings, mac and cheese, meatballs, a medley of roasted vegetables.

Women in classic business suits and tough working gear flocked to the food, laughing and chatting as they filled their plates and found seats at the wide round tables.

In two of the corners, bars had been set up serving water, soft drinks, beer and wine.

Yet for all there were thirty women and one man in the large room, it looked almost empty. Petie understood now; she'd been brought in to fill a seat.

She scanned the faces; she recognized none of the women. Her mother was not here. Neither was former Chief George. Really, who else knew Petie?

A woman with a small, worn yellow notepad hurried up.

"Faye, I'm so glad you made it!" Stacey offered her hand and they shook briskly.

"This is my guest, Petie Jeenli. She's new to the area. This is Faye Miller."

"The reporter," Petie said.

Faye shook Petie's hand and summed her up with one sharp glance. "How did you know?"

"I read the paper."

"You're from out of town and you read the *Rockin Herald*?"

"I was coming here to work." Petie looked Faye right in the eye. "I wanted to know about the town."

"Hm." Clearly, Faye had her doubts. "Where do you work?"

"I'm self-employed."

Faye's focus shifted back to Stacey. "Thanks for inviting me to the kickoff of your campaign. Can't wait to hear your speech. What are you going to say that's different? How are you *really* going to make a difference?"

Stacey stepped back a pace, then forward. "Don't mince words, Faye. Throw down that gauntlet."

Faye nodded sharply. "You're a woman in a man's country. You're a challenger to the establishment. How are you going to shake things up?"

Wow. Plain speaking. Petie admired that.

Stacey's eyes narrowed. "I'm going to have to up my game to impress you."

"Not me. My readers. You know, the voters." Faye had a point, a good one.

"You'll have to listen to my speech. I promise it will be memorable."

"I'll record every word," Faye answered. As Stacey walked away, she muttered, "Every insipid word."

"Will it be insipid?" Petie asked.

Faye turned on Petie. "With Stacey, who knows? She's smart. Speaking to a group of women requires a different approach than speaking to men. It'll be interesting to see how and if she taps the feminine vote." Faye raised her notebook and readied her pen. "Petie Jeenli. How do you spell that? Have you visited Rockin before?"

Petie thought. Should she admit to having been here before? What could it hurt? "I visited once, briefly, about ten years ago." There. Honest and yet unrevealing.

Faye peered over her notebook at Petie. "What do you think of the changes to Rockin?"

"The town seems revived."

Faye scribbled. "In what way?"

"New stores, new hotel, and this seems to be a very vital gathering."

Faye scribbled again. "Thank you. Hope you enjoy your stay." Before she'd finished speaking, she moved to the next women, two tall, weary-looking forty-year-olds in Red Wing boots, jeans, long-sleeved plaid shirts and fluorescent construction safety vests.

Meanwhile, Stacey worked the room. As more women came in, she greeted the newcomers, shook hands, introduced the women and organized them into groups for her photographer to snap. A young female police officer came in and looked around uncertainly; in mere moments, Stacey was introducing her to the construction workers. Petie admired her smooth knack for bringing people together. In the hospitality business, that ability was gold—and in politics, Petie supposed.

At five-thirty, the one gentleman in the crowd climbed the stairs to the stage and stared around at the crowd of women.

General shushing started. Someone tapped their glass with

a spoon. All attention centered on him and on Stacey waiting at the bottom step.

"Most of you know me." He nodded around the room.
"I'm Marc Yazzie, the owner of Yazzie Rentals, so if you've
ever needed a compactor, we've met."

Everyone laughed warmly.

Petie thought Marc was pleasant-looking; dark hair reced-
ing away from his broad forehead, working man's attire and
an all-embracing smile.

"I'm also Stacey Collins's campaign manager. I'm not doing
this job because I need more work. I'm doing it because, since
Stacey got on the city council, Rockin's population has in-
creased by one hundred people. I hear what you're saying—
that isn't a lot. But that reversed a twenty-five year downturn.
With an increase in tourism, the city's income is up, and most
important—*my* income is up."

More laughter.

"I know who to credit—Stacey Collins. That's why I took
on the extra work. That's why my wife encouraged me to
help with Stacey's campaign. That's why my kids are willing to see less of me… Although as teenagers, I suspect they
haven't noticed my absence."

One woman nodded her head emphatically. His wife, Petie
supposed.

"But you didn't come to listen to me. You came to hear
our candidate tell you how she's going to continue to improve
your lives. Let's have a warm welcome for Stacey Collins!"

Enthusiastic applause. Some cheers. Most of the women
who were seated stood up.

Faye sank into a chair at a dining table up front, put her
phone on the table—Petie supposed she was recording the
speech—yet also kept her notebook and pen poised for action.

"I was born in Rockin." Stacey looked over the audience,

making eye contact. "My grandmother's family was one of the original Alaska settlers. My grandparents, God bless them, raised me. They had to, because from my first memory, I knew my mother was mentally unstable."

Wow. So this was what Faye meant when she said Stacey was smart and knew her audience. She hooked the women with the personal, emotional story, and…it would be interesting to see how she turned it into a sales pitch for her campaign.

"My grandmother and grandfather were good people, dealing with their difficult daughter and bewildered granddaughter. When I was six, I decided Santa Claus was my father." Stacey gave a crooked smile. "When I was a freshman in high school, in front of everyone who mattered, one of the other girls asked me, 'This morning, was that your mother digging through our garbage?'"

All around the room, women winced in sympathy.

"Of course, it was. I might have been beaten down, but one of the popular girls said, 'I'd dig through garbage, too, if you'd toss your blue sweater out. I envy you that sweater!' She linked her arm with mine and we went to lunch, the whole crowd of popular girls trailing after." Stacey smiled at someone in the crowd.

A construction worker stood close by. Petie heard her murmur, "Who's she looking at?"

Behind her, Petie heard the scrape and clatter of a chair being pulled out.

A smoke-roughened, sarcastic voice answered, "Stephani Terwilliger. Married to the bank president, who our lovely Stacey Collins loves. Stacey and Stephani are best pals. It's so Greek tragedy as to be nauseating."

Petie stiffened. She knew that voice.

Chief of Police Gretchen George.

20

OR RATHER—*EX*-CHIEF OF POLICE Gretchen George.

Petie half turned.

Wretchen Gretchen wore ironed khaki pants, a starched white button-up shirt with the sleeves rolled up and black boots. Her harshly tanned face was more wizened than Petie remembered. Before her on the table she had a full plate of food, a full wineglass, and ignoring the No Smoking signs, she lit a cigarette and balanced it on her bread plate.

In her surreptitious survey, Petie realized—the woman was actually as weird and warped as she appeared in all those nightmares.

All around, Stacey Collins supporters scowled and moved away.

Faye appeared at Petie's side.

Petie raised an inquiring brow at her.

Faye tilted her head toward Chief George. She had her notebook and pen in hand and her phone in her shirt pocket.

Stacey ignored the ex-chief's appearance and continued

unabated. "My new friend's father worked at the bank. He gave me a part-time job, taught me the rudiments of finance and economy... My grandparents died while I was in college. My mother disappeared not long after."

The women murmured in sympathy.

Wretchen Gretchen said loudly, "I love to hear a touching load of crap," and dug into her dinner.

The construction worker swung on her. "If you don't like Stacey, what are you doing here?"

Wretchen Gretchen smiled, her teeth uneven and yellowed. Picking up her cigarette, she took a long drag. "Free food. Free drink. She owes me."

Petie murmured to Faye, "Why does Stacey owe her?"

"She used to be the chief of police." Faye spoke so quietly Petie had to lean closer. "Six years ago, Stacey drove through the funding for law-officer body cameras. Within the first week, Wretchen Gretchen was caught on video sexually harassing an underage female in custody. There'd been rumors for years."

"I'll bet." Petie knew firsthand the truth of those rumors.

"It was like she didn't think anyone would watch the video. Or take the issue seriously." Faye was clearly incredulous. "Next thing, Gretchen is out of a job and barely scraping by. She's got a real case of the ass about Stacey Collins."

Stacey's voice grew stronger, her message more sincere. "You're wondering why I'm dragging you through my early life, but I want you to understand my devotion to Rockin. Rockin is like me, and I'm like Rockin. Rockin was the town the other football teams beat. Rockin was the town all the shiny-teethed other town cheerleaders picked on. Corruption oozed through the government and law enforcement."

"Fuck you, bitch." Ex-Chief Gretchen didn't bother to keep her voice down.

From behind her, Petie heard a thump, something firm hitting something hollow.

"Whoops. Sorry. My elbow flew out as I was walking past." It was the construction worker who had spoken before. "Hope you're not hurt."

"Good shot, Ava."

Without shame, both Petie and Faye turned to look.

Faye pulled a small camera out of her pocket and snapped photos of Wretchen Gretchen, rubbing the bump on her head while one of the construction workers stood towering over her, fists on her hips.

Wretchen Gretchen was hopping mad. She was also five foot almost nothing, skinny and in her sixties.

Ava was just as mad, six feet tall, well-muscled and twenty years younger.

At one time, out of sheer orneriness and exerting her power as a law officer, Ex-Chief George might have been able to take her. But not now.

The police officer moved toward the confrontation.

Wretchen Gretchen glanced at her, reached for her cigarette, took a puff and blew it toward Ava's face.

Ava reached down, plucked the cigarette from Wretchen Gretchen's fingers and ground it out in her gravy. "You could light another one," she said, "but I know Officer Donatti. She'll throw you out, and I'll help."

Wretchen Gretchen turned so red, she looked like a cartoon character about to blow steam out her ears. Then the quiet must have caught her attention. She looked around.

So did Petie.

Stacey had stopped talking. Every eye was on the drama between Ex-Chief George and Ava. Silence crowded the room.

Wretchen Gretchen subsided. She pushed the plate away. She stood and stalked out.

Satisfied, Ava returned her attention to Stacey.

"Ahem." Stacey cleared her throat and picked up without a hitch, and Faye moved back to the dining table near the stage. "When I returned from college, Rockin was the same feeble, dying town with empty retail space and sordid motels. The people in Rockin deserve better." Stacey had the crowd gripped by their throats. "I could always see Rockin's potential to appeal to tourists visiting Denali. I ran for city council, and when I was elected, I spearheaded the Rockin revival." She lifted a hand and gestured at the ballroom, the chandeliers and the waiters waiting to serve flutes of champagne. "This is the result. This, and the weekend market in the town square, and the spa, and the new stores. When I am elected mayor…"

An arm slid around Petie's waist and hugged tightly. A head rested on Petie's shoulder. A familiar scent enveloped her. "Mama," she whispered.

21

FOR ALL PETIE'S WORRY about meeting Ioana after so many years, nothing could have prepared her for the warmth that swept her, the primal joy of once again being with her mother, the woman who had carried her, sheltered her, loved her.

Ioana's warm, husky voice murmured, "Darling girl, what are you doing here?"

"Looking for you. I want to warn you—" Petie stopped.

Stacey observed the two of them while never missing a word of her speech.

Petie couldn't tell Ioana about Donald White here, now, in the ballroom.

"Later." Ioana withdrew her arm and stood shoulder to shoulder with Petie. After a moment, she whispered, "You look fabulous. Where have you been? I hope Paris or London or Tokyo."

"Remember? I told you. At that fishing camp in western Alaska."

A startled inhale, then Ioana wrapped her arm tightly

around Petie's shoulders. "Still? No. That's not what I wanted for you!"

"I didn't have a lot of options."

Ioana's arm tightened. "After the landslide, I should have somehow sent you abroad."

"Mama, I had no identification." Petie kept her voice low.

"No, and I didn't know where you'd be safe, I couldn't leave your sister to go on the lam with you, and I knew...I knew you were strong."

"I don't bear any grudges, Mama." For a long time, she had, but the years had worn it away.

"Thank you for that. Thank you for finding me. This is the best day of my life."

Petie smiled. "Thank *you* for that."

"Evie—"

"It's Petie now. Petie Jeenli."

"Of course. I understand. I will remember."

It was true. With Ioana's background, she would remember. "Petie, you do look as if you've prospered."

Petie thought of all the investments. "Actually, I have." She took the opportunity to glance at her mother, seeking changes, hoping to see none.

The years had been good to Ioana. She was, as Petie had noted, trim and fit, her petite, curvaceous figure was clothed in a swirl of peacock blue that gave depth to her blue eyes and richness to the upsweep of her blond hair. She wore heels so high that Petie in her sandals winced in imagined agony, and a clunky antique gold bracelet and choker studded with fake cabochon sapphires so large they were tacky.

Petie did a sharp double take that almost dislocated her neck. She grabbed Ioana's wrist, lifted it and looked hard at the bracelet.

Those were *real* sapphires. This was real gold. The antique choker and bracelet were genuine—and worth a fortune.

22

"MOTHER! WHERE DID YOU get those?" Petie knew the answer.

She dreaded the answer.

"I am listening to our speaker. Please have the courtesy to do so also." But Ioana smiled secretly, like a woman in love.

Oh, no. He'd given her jewelry. He'd wooed her so well, she'd fallen in love. Petie had hoped so much the photo she'd seen had been a single incident. "Your *boyfriend* gave them to you?"

Ioana turned to Petie, put her hand on her hip and in a voice that was a little louder than it needed to be, she said, "Are you criticizing me for dating a man? The first man I've bothered with since I left your father? You two children are adults. You're out of the house. Why shouldn't I go out for a meal and some conversation?"

"And sex?" Petie might have been a little too loud, too.

The construction workers hushed them and glared furiously.

Petie put her hand to her forehead. She hadn't meant to say that. In the lowest possible tone, she said, "I'm sorry, Mother. I meant—"

Enthusiastic clapping cut her off.

Stacey Collins had finished her speech.

Marc got up on the podium again. "What an inspiration! Let's give Stacey another round of applause."

Shoulder to shoulder and stiff with anger, Petie and her mother faced forward and clapped.

"Everyone here wants Stacey Collins to win the election," Marc said. "We are all agreed it's time for a change, time to let a new vision direct Rockin."

Petie noted that Faye was drifting around the room, listening to the conversations, and shivered at the thought that Faye had heard the exchange between her and her mother.

Marc was still talking. "If we are to defeat the incumbent, we need funds. Open your wallets and your hearts…"

"Mama, let's go," Petie murmured, and tried to ease Ioana toward the door.

Ioana planted her high heels in the plush carpet and refused to budge. "I'm going to contribute to Stacey's campaign. She has my complete support. Do you know she ousted that wicked old woman who ran the shoddy investigation that led to your conviction? I suppose you have a complaint about that, too?"

"No, you're right. Thank you for supporting her. And me." Ioana believed Petie about the murders. She would believe her about Donald White…once she regained her temper. Petie began her retreat. "My room should be ready."

"You're staying *here*? At the *hotel*?"

"Yes. I'm going to take my luggage up. I'll give you a call in an hour. Is that enough time? Then we can meet—"

"I have a date. I'm going out to dinner. And no, not for

sex." Ioana was still spitting mad. "You can keep your prudish concerns to yourself. Derrick has been the perfect gentleman."

Petie stepped back and looked her mother over from top to toe. "Mama, if Derrick has been a perfect gentleman, that should make you suspicious. Because you're a knockout. Mother, you know that. You've always had a solid sense of your own worth. Think about it."

"Suspicious of what? He's retired with money." Ioana shook her finger in Petie's face. "Our date tonight is here in the dining room. It's the only nice restaurant in town. I'll call you. You'll come down and join us for dessert. You'll meet Derrick. You'll like him."

Petie tried to think beyond her fear and revulsion. "If I do that, you'll come up to my room afterward? And listen to me? Mama, what I've got to say…it's a matter of life and death."

Hearing Petie's earnest intention, Ioana's ire faded. "Sweetheart, what is wrong?"

There. There was Faye standing close, ears perked, listening in on what was all too obviously a heated confrontation.

Ava and her friend were eyeing them, too, and Stacey Collins was still glancing toward them with concern.

In careful Belarusian, Petie said, "I'll tell you afterward. Okay?"

Her mother froze, her fury derailed. In a Belarusian that sounded more fluent, less formal, she asked, "How do you know the language?"

"I have had much time alone. I learned many languages. I learned Belarusian to honor you."

As if bewildered, her mother stepped back and again in Belarusian, she said, "I haven't heard my language since I left Belarus at sixteen. You did this for me?"

"You are my mother. I honor you, your past and your present." Petie saw Faye watching them as if trying to decipher some meaning from the conversation. "Mother, I love you."

"I love you, too, my darling girl." Pulling Petie close, Ioana hugged her. "I will listen to you. But you have to promise you'll meet Derrick with an open mind."

"I can't promise that, but I can promise I will explain." Petie pressed her mother's hand, swiveled and walked toward the lobby, her luggage, the key to her room and a moment of peace before the storm.

"Dress nicely." Ioana had that implacable tone in her voice.

Petie stumbled on the edge of the carpet and kept going. Of course she had to dress nicely. To impress her mother's killer boyfriend.

23

JIMI HENDRIX SHOWED PETIE to her suite. He explained the thermostat and the controls for the TV and promised to send housekeeping with a shower cap. She thanked him, tipped him, waited until he'd closed the door behind him, then flung her backpack across the room at the desk. "Damn it." That hadn't gone well. The first time she'd seen her mother and she'd alienated her.

Petie's phone rang.

Jeen Lee wanted a video call. Of course.

Petie picked up.

Although it was very early Saturday morning in Quemada, Jeen was perfectly groomed and wore her business suit. Did she never leave the office? "Please report." She made the demand as if she had every right.

Which Petie supposed she did, since she'd bankrolled Petie's flight from Midnight Sun Fishing Camp and arrival in Rockin. "Tonight I'm having dessert with Donald White and my mother. Derrick Black." She put her hand to her aching forehead. "Whatever his name is this time."

"An interesting turn of events. What do you hope to accomplish?"

"Poison in his food?" Petie was joking.

"That seems a precarious decision." Jeen didn't comprehend the humor; perhaps to her, if possible, it was an acceptable option. "I sense your frustration. Without a detailed plan, this will not be as easy as you'd hoped."

"Taking him down should be straightforward."

With some humor, Jeen Lee said, "Where humans are involved, nothing is straightforward."

"I suppose," Petie muttered.

In a carefully neutral voice, Jeen said, "For instance, I was wondering if Matella is with you."

"What? Why?"

"She did not return with the plane."

"You're kidding!" Petie remembered Matella's touristlike interest in Alaska. But— "She didn't have a passport. How did she get away from the plane? Anchorage is an international airport. You can't stroll in and out without a passport."

"How do you know she didn't have a passport?"

"She said so." Then Petie remembered. "No. Wait. That's not what she said. She said, 'Miss Lee did not give me a passport.'"

"A cautious way of speaking."

Petie made the logical leap. "So she had a passport which you did not give her. Where did she get it?"

"I do not know. I intend to find out. If you see her, please let me know."

Petie didn't envy Matella when Jeen found her. "If she wished to smuggle herself into the United States, she's not going to follow *me*. She's heard everything we've said. She knows we're friends."

Jeen's voice warmed, and she inclined her head. "We are indeed friends, and you're right. Matella knows that. But she has no money. Or at least none that I gave her. She is very capable. She can cook. She can care for all your physical needs. She might in fact follow you in the hope you will hire her."

"Jeen Lee, I swear to you, I haven't seen her. Furthermore, should she approach me, I will do what I can to detain her."

"Don't do that, I beg. She is trained in martial arts and in weaponry. My friend, she could hurt you."

"Then if I see her, I'll let you know ASAP."

Jeen Lee laughed softly. "*As soon as possible.* Of course."

"I'm sorry, Jeen. I know you depended on Matella and her loyalty."

"For most people, loyalty is for sale, yet in this circumstance, I am uneasy. She is always with me and Tziamara. I have spoken with Tziamara, and she insists whoever bought Matella's loyalty did so after she left to board the plane."

"So the question is—who?"

"And for what purpose?"

"What did she want so badly she would abandon and betray you?" Which seemed a risky proposition to Petie.

"I rescued her, educated her, trained her, so of course she wants to be free of any obligation to me." Jeen didn't sound angry or surprised, merely thoughtful. "But what does it have to do with you?"

"With me?" Petie was taken aback. "Why would it have anything to do with me?"

"The timing is suspicious. You leave Midnight Sun Fishing Camp. I send Matella. With the help of some anonymous person, she disappears. As you pointed out, if I could figure out who you are, anyone who was interested could also figure it out." Jeen expressed her worry with absolute stillness. "That is ominous."

"Sure. Make this look like a conspiracy." Petie held her phone and paced.

"Dark forces are at work. What do we dare hope?"

"That Matella heard there are a lot of men in Alaska desperate for a woman, and she wants to find one for herself?"

"That would make my worries look silly." Reflectively, Jeen said, "I would be glad of that."

"We could also hope that I take care of Donald White before word gets out that the convicted murderer Evelyn Jones has returned to town." Petie gestured, then brought the phone back to see Jeen's reaction.

"I'd like to think we can hope for more than that."

"I'd like to think that, too. But let's start with that."

"Speak to your mother. Tell her all the facts. She's an immigrant and a survivor. She is not easily led astray."

"Yes, but she…" How to express this? "She and I are so much alike. We go head-to-head on everything, and in the past, I've disappointed her. She still thinks I'm that young, foolish person who took the wrong path."

"She hasn't met the Evelyn Jones you have become."

"No." The reminder calmed Petie. "Will she be surprised?"

"Most surprised, my dear friend. You have become a formidable adversary."

24

PETIE DIDN'T KNOW ABOUT being a formidable adversary, but she thought she might be able to talk to her mother reasonably. Never mind that the most popular social-media post she'd ever seen said, *There are no functional families.*

She didn't want to unpack. She had hoped to quickly resolve everything—remove her mother from Donald White's influence, alert the authorities to his identity and return to Midnight Sun Fishing Camp where she could smooth things over with Hawley. Then she'd have a familiar place where she could figure out her next move, clear her name, regain her freedom and a place in society.

But one thing the hospitality business had taught her: everything took longer than planned. And the argument with her mother had illustrated that truth.

She flipped open her suitcase and—oh, my. The clothes! And the shoes! They'd been chosen with an eye to creating the image of sophistication, to give her all the respectability money could offer.

She'd never worn clothes like these. She unpacked, placing them in drawers and on hangers. She removed Tuddy from her shoulder bag; she pulled him out and sat him on the desk. "We're almost there, right, buddy? We've almost caught up with Timmy's killer." She wanted reassurance, but Tuddy remained stubbornly silent.

Damned uncooperative bear.

She tried to decide what *Dress nicely* meant, decided on a navy business suit, because it looked intimidating, and a peach cotton T-shirt, because she knew the casual top would irritate her mother.

She couldn't help it. She was hardwired to irritate her mother.

She hesitated about strapping on the holster and pistol. Donald White would never make a move in such a public place, but she couldn't take the chance of leaving the Ruger behind. She loaded the pistol and, making sure the safety was on, she slid it into the side pocket of her horrifyingly expensive backpack.

It fit perfectly. No wonder Jeen Lee had sent this particular bag.

Petie was touching up her makeup when Ioana's text came in.

Derrick excited to meet you. Come to the restaurant for dessert.

Petie texted back a thumbs-up.
The next text came in.

Behave!

Petie did not text a thumbs-up for that.
The restaurant surprised Petie: white tablecloths, crystal

and flowers. It seemed so unlike Rockin, yet the place was full. The diners *dressed nicely*...some of them. Others wore jeans, Aerosmith T-shirts and flip-flops.

There. That seemed more like Rockin.

From a round table in the corner, Ioana waved.

Petie indicated her to the host and headed over, and as she walked, she concentrated on assessing Donald White. He was one of the *nice* dressers—black designer suit, starched white shirt, red striped tie.

Suddenly Petie hated her choice of clothing. She looked old and staid, like him.

He was thin, almost gaunt, and pale, as if he spent far too much time inside...

Petie flashed back to her memories, of him sitting on the couch in the windowless den, avoiding contact with anyone who could bear witness to his presence, glued to his computer.

His face was so smooth, it looked as if it had been starched and ironed. His eyes had been pulled, his neck lifted and some kind of alteration had been done to his nose and jaw. She judged there had been multiple surgeries, some recent, to hide his age and change his appearance.

As Petie arrived at the table, Ioana, in her swath of blue silk dress and her glorious jewels, rushed to hug her.

For one moment, Petie relaxed in her embrace. This was her mother. This meant comfort and reassurance. When they were together, it seemed as if everything would be okay.

Then Ioana released her, and Donald stood to be introduced.

Smooth manners, yes. The eyes hadn't changed: green, cool and still like a stagnant pond. She remembered that, too; his gaze only became animated when he had made all his contacts to sell his stolen goods.

How could she have not at once recognized his photo?

"Derrick, this is my dear young friend, Petie Jeenli." Bubbling excitement gave a vitality to Ioana's petite figure. "Petie, this is Derrick Green!"

He offered his hand.

Petie pretended not to see, seated herself next to Ioana and picked up the dessert menu. "What's good?"

As Donald and Ioana sat, Ioana said, "We've eaten, although Derrick ate sparingly as he always does. One bite of salad. One nibble of steak."

"Three green beans!" Donald chuckled.

"Of course." All too well, Petie remembered his disinterest in food, at least until he finished his current job.

Ioana continued, "He has leftovers. For dessert, we're having the baked Alaska. It takes a while to make, so we ordered it when we sat down. It's such an appropriate dessert, and, Petie, I know you like ice cream."

Touched by her mother's thoughtfulness, Petie said, "I knew a chef who made baked Alaska, and you're right, it is a fun dessert for people visiting Alaska."

"You work at a…restaurant?" Donald visually assessed the cost of her clothes.

Petie needed to consider her words carefully. "I'm an accountant."

"Good Lord. Are you really?" Ioana sounded more than a little appalled.

"Among other things. I'm a huge proponent of learning in any spare time I might have. Investments, investigations, languages…" With a significant glance, Petie reminded Ioana of her proficiency in Belarusian.

"Studying has obviously proved a success for you," Donald said.

Ah, that voice. It handed out exactly the right amount of interest mixed with admiration. He hadn't lost that gift.

Petie smiled at him, a smile so false any human with the slightest bit of intuition would know she was mocking him. "What brings you to the little town of Rockin, Mr., um, Green?"

"I'm originally from Alaska. I like to return occasionally to visit the old stomping ground." Now the voice conveyed humor and affection.

Ioana had seen Petie's false smile and intervened. "He flew into Anchorage from Hong Kong. He's been living abroad for how long, Derrick?"

"Several years, but apparently I'm like a salmon." His voice might be beguiling, but with all that plastic surgery, his self-deprecating smile looked painful. "It was time to come home."

"So you've been in Rockin before," Petie said.

Ioana cleared her throat and glared.

He answered readily enough. "I've passed through, I think. I must have, but at the time it was not a memorable town."

"So about ten years ago." Petie might be a fool for attracting his attention, but if she could deflect his attention from her mother, she considered it worth the risk.

"What makes you say that?" The voice changed, became crystal clear and demanding.

"I was here about ten years ago, too. I thought the same as you—the town was not memorable." Before he could reflect too much about that coincidence, Petie asked, "What do *you* do for a living, Mr. Green?"

"I'm retired."

"You're young to be retired."

"Success makes one appear to have the illusion of youth." He'd eloquently said nothing.

Better than admitting he was a thief and a killer of innocent people.

Ioana frowned at her daughter in warning. "He was an antiquities dealer," she informed her.

"Buying and selling?" Petie asked.

"Selling. I still dabble when I have the opportunity." The pocket of his suit coat chirped.

"Like now?" Petie asked.

He ignored her. "Excuse me. This may be the news I was waiting for." He read the message and looked up. "It is. I must go and handle this. Please stay and enjoy the dessert. I'll collect my leftovers and sign the tab on the way out." He strode to the host desk, stopped and spoke.

The host smiled, and without hearing, Petie knew Donald had used that talented voice on her.

The host gestured to one of the waitstaff, who hurried into the kitchen.

His gaze returned to Ioana and lingered.

"He has the most beautiful voice," Ioana said in a dreamy tone. "So persuasive."

"Like a used-car salesman," Petie retorted.

Ioana's spine snapped straight. "You're being a toot."

"A toot? Really? That's the best you can do?" A rhetorical question; it was the best Ioana could do while she was mooning over Donald.

He smiled at Ioana and touched his neck and wrist.

She repeated the motion, touching the necklace and bracelet. "I don't understand why you've taken a dislike to him, Evie. He's kind and generous."

"Mother, I have something important to tell you." Petie caught Ioana's hand. "Please listen."

"Of course, dear. I always listen to you." Ioana had had a lovely dinner and good wine, and she was feeling mellow.

"Mother, you are dating—" Petie lowered her voice "—Donald White."

She gained Ioana's full attention. "What? What? What are you talking about?"

"Do you remember Donald White?" Petie lowered her voice even more. "Do you remember the man who set me up when I was convicted of a gruesome double murder?"

"Of course I do. But what are you saying?"

"That man—" Petie nodded toward the tall figure "—is him!"

25

IOANA DIDN'T SHRIEK OR gasp or clasp her throat in horror. Instead, she contemplated Petie with concern. "Dear, that's ridiculous. What kind of coincidence would it be if the same man who framed you asked me for a date?"

"Several dates. I don't know why he came back here. Maybe because he'd been successful here before. Maybe he's hiding from someone."

"If he's a big, bad murderer, who would he be hiding from?"

"Someone he stole something from. Someone whose wife or child he's killed. Those are the kinds of things that make some people really mad." Petie couldn't believe she was having this conversation. Petie gripped Ioana's hand more urgently and whispered, "Mother, he's Donald White!"

Ioana freed her hand to make a gesture that brushed that aside.

Leaning across the table, Petie laid out Jeen Lee's theory.

"Maybe he knows you're the mother of the girl he framed and he's taking fiendish delight in escalating this horror."

"Is this *The Twilight Zone*?"

"Mother, maybe not." Petie remembered how he had looked before his phone call, genial, casually interested, an actor playing a lesser part. "Probably not. But his motivation doesn't change the possible outcome!"

"Dear. Dear, think about this. It is a coincidence beyond the realm of belief. You've been in a fishing camp in western Alaska… Maybe you've been alone too much? Maybe with what happened to you here, you've become obsessive about certain—"

Petie could not believe it. "Are you trying to say I'm crazy?"

"That's too strong a word." Ioana was trying to soothe her.

A smiling waiter appeared from the kitchen carrying the beautifully browned baked Alaska.

"Mother, no one in this dining room is crazy." Petie pointed a discreet finger. "But someone *is* a thief and a serial killer."

"Dear, think about it. What you say is—"

Petie whipped her head around and fixed her mother in her gaze.

Ioana changed course. "Sweetheart, listen. All men should be as generous. Derrick has given me gifts, small antiquities."

Petie grabbed Ioana's wrist. "Gifts like this?"

"Yes, and things that require me to dust them." Ioana sounded less than thrilled. "Now there's our dessert. Behave!"

With a flourish, the waiter placed a magnificently golden baked Alaska on their table.

Ioana and Petie gave a little round of applause. The waiter

cut through the crusty meringue, the cold ice cream, the buttery pound cake, and conveyed two pieces to Ioana and Petie.

They were the center of the restaurant's attention.

Donald White stood at the host's desk, watching with apparent delight.

And her mother didn't believe a word she said.

It was, without a doubt, one of the most surreal moments of Petie's life.

Ioana and Petie thanked the waiter, hefted their forks, took the first bites and oohed and aahed.

The beaming waiter took the remaining half of the dessert to box up.

As soon as they were alone, Petie asked, "How many gifts?"

"I have three at home and this jewelry." Ioana took a bite. "This is excellent. Do you like it, dear?"

"Of course I like it!" Exasperated, Petie pushed the baked Alaska away. "Mother, look at these jewels. *Look* at them. They're real!"

Ioana glanced down at the bracelet, then up as the waitress returned to the host's desk with a to-go box and handed it to Donald. "Good, he's taking his dinner. Usually he leaves it. I don't know how the man survives. But tonight he agreed to take his meal in a to-go box, and he's actually picking it up!"

"Now that he's received that phone call, he's hungry?" Petie's blood chilled. "Mama, that means his business here is complete."

"Yes, dear." Her mother watched her out of the corner of her eye as if worried about her. "He said that just now."

With a wave in their direction, Donald White left the room, his full to-go box in his hands.

Petie watched, then turned back to her mother. "No, I mean—he's made his sales and he's about to skip town. He'll be coming for the stuff he gave you, and he doesn't leave witnesses behind."

Ioana rose from her chair and placed her fingertips on the table. "Those things were gifts. He's not going to ask for them back!"

"Give them to him, Mother." Petie rose also. "He'll kill you for them."

In a low, intense voice, Ioana said, "Derrick Green is not Donald White. He's not a killer!"

Petie could scarcely breathe. "Why would you believe in him and not me?"

"You're being absurd." Which was not an answer.

"Will you listen to Marya?" Petie went nose to nose with Ioana. "Because I'm going to tell her!"

Ioana flushed, and her blue eyes lit with fury. "Evelyn Angelina, you and I are not siblings. You do not *tell* on me." Picking up her wrap, she marched from the restaurant.

Petie followed her into the lobby. "Ioana!"

Ioana swung back to her.

Petie got close and spoke in an undertone. "No, we're not siblings. You're my mother, and I'll do what I can to save your life, whatever the cost."

Ioana gave an irritated huff.

Like duelers, Ioana and Petie turned on their heels and strode in opposite directions, Ioana to her car, Petie to the elevators.

As Petie passed the almost-empty hotel bar where a pianist played a slow jazz tune, she glanced in.

Stacey sat tall and alone on a stool, staring into the depths of a perfect, pale martini decorated with one perfect, green olive. Petie balanced for one second on an upraised toe, then headed in to join her. She slid onto the seat next to Stacey.

Stacey lifted her martini between her upraised fingertips. "Is your mother gone?"

26

PETIE CLOSED HER EYES. She knew. Stacey knew.

"When I saw you, I got that twinge of recognition. But I didn't connect the dots. I mean, how could I?" Although the piano muffled all conversation, Stacey lowered her voice to a murmur. "You were dead in a landslide. Buried alive."

Petie winced.

"Not until I saw you and your mother together, arguing, did I know. Evelyn Jones. You're Evelyn Jones. I should have guessed." Carefully Stacey placed the delicate glass on the bar and, without looking, reached out one hand and grasped Petie's wrist. "All these years, during the trial and after the trial, I kept thinking, *I've killed her. I've killed her.* Now you're alive again, and I have a second chance."

"I never blamed you for testifying against me in the trial. Donald White set me up. You only said what you knew." Grimly, Petie said, "We were both pawns."

"Were we?" Stacey swiveled on the bar stool to face Petie. "How could I be so stupid?"

"You weren't stupid. You were played."

"Stacey Collins does not get played."

Petie realized she had slammed into an ego that could not accept defeat. "I guess not, because I wasn't killed and Donald White is still at large."

"Is he? Do you know that?"

"He's in town now."

Stacey's expression changed from regret to horror to stern demand. "Are you sure?"

"Without a doubt. He has had some wonderful facial surgery."

"Like you."

"Yes. For different reasons, perhaps." Although maybe not. Maybe someone had caught up with him and beaten the snot out of him. Petie could only hope. "Nevertheless, it's him. I just met him for dessert…with my mother."

"The man your mother's been dating is Donald White?" Consternation colored Stacey's voice and expression. "I've met him! Derrick Green. I've met him! She introduced us. I've taken money from him for my campaign. Are you saying there's danger?"

"Most definitely."

"Are you sure it's him?"

"There can be no doubt."

"How can there be no doubt?" Stacey pounded her with logic, demanding answers. "During your trial, he didn't exist. A chimera."

"He looks very different, but he has the same mannerisms. His eyes glint as they did before. He has the same fascinations and the same indifferences. And there is that voice." Petie put her elbow on the bar and sank her forehead on her up-raised palm. "He's a sociopath. Nothing matters except him and what he wants."

"A sociopath. I don't understand."

Petie lifted her head and recited, "*A personality disorder manifesting itself in an extreme lack of interest in others and a total lack of conscience.*"

Stacey digested that. "Are you going to turn him in to the police?"

"How? He has no criminal record, I don't exist and I don't trust law enforcement." For someone who didn't exist, she was breathing heavily. "But I'm going to save my mother."

"Would he hurt her? Your mother? He seems enamored."

"He's given her things."

"What kind of things?"

"Things worth a lot of money."

As if less concerned, Stacey leaned away. "Valuable gifts are not a bad thing in a relationship."

"Remember? At my trial, I said he'd stolen things from the house? That's what he does. Acquires valuable antiques from one home and sells them for a lot of money."

"How much money?"

"Tens and hundreds of thousands."

Stacey sucked in air.

Petie continued, "He's using my mother to keep the current valuables safe until he can make contact with a buyer."

A text came into Stacey's phone. She looked at it, grimaced, turned on the bar stool to face the room. "I've got to go. Marc wants to talk again about what the fundraiser brought in. Thanks for the heads-up about Derrick White."

"Derrick *Green*. This time he's Derrick *Green*."

"Right." Stacey slid off the stool. "Although if you're not going to the police, I still don't understand what you're going to do about it."

"I have connections who will be interested in what he's

selling. Now that I know for sure it's him and what's he's got, I'm going to contact them." As soon as she got to her room.

"Don't bring the mob to my town," Stacey warned.

"You're safe from that." Petie smiled as she remembered the people at the MFAA, all so devoted to saving the world's heritage from looters. "All my connections are legitimate."

"Good to know." Stacey gestured toward the entrance. "Someone's coming for you."

The waiter hurried across the bar to Petie. "Miss Jeenli, I thought you might like to take your slice of baked Alaska to your room."

Petie stared at the to-go box in his hands. "Yes. Thank you."

"If you speak to Mrs. Jones, let her know we have her piece and the rest of the baked Alaska in the freezer."

"Thank you again." She accepted the dessert. "I will definitely be speaking to Mrs. Jones, and soon."

27

IOANA WALKED IN THE back door of her house, threw her keys on the kitchen counter, locked the door with a decisive click, set the alarm…and stood with her fingers pressed hard to her lips.

Damn it. Every single time she saw her baby girl, she said the wrong thing, acted the wrong way, doubted when she should have trusted, believed the worst when she should have known that at Evelyn's core was the pure heart of a dragon girl.

They were too much alike. Too much alike!

But she was the mother. She was supposed to be wise and mature. How could she be exactly the mother that Marya needed, but such a failure with Evelyn?

Yet for all the prickly hostility and hot words between them, Ioana loved her daughter from the depths of her heart. Evelyn was a woman who fought and worked and did what she had to survive—and always, always put her family first.

In her, Ioana saw the strength of her long-dead sisters.

In her, Ioana saw a chance for them to live again.

Ioana moved through the dark kitchen, skirting the table, heading for the living room. She flipped on the light for the stairway and began to climb…and glanced at the antique oak sideboard in her dining room and that damned Egyptian terra-cotta figure Derrick had given her.

Ioana backed down the stairs and picked it up.

She had blithely assumed it was a copy. A really good copy: all the sharp points had been worn away, leaving a figure that might have been human, might have been a creature and definitely was a god. Ioana only knew she liked the orange color and the statue felt warm in her hand.

Evelyn said it was real.

Ioana put it back down next to the reliquary which, Derrick had informed her, held the remains of the hand of the martyr St. Beliquist. He'd said so in a tone that gave her reason to understand he didn't believe it. But he thought it was pretty and she would enjoy it.

Ioana didn't care for it. But Derrick had presented it to her, so she had thanked him and displayed it, and now, in the shadowy light, the gilding on the hand looked real, as did the stones in the decorations of the sleeve.

She displayed the third gift he gave her, too, a copy of a Russian icon depicting the sorrowful Virgin Mary holding her blessed baby son, one hand extended as if offering to grant all prayers.

Ioana didn't believe in a higher power, hadn't believed in any divine intervention since her father had been taken, her mother had disappeared, her sisters had died. Still, she loved the burnished gold sheen of the Virgin's halo, the silver tear on her cheek, her son's loving arm around her neck. If Evie was to be believed, this was not a copy but a priceless icon, one that in its time had worked miracles.

On the off chance that was true…Ioana placed one gentle finger on the gilded frame. "Please." She wasn't sure what she was asking. For grace, for patience, for love, for family healing. For Evelyn to have whatever she wished: justice, freedom, the life she should have.

Opening the silver drawer, Ioana moved the spoons aside and placed the three gifts on the felt lining. She stared at them there, remembering how she had briskly dusted them, vaguely annoyed that Donald didn't realize she was a busy woman who didn't have time to care for such pretty, useless objects.

She shut the drawer, walked to the front door, checked that it was locked and the security set, walked to the back door and checked there, too. She went up to her bedroom, removed her heels and the jewelry. She carried the necklace and bracelet into the bathroom, flipped on the light and examined the gold and the stones in her magnifying makeup mirror.

No marks, none whatsoever. But they looked so old, the jeweler wouldn't have used a maker's mark. More important, the gold felt heavy and slick, and the velvety blue stones shimmered as if they had captured pieces of the sky.

She got ready for bed, carried the jewelry into her bedroom and spread them out on her nightstand. She hadn't cared for Donald's other gifts, but these she truly loved.

And…she'd thought of him as *Donald*.

She went to her bedroom door and locked it, then propped a chair under the doorknob. She opened the drawer of the nightstand, removed her pistol and placed it beside the jewels. A woman of her background knew how to keep herself safe.

Tomorrow she would decide what to do.

28

IN HER ROOM, PETIE told the bear, "It's not going well, Tuddy. Can't you help? Do I have to do all the heavy lifting?"

The bear didn't answer, which Petie figured meant, *Yes, you do. Hurry up and get it done!*

Housekeeping had turned down the sheets and put a chocolate on her pillow.

She took off her shoes, stacked the pillows against the headboard and, phone in hand, flopped on the bed. She dialed the head of the MFAA, Nils Brooks, and when she got his voice mail, she said, "Nils, it's Petie in Rockin, Alaska. Donald White is here. He's working under the alias *Derrick Green*. He has with him several pieces. One is a jewelry set that's worth... I can't imagine. Seven figures. He's involved with a woman." Petie hesitated to say it was her mother. "He's using her home to store them. Tonight I'm sure he made a deal to deliver. I can't go to law enforcement. Would you get the FBI here ASAP before someone is hurt?" She waited to see if Nils picked up. When he didn't, she ended with "This is real. Call me," and cut the connection.

One thing about Nils Brooks: unless he was on a mission, he was never far from the phone, and if he was on a mission, he had someone checking his messages. He would get back to her soon.

Petie ate the chocolate and wished for more. Chocolate eased the anxiety as she tried to decide how she was going to explain this to her sister. Her baby sister, the lawyer, who had grown up to be a forthright, powerful woman who in court made grown men cry and strong women cower.

Not chocolate but—the baked Alaska!

She fetched the to-go box from the desk where she'd left it, popped it open and took a bite of the softened raspberry ice cream.

That helped.

She called her sister's number.

It was after eleven in California, but when Marya answered, she sounded wide awake and chipper. "Hi, Evie, I was just thinking about you!"

"Why?"

"I don't know. Because you're my sister?"

"Has Mother told you she is dating?" Petie blurted.

Better have another bite of ice cream. And cake. And meringue.

"No… Really?" Marya sounded pleased, then uneasy. "Why do you say it like that? Isn't it good news that she's finally dating?"

"It's who she's dating." Petie put down the container. She'd lost her appetite.

"What's wrong with him?"

"He's Donald White."

A long pause. Harsh breathing. "Are you sure?"

"Of course I'm sure."

"You have to tell her!"

"I did. She won't listen. We had a fight in the restaurant, and she stormed out."

"In...the restaurant? Where are you?"

"Oh." This conversation was about to get uncomfortable. "When I saw a photo of Mama and Donald in the Rockin newspaper, I flew to Rockin. I'm in the hotel, registered under the name of Petie Jeenli."

"And you didn't think to tell me?" Marya's voice rose.

"There's been no time." Not strictly true, but true enough. "I saw the photo early yesterday morning."

"Let me see if I got this right." The words sounded patient. The tone did not. "You saw the photo. You flew to Rockin."

"Anchorage, actually, and drove to Rockin."

"You got there. You found Mama. You told her she is dating the murderer who killed Michele and Timmy Jameson. And she *argued* with you?"

"You missed the part about me having dessert with her and Donald." Which was funny in a film noir sort of way. "And her suggesting I was delusional because I'd been alone so much."

"You two. You always had the most difficult relationship!" Marya's tone changed from exasperated to frightened. "But I don't care. How can she not take this seriously?"

Petie found herself defending her mother. "It's him. He's charming. He's mesmerizing. That voice would lull a baby to sleep...right before he smothered it with its own pillow."

Tuddy sighed *Yes.*

Petie flinched.

"Why would he pick her to date? *Your* mother, of all people?"

"You mean, the mother of the baby killer Evelyn Jones?"

"That's exactly what I mean!"

"Maybe he doesn't know." Which might be true. "It is Alaska. There aren't that many women in Rockin, especially not women who look like Mama."

Marya briskly dismissed that. *"Everybody* knows. And they don't forget. She still gets death threats."

Petie came to her feet. "What? Why haven't you told me this before?"

"What are you going to do about it? Come back from the dead, tell the truth *again*, be arrested and convicted *again*—"

"Yes!"

"No. You know Mama. She can handle herself. If anyone actually says something to her face, they only do it once. She stands on her toes, shakes her finger under their nose, tells them Gretchen George was a child abuser and a lousy cop and that someday your reputation will be cleared."

Petie could picture it: her mother taking down a big, nasty bully with the sharp edge of her tongue. But she also knew what bullies were like. "Not everyone gets in her face, do they? Most of the threats are anonymous, aren't they?"

Marya set out to comfort Petie. "Yes, but Mama has a pistol, and she's a sharpshooter. She keeps in shape. She takes self-defense classes. The house has a *great* security system. She has it reviewed every year and keeps it up-to-date. Plus most people know not to mess with Mama. She's charming, but she can be scary."

"None of which does any good if someone sneaks up on her." Even dead, Evelyn Jones was a threat to her family.

Marya started to speak. Stopped. Started again. "Listen, Evie, I haven't said anything because I didn't want to get your hopes up. But for months, I've been reviewing the case."

"My case?"

"Of course your case! When I visited Rockin, I requested

to see your case evidence from the Rockin PD. Chief Dumas granted permission. I scanned in the paperwork, took photos of the hard materials, and to no one's surprise, there are discrepancies."

"And...?"

"I've found a partial fingerprint. *Not* yours!"

29

PETIE FELT SOMETHING STIR in the pit of her stomach and rise toward her brain. Whatever it was, it better not be hope. Hope was a bitch who betrayed her every time. She had strangled hope, and by God, it better stay dead.

"That POS chief of police buried it in the evidence, but tonight I found it. Evie, I'm going to get you off!" No wonder Marya had sounded chipper.

Petie felt the warm glow of knowing her sister had believed in her so thoroughly and invested so much time in her exoneration. "I would like that." But she wouldn't hope.

"In the meantime, we've got to deal with Donald White. Maybe him dating Mama is a horrible coincidence."

A thought occurred to Petie. "Wait. No. You said she has a good security system."

"Yes... Why?"

"He gave her the artifacts because he knew they'd be safe until he came to fetch them. She was wearing the jewels, but she said the other stuff is at home."

"Where is she?"

"At home."

"Why would you let her go alone?" In Marya's voice, Petie heard the echo of her mother's domineering personality amped up as far as it would go. "I know. Because you two had a fight. Not good enough, Evie! Where's Donald White staying?"

"Here, I think. At the Rockin Hotel."

"What name is he using?"

"Derrick Green."

"Hang on." Marya put her on hold for three minutes, came back and proudly said, "I woke him up."

"Woke…? Donald? You called him?"

"I called the hotel, asked for his room, it rang and he picked up. His voice isn't so wonderful when it sounds like he's got spider webs in his throat. He yelled, 'I told you I'll handle it in the morning.' Then he hung up."

The two of them contemplated that.

"That sounds right," Petie said. "When he set me up, when he finished making the deals, he ate and he slept. That's the pattern. He works nonstop until he's finished, then he collapses."

"In that case…Mama *always* locks the doors and windows, and she *always* sets the security system. She's got her pistol, and she's religious about safety. I say we leave her alone tonight, let her get over her bad temper. She'll be better in the morning." Marya sounded relieved at not having to send Petie into the lion's den.

Petie felt the same relief. "She always is."

"Meanwhile, I'll make arrangements to fly to Alaska. I'll catch the earliest flight. It'll get me there tomorrow afternoon. You hold the fort until then. No one has recognized you, have they?"

Petie didn't answer. She didn't want to tell Marya about Stacey Collins and didn't want to send her into a bigger tizzy.

"No one will." Marya was talking to herself now. "You don't look at all like Evelyn Jones." Sounding more like Evie's younger sister, Marya asked, "Evie, are we doing the right thing? Are we going to be okay? Is Mama going to be safe?"

Petie got her leather jacket out of the closet. "Right now, I'm going out to drive past the house, make sure she's there and is safe. How does that sound?"

"Like a good idea. When I get up to catch my flight, I'll call Donald White again and make sure he's still in place." Marya's voice got a note of excitement. "Oh, Evie, after so many years, I'll see you tomorrow! Tonight, get some sleep. Try not to worry. We're going to make this thing turn around!"

"You're tempting fate." But Marya had hung up.

Petie went out. She drove to her mother's house, parked and watched long enough to see the shadow of her mother move back and forth across the bedroom shades.

She noted, also, a gray Subaru Outback that seemed to follow her from the neighborhood back to the hotel. But when she turned into the parking garage, the Outback continued on toward Walmart.

She shrugged and forgot about it.

By the time she reached her hotel room and swiped her key card, hope had established itself in her heart and mind and sang a cheerful song in her head.

Maybe that's why she failed to realize that she was not alone.

A man's voice spoke from behind her. "Evelyn Jones, I presume?"

She stiffened.

She turned.

She saw him.

She knew him.

Tall guy. Burly guy. Dark hair, strong chin, dark angry eyes.

"Zone Jameson." She held the door and gestured. "Won't you come in?"

30

WHEN FAYE MILLER COVERED an event like today's fundraiser, she kept her Reporter's Notebook and pen in her hand and her phone recorder on. She considered the notebook and pen her best tools. A scribbled word triggered memories and whole stories.

But she always had the recording transcribed for reading later. Some of her best stories had come from following up on a line of conversation she'd missed but the recorder had picked up.

That night, while she sat at her coffee table and ate the dinner she'd picked up at Taco Joint—she understood the *Herald* rule about not accepting food bribes, but passing up that crab dip had hurt—she scanned the transcript for anything interesting. She got to the part where Petie Jeenli and Ioana Jones switched into a language that sounded vaguely Russian.

Wasn't that interesting? The transcription guessed at the mishmash of sounds, and Faye jumped back and forth with an online translator until she hit the jackpot. "Belarusian," she muttered. "Really?"

Then she looked up Ioana Jones's online business bio and discovered she had immigrated from Belarus. That explained her accent, but nothing could explain why Petie Jeenli could speak such a specific language. They didn't look alike. In fact, Petie had one odd-looking face. But clearly they were having an argument, so between that and the language—good possibility they were somehow related.

A quick online search yielded nothing on Petie, which was interesting in itself and warranted further investigation.

But first, the rest of the transcript.

Faye got to the end without finding anything else of interest. She was about to toss the printed pages in the trash when she saw one line that stopped her short. Aloud, she asked, "Who said that?"

No one answered. Of course not. She was alone, so no one complained when she scrambled to her feet and knocked her chili tots on the floor. She returned with her phone and brought up the recording app. She clicked on to the last two minutes of the fundraiser. Absently she brushed lint off one of the tots, popped it in her mouth and replayed the scene in her mind.

The event had been finishing up. She had stood at her table in front of the podium, packing up, stomach growling, ready to get out and get food. On the recording, she heard the rustle of paper as she slid her notebook into her pocket, her comments to Stacey's fervent supporters offering their help writing her article, her edged reply to the one woman who confided she wanted to be a reporter, too, because she could do the job while the kids were in school. Then there in the background, those words, that partial sentence that—

Whoa. Unwise, to say the least, and if that was true…

She recognized that voice.

She recognized the voice that answered, too, although those quiet words were indecipherable and so hadn't been included in the transcript.

This was a *story*.

She looked up a number and dialed. When her contact answered, she said, "This is Faye Miller from the *Rockin Herald*. I overheard you say the most fascinating thing." She explained what had piqued her interest, listened to a gush of panicked backpedaling, then said, "I'd love to interview you so you can explain further. Tomorrow. What time would be convenient?"

31

ROCKIN CHIEF OF POLICE Rodolphe Dumas had been on the job two years. The old chief, known as Wretchen Gretchen, had been caught in the act of sexual abuse with a minor and precipitously fired. There'd been a string of appointed replacements, her officers who were briefly promoted, then removed. She had created a corrupt organization, doing sloppy police work, and everyone under her supervision was there for a reason—mostly bribes and bullying.

For eight years, Chief Dumas had been coming to Rockin in the summer, using it as a base to fish, explore, hike.

He was from Houma, Louisiana, Cajun to his bones, five foot five on a good day and, he was told, mellow-looking. Whatever the hell that meant. He'd found in the frigid north his accent convinced people to drop ten points off his IQ and assume a few egregiously wrong facts, like they could easily flimflam him. He'd been in law enforcement thirty-three of his fifty-two years, and liars were easy to spot. The only lies he ever believed were the ones people believed themselves.

So the sixth summer he came to Rockin and read about the current scandal in the chief of police's office, he started thinking.

His kids were grown.

His divorce was final.

He liked this place, and he liked the way the city council was trying to head Rockin out of its decline.

He figured Rockin desperately needed stable law enforcement. So he put his name in front of the city council, and they gave him the job. Not too surprising: he usually succeeded at what he set out to do.

He'd spent the first year weeding out the corrupt officers, scaring the halfway honest ones onto the straight and narrow and hiring some new folks, including a few women because, dang, he wasn't supposed to generalize but they sure knew how to talk to criminals and victims better than the guys did.

The gals treated him pretty warily for a while, but he liked to keep a big ol' pot of gumbo simmering on a burner in his office, with rice in the cooker beside it. They'd come in frozen from some accident—there weren't a lot of serious crimes in Rockin—they'd come in to get their bellies warm, and while they ate, they'd tell him everything that happened on the streets and in their lives. You might say he won those young women over with his cooking. The boys soon followed.

He was at home, in his bed sleeping pretty hard when his phone rang around midnight. He picked right up—he needed to take a piss anyway—and heard his dispatcher tell him Faye Miller, the reporter down at the *Rockin Herald*, had been shot in the back in a dark alley up by the old furniture warehouse. She was being transported to the hospital in critical condition.

He knew Faye pretty well. She was one of six reporters at the *Herald*. He'd no sooner put his name into the pot for chief of police when she called asking for an interview. Of course he'd cooperated, and right away he'd pigeonholed her as *the* official pain-in-the-ass Rockin reporter. She liked to ask questions the way he liked to ask questions…get the person all relaxed, let them babble and wait for them to slip up and say too much. It was a great law-enforcement technique, and it annoyed the hell out of him when she used it on him.

But she must have liked what he had to say, because she wrote him up good.

Then after he got the job, she turned on him like a mad dog and demanded to be the first to get to the bottom of stories.

Now she was shot? In the back? Left for dead in an alley?

That girl had asked the wrong person the wrong question.

He sure hoped she survived.

32

"**AFTER YOU." ZONE IMITATED** Petie's gesture. "Call me a fool, but I don't turn my back on convicted murderers."

Petie walked in ahead of him, the back of her neck crawling. He was watching her, hating her. She didn't need to see it. She could feel it. When the door shut, she turned to face him and found him studying her like a particularly loathsome and deadly insect.

He was tall, muscled at the shoulders and skinny at the waist, wore somber black, and his dark, barely grown beard accentuated the slopes and shadows of his face. She remembered his wedding photo; once he'd been young and happy. Now all his pleasure in the world had been burned away by tragedy.

She spread her hands, showed him she was unarmed, not dangerous. "I am not who you think I am."

"You're not Evelyn Jones?"

"I'm not the one who killed your wife and child."

"Tell it to the jury." He was savage in his skepticism. "Again."

"I didn't... I'm not..." The need to have him believe choked her.

"I saw the photos. Do you think I could ever forget that sight? My wife and my son rotting in..." He choked off the words, and his dark eyes grew wild with rage and horror. "You make my skin crawl. You killed my family, lady. They're dead, and you're alive."

"I was almost killed getting free, and I've spent my time since trying to find Donald White. You know who he is. Surely you read transcripts of the trial?"

He gave a jerky nod. "I know who you said he was, and I know he was a chimera you created to exonerate yourself."

"Not a chimera. I have found him! If you would listen to me—"

He talked over her. "If you think I feel sorry about your battered face, you—" Something distracted his attention. Something behind her.

She turned to look.

Zone bounded to the desk, snatched up the teddy bear. "Tuddy." He squeezed its belly, put it to his nose, closed his eyes and smelled it. His eyes popped open, and he glared at Petie. "If you're not Evelyn Jones, the woman who killed my son, why do you have Timmy's teddy bear?"

Petie wet her lips. That damned bear. First it drove her to seek justice, then it betrayed her to Timmy's father, to the man who quivered with the need to hurt her as he believed she'd hurt his family.

Zone reached out one big, rough hand and grabbed her arm. "Don't tell me again you're not her."

"I didn't say I wasn't Evelyn Jones. I said I didn't kill them!"

"Evelyn Jones. You bitch. You killed my child and stole

his teddy bear. How sick is that?" He bared his teeth, white in his darkly tanned face, and dropped the teddy bear on the bed against the headboard. "What? Is Tuddy a memento of your first real bloody murder?"

"I didn't kill Timmy. I didn't kill him!" Petie put both hands on Zone's chest and pushed.

He stumbled backward and rebounded in a moment. "Liar!"

"Donald White killed him."

"Donald White? Have you convinced yourself he really existed? Does it ease your conscience to tell yourself you didn't do it, it was him?"

"Donald White, the man who murdered them both and set me up. Donald White, the man who's pulled the same con time and again. Wait!" She pulled open her backpack and shook its contents onto the bed. Snatching her computer tablet, she flipped it open, brought up the photo she took of Weezy's sketch and shoved it at Zone. "There. There's his picture!"

Zone slammed the tablet on the desk. "I don't give a damned about your—" He stopped, mouth open, and pivoted back to the tablet.

Petie didn't like the way he looked, pale around the eyes and sweaty, like he was going to faint. She almost shouted, "What?"

Zone's voice was half an octave higher. "I've seen that man before."

33

NOW PETIE BROKE A SWEAT. "Here? Since you got to town? Or before?"

"Before. At our house. Our home. Outside of town. We were isolated. Michele loved company. If someone wanted to stay in Rockin, there weren't any places. Fifty-year-old motels. We ran a bed-and-breakfast. Not for everyone. We were choosy. But this guy..." Zone's voice trailed off. He picked up the tablet. It had switched off. "I broke it," he said, and his voice broke, too.

"No. It's okay." She took it, turned it on, used her fingerprint to get in. She handed it back to him. "Anyway, that's a scan. I've got the original sketch."

Zone looked at the picture again. "This guy stayed with us. Clean...clean record. Name of...um, Dylan Something."

"Orange, Black, Purple, Yellow?"

"I don't know. I don't remember. But I personally ran the background. Clean. Really! He was affable. Charming. Said he'd recently gotten a divorce. Nice guy. Interested in the antiques. Asked a lot of questions. He really listened when I talked, and I—" He stopped, stricken.

Petie filled in the blanks. "You told him stuff. Stuff that made him think about how much your valuables were worth."

"Yes."

"But you were a good-sized guy with boxing trophies."

"And we had a top-notch security system in the house."

"Right. So he didn't make a move on you. But when he heard you'd been captured, he returned and convinced your wife to let him stay again."

They were building the correct scenario brick by brick.

"Michele was a smart woman, one of the most intelligent women I ever met." Even now, his voice rang with pride. "And she was kind. She believed the best of everyone."

"She wasn't careless, but he'd stayed before. She felt like she knew him."

"Right. He slept in the guesthouse."

"She was scared about you. All her mind was bent on ransoming you."

"She wasn't thinking straight."

Petie realized she had been angry at Michele. What woman would allow a murderous psychopath into her home?

Together, she and Zone had answered the question: someone with an innate belief in the goodness of humanity, someone panicked at the fate of her husband, someone who was lonely and believed that Donald White was a friend.

Zone drew a shaky breath. "Okay. That explains a lot. Okay."

Petie realized he'd been angry with Michele, too. "Yeah. She was betrayed. Yeah."

"Sometimes I dream about her, telling me to make it right." His fingers shook. He was a man caught in the throes of never-ending grief and remorse. "I would if I could, but—"

She couldn't bear to watch his pain. "Together we will make it right."

Icy guilt clutched him, then dissolved in a rush of hope. "You said you found him? Dylan? Donald? Whatever his name is?"

"I did. And I know you had a security system in your home. Did it include security cameras?"

He caught on immediately. "Yes. Right. There has to be video of that bastard from his visits."

"If you can find him, that's all the evidence we need. But…"

"But?"

"But the police claimed they had looked at the video recorded while I was there. They said he wasn't on there, that I'd made him up."

"I looked, too, when I got home. That's why I knew you were guilty. But he was there a couple years before. He couldn't have erased his earlier visits." Zone pulled his phone out of his jacket, tapped at the screen, waited, tapped again. "Here it is. I've got to get to the right time." He massaged the bridge of his nose with his finger and thumb. "Had to be summer. First visit was twelve years ago. We had garden-fresh tomatoes for dinner. So…August."

Petie laughed a little. Having Zone here, seeing the chance to be exonerated in his eyes, made her almost buoyant, as if after so many years the horror might end in justice. She joined him where he stood by the desk. "You remember what you had for *dinner*?"

"I remember garden-fresh tomatoes." He typed in *Visitors* and pushed Play.

For twelve years ago, it truly was a sophisticated system. One camera was mounted on the front porch, one on the back porch, recording every person—mail carriers, package couriers, friends, relatives—who walked up the steps and to the door. The video leaped from person to person, one after another.

None of them matched Donald White.

"So maybe early September," Zone muttered and kept the video moving until they saw a delivery made in blowing snow.

"Maybe you got early tomatoes?" Petie suggested.

Zone snorted. "Sure. In Alaska." But he backed up the video, all the way through July, June, May and another shot of blowing snow in April.

"Sure you got the right year?"

"Yes." Zone's mouth was set in a grim line. He sat on the corner of the bed and moved to the previous year.

She pulled the desk chair close enough to watch, too, and saw him repeat the process.

"He's nowhere." Zone couldn't lift his gaze from the phone. "He wiped himself from the system. All the time he was there with you. All the previous times. We've got no record that he was ever at the house. He fixed it."

"He really did."

Zone looked her in the eyes. "You know what this means?"

Petie got a nerve buzz along the outer rim of her ears, like feeling returning to frostbitten skin. "What? I mean, yeah. You believe me."

"Of course I believe you." He brushed that aside as if a half hour before he hadn't been accusing her of murder. "When I go to court and say this man visited Michele and me at our home and yet there's no record of him in the security archive... we can prove your innocence."

"And his guilt." This buzz wasn't painful. But it did spread down her neck and chest. Her lips and cheeks heated and made her realize...Zone was an attractive man.

She hadn't thought of him that way. He looked rough around the edges, like a man who'd stared his own death in the face and won, but at a cost. He was an adversary, an obstacle to her search for safety for her mother and justice for herself.

But sitting this close to him…

His black hair had a curl to it that gave the illusion of life. She couldn't take her gaze away from his chapped lips as they formed words.

She would enjoy kissing him. At least, she was pretty sure she would. She hadn't kissed a man for so long…

"Evelyn." His tone had changed from one intensity to another. He looked deep into her eyes. "Before I left for Magara, Timmy was crying. He was afraid of the monster who had come to the house, and I was the only one who could vanquish that monster. I told Timmy that Tuddy was a protector teddy bear. I promised him that Tuddy would always care for him." He wiped the back of his hand across his eyes and looked at the bear perched on the bed pillow. "Tuddy failed us both."

Petie was horrified. For one fleeting moment, she'd wanted to kiss Zone.

While he was focused on the memories of his dead son.

She couldn't spend her time wallowing in her own emotions. She'd done enough of that while at Midnight Sun Fishing Camp. Now it was time to think of someone else. Everyone else.

She put her hand on Zone's arm. "No, he didn't. Tuddy's still protecting him. The monster man is in town. He's using my mother to keep his valuables safe until he's made contact with the clients who will buy them."

"Your mother?"

"My mother. Ioana Jones."

"The clients?"

"Private collectors, probably. People who will pay top dollar and absorb the treasures into their hoard, where they'll never be seen again."

She observed as he assimilated his personal knowledge of this racket. The calculator in his brain tallied up the profits, and she saw his anger at the realization his wife and child had died for monetary gain and collectors' greed.

Softly she said, "I promise I'm going to catch Donald White. Tuddy won't let me fail this time."

Her words must have caught him, captured him, given him a release from the grinding guilt of years of his life, lonely and warped.

But life! Life while his wife and child rotted in the earth.

His loneliness pulled at her. They were like two black holes, broken stars spinning alone in the nothingness of space, irresistibly dragged toward each other by some great gravitational pull. They shared so many events, so much pain…

He looked at her hand, strong, warm, gripping him with the urgency of old injustice and new, startling desire.

He grabbed her arms and kissed her. Kissed her and kissed her and…

She sank into him.

They fell back on the bed.

They wrestled each other out of their clothes.

They had sex.

Because it most definitely wasn't love.

But the act they performed was a connection neither of them had experienced for too many years.

It was a joy.

It was a release.

It was the best thing in all the years of loneliness and grief.

And Tuddy approved.

Petie knew it.

34

AT ONE IN THE MORNING, police and ambulance sirens wailed.

Petie woke with a start and waited until the racket died down.

Beside her, Zone was awake. She could tell by his breathing. "I'm sorry," she whispered. "I've lived in the wilderness for so long, I can't sleep through that."

"Me, too." He pulled Petie into his arms, and they slid back into slumber.

At four, the hotel room door opened a crack.

Zone came up on one elbow and protected his eyes from the light. "What the hell?"

A woman stood silhouetted. Her soft, accented voice said, "Sorry, wrong room."

She shut the door.

"What the hell," Zone muttered again. He got up and flipped the security bolt. He came back to bed, and his hand groped for Petie's.

She rolled toward him.

They made love, slow, hot and sweet.

At five-thirty, Petie's phone rang.

"What the hell?" Zone's outrage was stronger this time.

Petie fumbled, answered and listened. "Okay. That's good…Thanks, Marya…No, it's okay, I was almost awake."

She hung up.

Dawn had begun to light the sky.

She reached for Zone.

Zone rolled away, flipped on the bedside light and sat up, his bare feet on the floor beside the bed.

She watched him, his hunched shoulders, the way he ran his fingers through his hair and his palms over his face. She'd spent years observing others for clues of their feelings. It had been a vital survival technique in JDC and in jail. In the hospitality business, it had kept trouble at bay.

She could have predicted that he would feel confused. Guilty. And he did.

She sat up, inched closer, her hand hovering two inches over his shoulder. She wanted to touch him, but she knew… she knew this wouldn't be easy.

How could it be? They were both here, on earth, struggling toward a new existence.

The sex between them had been desperate, needy, generous, quick and then slow, all the things a human could want, filling all the spaces with satisfaction…and between them would always be the deaths of his wife and son.

Zone knew now she hadn't killed them.

Yet Petie had been there, a witness to the atrocity…and he'd slept with her.

She allowed her hand to descend onto his shoulder.

He came off the bed as if electrified. "No!"

Okay. So all the guilt.

"I can't!" He drew breath.

Focus on something besides the knowledge that, after she had given her whole self, she was being forcefully rejected. Focus on the next step of what needed to be done to stay free and prove her own innocence, to keep her mother safe and prove to the world Donald White was a murderous thief who should be held forever in a prison cell.

"I need to leave." His voice sounded as if it was clogged with emotion. "I can't be here with you. This isn't right."

"It feels right to me, but…" She waved that away. "No matter. Listen…leave? What do you mean, leave? Go where?"

"Away from here."

"Leave town?" He stood half-turned away from her, and in his profile she could see the longing to get as far away from her, from this, as possible. In a panic, she said, "You can't leave Rockin. Things are occurring here, now."

"I got that, Evelyn."

"No. Please don't call me…" She swallowed. "Call me Petie. That's who I am now."

"All right. Petie." He glanced at her, and the idea of leaving the name Evelyn behind seemed to comfort him. "Petie, I got it. You're in Rockin because Donald White is in town." Zone gathered his clothes, threw them on. "You need me to stay and help you."

"No. No, I don't. That wasn't what I meant at all." She got out of bed, found the hotel bathrobe and slipped it on. "Last night I called my friend Nils—"

Zone turned on her. "Nils Brooks? Of the MFAA?"

"How do you know that?" She caught on. "Of course. You're the expert he uses to authenticate antiquities. I should have thought…"

"And you? Who are you?"

"When I went looking for Donald White, to bring him to

justice, it was his sale of stolen art and antiques I watched for. He is especially fond of ancient artifacts, so I learned about them, and when I needed someone to help me rescue them, I found Nils."

"Now you help him."

"We help each other. When he needs someone to find a stolen object, he calls me." How strange to realize the connections she shared with Zone. So many threads woven together...

"Nils Brooks is a pain in the ass," Zone said, "but if you called last night, he should have been on it."

"Yeah. I don't know how it slipped my mind." At a time like this, a girl was allowed a little sarcasm.

Her phone rang. She looked. "It's him."

Nils was as annoyed as she'd ever heard him—and with his job, Nils was annoyed a lot, rescuing the world's history from looters while trying to explain to obtuse senators why it was important not to allow terrorists to fund their campaigns.

This time, while he'd been at his mother's birthday party, his new assistant had gone out, got drunk, got rolled by a prostitute and spent the night in jail. Nils's messages had gone unchecked, and when he'd heard Petie's call...

Well. He now had a new assistant, and he'd handled the matter himself.

His contact at the Alaska FBI office had promised they would call the chief of police and tell him the suspected thief and serial killer Donald White was in Rockin. They had also promised they would have agents in town by this afternoon, and Nils made her swear she'd call him if no one showed up. "You wouldn't believe it, Petie, but sometimes the individual FBI field offices don't appreciate the MFAA helping them catch criminals. Sometimes these guys think getting tips from a bunch of sissies who like to play with pretty pottery is embarrassing."

"I'll call you if they don't arrive," she said for the third time.

While she was on the phone, Zone used the bathroom. When she cut the connection, he returned with his face damp and his black hair wet and pushed back off his forehead. "Well?"

"The FBI's on the way. You can go wherever you want."

His shoulders relaxed as if she'd removed a weight from him.

She couldn't help it; she had to ask. "But can you stay close in case things don't go well? So you can speak on my behalf?"

"I am close. I've got a room in the hotel. Hawley got it for me. I just… I didn't use it last night. I'll use it tonight."

Each of them had cut themselves on the jagged edges of unfamiliar emotion. In her gut she knew they shouldn't leave the issues of family, guilt, love, passion so unresolved.

But what could she do? Perhaps a little time and a little distance would bring clarity to them both.

"I'm not going to leave Rockin. I'll bear witness to your blamelessness. Just not while we're—" he groped for a word "—together. You have to understand that?"

"Sure. I do." Sadly, she did. She even sympathized with him. Sympathized while her body ached from good sex and she began the slow process of gathering the pieces of her shattered soul.

At least he was sticking close. She tried to be glad of that. Gesturing him toward the door, she said, "I'll see you around. I hope you find peace in your own room."

"I don't hope anything for you. I know you'll find justice and freedom. I'll help you make it happen. I will, Petie. I promise." Zone picked up his backpack and walked out.

The door closed with a firm click.

Petie sat, breathing hard, thinking nothing, until Tuddy's black plastic gaze captured her attention. Reaching for him, she held him up and looked into his one black eye. "You'd better be helping me find all the truths," she said. "Otherwise I'm going to die."

Tuddy didn't answer.

Of course not.

That damned bear. He never said he cared about her safety. He only cared about Timmy, and justice.

35

OFFICER GABRIELLA DONATTI RAPPED on the sidelight beside the door of Chief Dumas's office.

He waved her in.

"Chief, it's Paolergio at FBI Anchorage on the phone for you. Line four."

Chief Dumas gratefully turned away from filling out the report on Faye Miller's shooting—nobody had seen a damned thing, but she would survive because that homeless guy had found her and called it in—and punched line four. "Dumas."

"Hey, Dumas, it's Paolergio. I've got a tip about a serial killer in your neck of the woods."

"A serial killer?" *Here we go again.* "Name of Donald White?"

"Yes." Paolergio sounded startled. "How'd you know? Did you get him?"

"No. No, that's kind of hard to do."

Paolergio's voice got low and wary. "What are you talking about?"

"Do you remember ten years ago when some girl killed a woman and child outside of Rockin, then claimed a Donald White did it?"

"I didn't live in the area then."

"Yep, she claimed he set her up—only there was no trace of Donald White anywhere. No fingerprints, no video, nothing. She was convicted. Got killed in the landslide."

"Justice."

"Sure. Now, in Rockin, the name Donald White is synonymous with the boogeyman."

"You're kidding me."

"Every Halloween, we get calls from the good citizens of Rockin telling us Donald White is in town and we need to come and get him. Sometimes someone else set them up and scared them to death. Mostly it's some sick bastard who thinks it's funny."

"Are you saying I've been scammed?" Paolergio was outraged.

"I can't say that. I'll take down whatever information you have and check it out. You know I will."

"That worthless prick Nils Brooks pulled one over on me? Because I made fun of his pottery?" More than outraged. Paolergio was livid.

"I don't know who Nils Brooks is, but—"

"He's from the sissy-ass MFAA."

"Son, I don't know what that is."

"Some federal agency that collects antiques."

"Sounds like something the federal government would do."

"That's it." Chief Dumas heard Paolergio rummaging around with some papers. "I'm calling back my agents."

"You were sending agents?"

"Serial killer? Of course. Can you imagine if I didn't and it turned out to be real?"

Good point. "Tell you what. Send me any details about Donald White and where he is, my folks will follow up, and we'll call you in if we need help."

"I'll get even with that prick Nils Brooks. I'll make him sorry." Paolergio slammed down the phone.

But he sent the information right away.

Chief Dumas called Donatti into his office and politely requested she follow up.

"Donald White is checked into the Rockin Hotel?" She got that super-patient expression she did so well. "That should make catching him really convenient."

"That's what the Rockin police office is all about." Chief Dumas turned back to his paperwork. "Catching criminals the convenient way."

36

ZONE WENT TO HIS hotel room, dropped his backpack on the bed and headed into the shower. In record time, he was in and out, dressed and down at the valet desk getting his rented car. For a few short, sweet moments, he needed to get away from Rockin, away from his memories and, mostly, away from Petie.

As he drove out of town, he wondered...

What had he been thinking? What kind of man fell in bed with the woman who had...had discovered his wife's and son's bodies? Who had spent years of her life paying for a crime she didn't do? Who had come to Rockin to find the real killer and...

She'd call him in case she needed help. Right? Not that she would. Even after a few minutes' acquaintance, he'd realized what a capable woman she had become.

But she couldn't call on law enforcement. She was going up against Donald White. She needed backup!

He had to return to Rockin. And he would. Just a few more miles...

Then although he tried not to, he saw the turnoff to his old home. There was a signpost—and it read *Michele and Timmy Road.*

Seeing that made Zone feel a little light-headed, so he pulled onto the shoulder, gripped the steering wheel and sat with his head on his hands.

Who had renamed it? The neighbors, maybe. Or his in-laws. Michele's family had owned the house and all the land and developed it into the sprawling estates. Here everyone lived in privacy—and for more than a week, no one had realized a woman and her little boy had been murdered.

He was not going there. He was not returning to that house. He'd had all the pleasure and heartache, all the horror and joy, he could handle in one life.

Lifting his head, he pulled back onto the highway, turned and headed back, driving fast as if something terrifying chased him. The wheels of his rented SUV squealed when he made the corner onto Michele and Timmy Road. He didn't want to be here, recognizing the landmarks and amazed at the changes. He did not want to be here...

Abruptly, he was.

The road ended in the driveway of his home, the house he had shared with his family: two stories, three-car garage, a broad porch, all surrounded by pines that towered higher and higher as the years passed.

When he and Michele bought the home from her parents, it had been in her family for three generations. To the two of them, settling here had felt good, like security, like a nest created of time and tradition. They had celebrated her getting her medical license here. They had conceived their son here. They had loved each other here.

Here he had left Michele and Timmy alone to be murdered.

As he stared at the house, a small boy catapulted over the bannister onto the porch, shrieking in terror.

Zone found himself standing on the gravel beside his vehicle, seeing…seeing that the little boy was a little girl, about four, who was running from a woman who gently tackled her, rolled with her, picked her up and held her in the air.

He started forward, heart pounding.

"Got you!" the woman bellowed. "You dared think you could escape the dread mother, Berthorina!"

Zone stopped in midstep.

Oh. Yeah. The past was past. Michele's family had sold the house. A new family lived here.

Another kid, about eight, charged out the front door, screaming, "Berthorina must be punished!" And pounced on the two rolling around on the porch.

From all the corners of the hemisphere, more children appeared, calling for vengeance, for victory, for…

The front screen door opened with a slam that stopped all the action. "Are you going to spend the afternoon running around like a bunch of heathen banshees, or are you going to come in, clean up and eat your lunch?" The woman who stood in the doorway was not tall, but she was formidable. "I'm not going to ask twice!"

Berthorina spoke quietly, but her voice carried. "Rumor has it there's bread pudding for dessert."

The swarm of children around Berthorina broke apart and roared through the entrance, driven by hunger and laughter and love.

Berthorina got up from the porch, hand to her back, groaning.

The woman in the doorway shook her head. "Don't even

give me that. While I was cooking, you were playing with the kids. You can clean up."

"I will." A pause. "I have staff."

The other woman slammed the door behind her.

Berthorina rolled her shoulders and looked out at Zone. "Can I help you?" she called.

He'd been spotted earlier, he realized, but not considered a hazard. *Don't believe in the goodness of mankind*, he wanted to say. *Evil is everywhere.*

But this woman watched him with wise, wary eyes as if she was used to assessing men, who they were, what they were, whether they were threats.

"I used to live here," he said.

She straightened. "You did? You...you did? You're Jameson? Your wife and child...?"

"Yes, but I'm glad to see that you...that your children..." He didn't know how to say what he felt. He took a step toward the porch. "There's life here. Food and air and laughter. The shadow is gone."

She stepped off the porch, looked back at the house as if viewing it afresh. "When we came and saw the house, the shadow was here. But this place was big enough for the children we wanted to foster, and because of the murders, it was cheap. So we bought it, and yes—our kids have heard someone died here. But their parents dumped them, and they also hear their mothers—that's us—are lesbians, so those past deaths are minor in their worldview." She offered her hand.

Maybe she put a little extra force in her handshake, a warning to him, but he understood, and that was fair.

In a lower tone, she said, "Before we took possession of the house, my wife and I went down in the cellar with a steel firepit. We took branches of fresh sage, lit them and cleansed the air. We added lavender for serenity and rosemary for remembrance." She laughed. "The smoke got so thick the alarm went off and the fire department showed up. We met a lot of the emergency response team that night, which was fine, because with eight foster kids who regularly break bones, it's good to know their names. The emergency team, I mean."

Zone nodded. "So no ghosts in the house?"

"No ghosts in the house. You want to come in? We always have plenty on the table."

Zone wanted to say no. Who was he, to intrude upon these people and their meal? Instead he said, "I heard you have bread pudding for dessert, so…yes. Thank you."

Berthorina said, "I'm Bernadette. My partner is Signa. Welcome to our home."

37

AFTER ZONE LEFT, PETIE alternated between anger, terror and rejection. Here she was, trying to save her mother's life from a murderous career criminal, and her mother didn't believe a word she said.

Nearly ten years Petie had stayed away. If she was caught, she'd be incarcerated forever, and that was only because Alaska didn't have the death penalty! Couldn't Mama comprehend that only something of the greatest importance could have brought her out of hiding?

The swing into terror was briefer; her mother faced the worst kind of danger.

Distracting herself from her mother's peril did no good.

That path led right to Zone. That bastard. That cad. That cowardly son of a bitch, running away, leaving her alone to face a serial killer.

Okay, he hadn't run very far. But that wasn't how it felt. She couldn't lean on him for support. She didn't want to call on him for help. She wished she could hate him.

She *did* hate him.

Except…she empathized with him, too.

To discover that he'd helped the man who'd gruesomely murdered his wife and child. That he'd welcomed him into his home, showed him the path to a fortune paved in gore.

If only Zone had been a selfish lover, she might be able to reject him and the memories. But he'd been eager, caring, needy, worshipping her and ready to be pleased. When she thought about how their two bodies had melded, how they banished the loneliness and became one…

Determinedly, she returned to thinking about her mother. She concentrated on anger and rejection, the day's schedule, and told herself repeatedly the FBI was on its way and everything would be okay.

According to Marya, her mother had a busy day planned.

*Work out with her Pilates group.

*Cut and color at the hairdresser.

*Book group at the Rockin Bookshop.

*Grocery shopping for the weekend's cooking.

Ioana would never be home, and she would never be alone.

Marya should get into town between two and three. They were going to meet at the house, and between the two of them, they could talk sense into Ioana.

At least, Marya could.

Not that Ioana would take this intervention graciously. She was a stubborn know-it-all.

Whether or not her mother infuriated Petie wasn't the point. What mattered was that Ioana should live to infuriate her some more.

Because they loved each other.

Petie didn't love Zone.

What had passed between them was not love.

But when Petie allowed herself a moment to think…she

knew it wasn't not-love, either. The sex had been good, and true, and honest, and for the first time in too many years, Petie experienced a connection that made her close her eyes and relive the moment.

But no, she didn't want to do that. She needed to keep busy until it was time to go to her mother's.

She spent the morning in the hotel pool, then at the hotel spa getting a massage that did her no good because she couldn't stop thinking and *relax*. Then she showered and dressed in one of the summer dresses Jeen had sent, then stripped it off and put on workout clothes. She shouldered her very expensive backpack, with its perfect-sized pocket for the Ruger LC9s, and headed out of the hotel to run the three miles to her mother's house.

Which was stupid.

But she couldn't sit still, and she couldn't show up before her mother got home from all her activities, and she figured someone would give her a ride back to the hotel. Maybe Marya, bossing Petie around, or maybe Ioana, driving too fast and shouting.

The first two miles went by quickly, and Petie was reminded of the meme she'd seen whip past online: *If you ever see me running, please kill whatever is chasing me.*

It had been funny, then.

Now it was a little too true.

She dropped to a walk, put a hand over the stitch in her side and walked the rest of the way.

38

LUNCH STARTED WITH GRACE, a prayer taken seriously by the family who lived at the old Jameson place.

"We got a couple of the kids off the street," Signa explained. "They didn't always have something to eat, so they are truly thankful."

As promised, the bread pudding was excellent, if stretched a little thin for so many hungry mouths. After the meal had ended, Bernadette gathered the kids into a cleanup crew and sent Signa, an earth mother if there ever was one, with Zone to view the changes in the home.

Everything about it felt different, looked different to him.

Signa took him on a tour of the house and grounds, made him think pretty deeply about what his life was, what it had been, what Michele and Timmy would have said to him about hiding in the mountains, helping no one, refusing to heal from his loss.

As Signa showed him the sizable vegetable garden, she asked, "What brought you back to Rockin?"

"A woman."

"Good. You're dating?"

"No." He thought about the night before; meeting Evelyn Jones after all these years, realizing she was innocent and getting lost in a morass of guilt all over again. A different guilt this time, knowing the truth about Donald White, knowing that Zone had educated his son's killer in antiquities and what they were worth, had allowed that man to become such a familiar entity that Michele had permitted him to spend time with them, cooked for him, given him wine and died at his hands.

And then...then... "I came here to render justice on the woman who murdered my wife and child—and I slept with her."

"What?" Signa softened her voice and repeated, *"What?"*

The whole story poured out of him, how the girl Evelyn had been falsely accused, convicted, saved and changed by the landslide. How she had been in hiding until the day she saw her mother with the real killer. How he'd been led first to her hiding place, then sent to Rockin.

Signa sank onto a bench between the tomatoes and the rhubarb.

He'd met Petie, and she'd showed him the picture, and he'd simultaneously realized the truth and, with her, betrayed the memory of his family.

Signa waved him to silence. "Let's break this down to its components. After your wife and son were murdered, you disappeared into the mountains and were no good to anyone."

He had enough sense to feel insulted. "I wouldn't go that far. I do the usual lookout stuff—watch for forest fires, rescue idiots who get lost or get hurt. I authenticate antiquities. I'm the best in the business."

"That's how you make your living?"

"No, I have money, so I do that pro bono."

She nodded.

"I've managed to rescue a few—quite a few, actually—pieces of the ancient world and get them routed to museums." For some reason, he wanted this woman's approval. "I'm good at picking out frauds."

"You're a hermit, but you're a busy hermit."

He shrugged. "I do some experimenting with inventions that help me live off the grid. I've got patents for solar-energy devices."

"Whew. The way you were talking at first, I thought you were worthless. But the whole time you lived in the mountains, you've been wallowing in guilt."

"Not wallowing." He didn't like that word, not when applied to him. "I simply don't form relationships."

"Why not?"

"It's easier that way."

She snorted.

Rude.

"You get mysterious texts bringing you to Alaska where you find the young woman who all those years ago escaped justice, and it turns out she wasn't lying, and the man who really murdered your wife and child is in town dating her mother. You have an affair with this woman—"

"It wasn't an affair. It was a one-night stand!" As soon as he said it, he knew he hadn't made it better.

"And in the morning, you leap out of bed and *run away*."

"She said I could go. She understood. She said the FBI was on its way. I went to my hotel room. I only drove out here. I told her I'd help her get justice!" Why was he trying to win this? He knew he'd been a jerk.

Signa stared at him like a Valkyrie about to smite a mortal.

He deserved it. He said, "There's a serial killer in Rockin, and the woman I now know is innocent—"

"And who you slept with!"

"The woman I now know is innocent intends to somehow bring the killer to justice before he murders her mother."

"But thank heavens the FBI is somewhere on the road heading for Rockin," Signa said.

"Excuse me. I have to leave." He strode through the vegetable garden, toward the driveway and his car. "I'm going to Rockin to find Evelyn Jones."

"I would hope to hell. Do you know where her mother lives?"

"No." He stopped. "Is that where she'd go?"

"How long has it been since you've thought about anyone but yourself?" Signa pulled out her phone while she walked and tapped at it.

He headed toward the car again.

She trailed after him and he heard her say, "Hello, Rockin Hotel? Could you put me through to Petie... Wait, Petie Something... I met her last night at the fundraiser, and I can't remember her name."

He got in, started the car and rolled down the window.

She stood, listening, then hung up. "She's not answering the phone inside her room. Hold on, I'll get her mother's address."

As he backed up, she yelled out, "In the old sawmill subdivision, 278 North Bayview! Do you need directions?"

He waved, yelled back, "No, when Timmy was a baby—" He stopped, steadied his voice and said, "When Timmy was a baby and had colic, the only way he'd stop crying was if we put him in his car seat and... So we drove him all over, and I know Rockin well. Thanks, and thanks for lunch!" And he drove like a bat out of hell back to Rockin and into town in search of Evelyn Jones.

He felt better about himself.

And scared for Petie.

What the hell had he been thinking?

39

IOANA GOT HOME FROM her Saturday morning's activities feeling good. She carried the groceries in from the car and placed the bags on the counter. She locked the back door with a decisive click and set the security system.

Her reading group had been canceled—after a car backed through their window, the bookstore had had to close—but something about a hard workout with friends cleared the tangle of emotions and gave clarity to the recent events of her life.

Evelyn was home, and she'd come with a dire warning. Which made Ioana mad because she didn't want to admit the first guy she'd dated since her divorce—the first guy she'd dated *ever*—was the most serious villain Ioana had ever met. And in Belarus, she'd met quite a few.

Ioana put the groceries away, leaving out the ingredients for her pork stew. Evelyn loved pork stew.

Evelyn wouldn't have come here, where she was in danger, if she wasn't sure of her facts.

While Ioana hated to admit it, she had begun to wonder about Derrick herself. This morning, at the salon, she had viewed herself in the mirror with a critical eye—and she was gorgeous. Derrick could hardly be bothered to kiss her, and when he did…Ioana was the one who drew back. It was cool, smooth, deliberate, like kissing a reptile.

Ioana gave herself a few points for good sense and made her plans. She would lure Derrick to a public place, return the so-called gifts, and when he had them in his possession and she was out of reach, she would call the chief of police.

She walked into the hall to the sideboard, opened the silver drawer and pulled out the antiques: the Russian icon depicting the sorrowing Virgin Mary holding her blessed baby son, the gold and jeweled reliquary holding the remains of martyred St. Beliquist's hand and the Egyptian terra-cotta figure. She set them on top and turned to go upstairs for the jewelry.

Shock jolted through her.

Derrick stood in the entrance to the kitchen.

Her heart jumped into the race, beating too fast. Her defenses snapped into place, ready to protect. "Derrick! How did you get in?"

"You left the door open."

"No, I didn't," Ioana said, then thought back. She remembered the snap of the lock and setting the alarm. "I didn't," she repeated.

He smiled.

Once again, she thought of a reptile, one with fangs that dripped poison and death.

She was in trouble. Real trouble. Not for the first time. *Play it calm. Play it smooth. Play it confident.* "Did you come to collect your treasures?"

"I did." He started toward her.

"Wait!" She held out the flat of her hand in a stop gesture. "I need to get the jewels for you."

"Where are they?"

"Upstairs. It won't take me a moment." She started toward him, all false assurance and strong intent. The stairs were behind him. She had a phone, a landline, on the second floor.

"In your bedroom or your bathroom, I imagine."

Of course, he was right. Last night when she took them off, after she examined them in the magnifying mirror, she had laid them carefully on her bedside table. The stones glowed so beautifully blue, the gold was so heavy and bright...

She got too close to him.

He caught her arm. "I can find them myself."

He was very tall.

She was not. But she worked out. She was strong. And in Belarus, she had faced her fair share of monsters.

He pushed her toward the sideboard.

She gestured at the icon, the reliquary and the Egyptian figure. "Here they are! I intended to return them to you, of course. But you shouldn't be in my bedroom. I'll get the jewelry for you."

"I wonder..." He tapped his lower lip and examined the pieces he'd given her. "What made you decide these were treasures?"

"You gave them to me." She fluttered her eyelashes. "Of course they're treasures."

He was supremely unimpressed. Petie was right; he was immune to everything that didn't revolve around him. "Why would you return my gifts?"

Glibly she said, "They look real, and I realized they were too valuable for me to keep."

"They are real, and...you intended to break up with me."

He sounded genuinely surprised. "Why would you do that? Was it something I said?"

"Not at all." She tried to step away from him.

His grip on her arm tightened. "Was it something that young woman said? The one who came for dessert and spoke so bluntly?"

"Yes."

"You're related, aren't you? You don't look alike, but your expressions, your mannerisms are similar. She's your daughter."

No harm in telling him now. "Yes, she is. She said I was too old to be making a fool of myself over a man, and I decided she was right."

"Right." He nodded.

He believed that, that she was too old to bother with a man. The *bastard*.

He said, "I sensed tension between the two of you. It's too bad that the last time your daughter sees you, you're having a disagreement."

He had just told Ioana he intended to kill her. Evie, too? Yes, of course, he would kill Evie. Ioana felt her bubbling fear cool to icy intent. "We'll see each other again soon. She's on her way here."

"Then I'd better hurry." With his long arms and man-strength, he held all the advantages. He caught Ioana by surprise, swung her against the wall against the stairway, grabbed her throat in both hands, lifted her off her feet and squeezed.

She had one chance. One, before she blacked out. She kicked him, a good hard kick fueled by fury and fear, powered by Pilates, and she hit the bull's-eye—right between his legs.

He yipped like the dog he was, dropped her, doubled over.

She kneed him in the face, whirled to run, took two steps—

He punched her between the shoulder blades.

She fell forward on her face, all the air blasted from her lungs.

He picked her up by her hair, her beautiful, newly colored and styled hair, stood her up and slapped her, a hard blow to the cheek. He demanded, "Do you know who I am?"

His outrage made her want to laugh. But she was in too much pain. She got her breath. "Yes. I do."

He pulled a knife from a holster under his jacket.

She saw a figure pass the window, moving fast, a pistol in her hand.

Evelyn.

Ioana got a bigger breath, wet her lips and said loudly, "You're Donald White."

He froze.

Another breath. She shouted, "You killed Michele and Timmy Jameson."

He let go of Ioana's hair, took a step away and stared into her face. With his knife still pointed at her, he asked, "How do you know that? No one saw me at the scene. Anyway, I don't look like him."

"That was *my* daughter you set up."

"I know that. But she's dead. That girl last night…she had to be your other daughter."

"No. That was Evelyn. She was convicted of *your* crimes. She knows who you were. She knows who you are. She came to warn me about you. She *knows.*"

"Evelyn… That was the kid's name." He laughed incredulously. "She's dead!"

"No. She's not. She survived the landslide." *Keep talking,*

Ioana. "She knows you're alive. She knows you're here in Rockin. She has you cornered."

"She's alive?" He chuckled. "She has me cornered? She was a smart kid, but she's not that smart. She could never corner me."

"Yes, she can." He wasn't listening. He wasn't afraid. Maybe that was better, probably that gave Evie a better chance. But his cocky disbelief infuriated Ioana. "You're going to be sorry."

"She's on her way here? How delicious. What a fitting finish." He adjusted his grip on the knife and started at Ioana again. "I suppose that means I'd better wait for her to arrive to—"

"Mama! Move!"

Ioana dove for the floor.

The pistol blasted.

Donald White paused as if suddenly at a loss for words. He looked surprised. He touched his chest, and his hand came away a gory red. He turned toward the kitchen, where Evelyn stood in the doorway. "You can't..."

"Yes, I can," she said. "There's no one who has more of a right to execute you."

He dropped to his knees, wavered...

Ioana stood up and kicked him in the shoulder.

He didn't even scream as he toppled. He was already dead.

Rage roared through Ioana. She wanted him to be alive, so she could trample him, hurt him as he had hurt her baby.

"Mama, are you all right?" Evelyn's voice trembled.

"I'm fine. I'm so mad. I feel stupid. I—" Ioana caught a glimpse of Evelyn's face.

Evie was shaking. She was crying silently. She couldn't take her gaze off the corpse lying on Ioana's oriental rug.

The girl had no stomach for killing.

Ioana forgot everything except her daughter. "Honey, it's okay." She hurried over, extracted the pistol from Evie's fingers and reached around the doorway to place it on the kitchen counter. "You did what you had to do. You saved me."

Evie looked at her, seemed to see her for the first time, saw the bruises on her throat. "I didn't get here soon enough. He hurt you!"

"I'm fine. I'll heal." Ioana's brain went into action. This was her fugitive daughter. She couldn't go back to jail now. Not for this. "Honey…"

Evie's gaze returned to the corpse.

"Evie…"

Evie shuddered, and shuddered again.

"Evelyn!" Ioana's sharp voice got Evie's attention. "You need to hide."

"I can't, Mama. I killed him. The police will come and take me away." Evie's pupils dilated to fill her eyes. "Again."

She was afraid.

A man's voice spoke from the open kitchen door. "Hide her. I'll handle the rest."

Ioana faced him and prepared to fight for her little girl.

But Evelyn sighed and sagged in relief. "Zone."

Ioana did not relax. "Who are you?"

"Zone Jameson."

She knew the name. She knew who he was. She recognized him from his visit. She remembered his threats, and his beard and his wild, dark, feverish eyes. "Why should I trust you?"

He plucked up the pistol and a kitchen towel and walked past them, bold and calm, a tall dark-haired man without a beard, yet still in need of a shave.

"Because he knows I didn't kill his family," Evie said.

"So he says."

He polished the gun, polished it as if he had all the time in the world. With his foot, he turned Donald faceup, aimed and shot him in his motionless chest.

Evie covered her face with her hands.

To Ioana, he said, "I saw him twitch."

Now Ioana believed in him. "So did I."

To Evie, he said, "Don't cry, Petie. It's okay. You're going to hide upstairs as far in the back of the closet as you can get, and stay there until someone tells you it's safe to come out."

Evie flung her hand toward the corpse. "But I shot him!"

"No, you didn't. *I* wiped down the gun. *I* have powder residue on my hands. *I* shot him."

"Oh." Evelyn sounded faint.

He walked over, wrapped one arm around her waist and pulled her close. He held her cheek against his chest, let her absorb his warmth, hear his heartbeat. "It's all right, Petie. We're going to make it through this."

"Are we? The police—"

"Will never know you're involved." Gently he moved her away. "Mrs. Jones, take her up. Go on, Petie. I'll call 9-1-1 and confess." He transferred a stern gaze to Ioana. "Then Mrs. Jones, come back down so we can get our stories straight." He watched Ioana lead Petie up the stairs, then pulled out his phone.

The back door opened.

He turned swiftly to face the beautiful young woman who walked into the house as if she owned it.

She surveyed the scene as if she had somehow anticipated a man's body on the floor, blood pooling beneath him.

Zone said, "You must be Evelyn's sister."

Marya nodded. "Yes. Are my mother and sister unharmed?"

"Your mother is bruised, but unbroken. She's hiding Petie upstairs."

"Evie was the shooter?" Marya's voice rose.

"No."

"No? You were? Who are you?"

"I'm Zone Jameson." He dialed 9-1-1. "I'm calling the police to confess to the killing."

Instantly, Marya understood what had really happened. She strode toward him and offered her hand. "I'm Marya Jones, and I'm a lawyer. It looks like you're going to need one." Her grip was strong, and she shook his hand a little too hard. "And on behalf of my family, *thank you*."

40

PETIE HUDDLED IN THE back of her mother's narrow walk-in closet, hiding behind the long dresses and coats, rigid with fear and remembered horror. She had shot. She had killed a man, a man she had hunted through the years, a man who had murdered and destroyed.

She felt no remorse. She would have killed a thousand men for her mother, her sister. And she had dreamed of killing the man who had taken the lives of Michele and Timmy and left them to rot in a basement.

But she couldn't get the scene out of her mind: the way the wound opened in his flesh, his surprise, his realization he would be dead. And then…death, the soul vacating the flesh, leaving the eyes cloudy and lifeless.

With Michele and Timmy, she had seen the results of death's visit.

That was so much worse than this.

But it didn't matter how many times she told herself she'd

done the right thing, the macabre scene continued to replay in her head.

Donald White. Surprise. Falling. Dying.

Then Zone Jameson, arriving, taking the pistol, cleaning away her fingerprints, deliberating shooting the body again at close range. Rescuing her from the horror of being arrested, taken to that jail where she'd been held before, knowing justice could fail…

And had.

It wasn't remorse that she'd wiped a cold-blooded killer off the face of the earth.

She couldn't wipe away the knowledge that she had taken a life.

The closet wasn't deep enough.

It could never be deep enough.

41

"**MY MOTHER IS INJURED.** She was almost killed. She needs a doctor, not to stay here in this noisy, cold, dreary police station all night." Marya gestured around at Chief Dumas's office, then out the door at the desks, the officers as they came in from patrol, went out to patrol, wrote up reports, poured mugs from the constantly emptying pot of coffee.

Damn, Chief Dumas hated lawyers. Not that Marya Jones was a lawyer of the Alaska bar. She practiced in California, and she had freely confessed to being an entertainment lawyer.

But she'd been to law school, knew the ins and outs of what governed police work. Mostly she knew how to make herself an irritant. He'd be even more annoyed…except that she was protecting her mother.

He couldn't fault her for that. He'd been darned fond of his own mother.

Wearily, Dumas leaned against his desk. "For the last several hours, I have told you to take her to the hospital and then home. I merely request that she agree to have a police escort until I've properly questioned her—"

"I cannot leave him here alone. My Zone. The son God never gave me," Ioana said.

Dumas transferred his attention to her.

Zone sat in a chair against the wall.

She stood beside him, her palm resting on Zone's shoulder. He awkwardly patted her hand.

Dumas couldn't quite decide if she was playing him. He'd met her before. She had always had an exotic accent, but now it was more… Just more. Her voice seemed husky, her gestures exaggerated, and the way she stood, shoulders back, spine erect, neck long, made him think of a petite model.

Of course, she had had a rough afternoon, she was excited, so maybe it was fatigue. Because how would she know he had a weakness for voluptuous women?

Dumas exerted himself to look authoritative and respectable. "I promise, Mrs. Jones, Mr. Jameson will be perfectly safe in my custody."

"You'll keep him up all night." Ioana got tearful again. "You'll brainwash him until he confesses."

Too loudly, Dumas said, "He already confessed!" He glanced out his office door.

His officers had paused to stare at him.

He took a breath, straightened to his full height and let his own accent strengthen, grow softer, slower, more Southern. "Ma'am, Mr. Jameson has already confessed. All we want is to speak to you both, separately, about the crime." Which had been impossible, because she'd been clinging to Zone.

"The death of that horrible man was not a crime!"

"Murder is a crime."

"Zone saved my life from a violent serial killer!"

"Serial killer?" Dumas went from weary to alert. "What makes you think he was a serial killer?"

"When I tried to break up with that man, he illegally entered my home."

That much was true. The lock and security system had clearly been tinkered with.

"He tried to choke me for the trinkets he had given me." Ioana touched the bruises on her neck.

"Trinkets." Dumas looked at the antiques lined up on his desk. Zone had insisted they take the things on Ioana's sideboard to the police station. He said they were too valuable to leave lying around. From what Dumas had heard about Zone Jameson, the guy would know.

"I wanted Derrick to remove them from my home, but he said no woman was allowed to leave him, to return his gifts! I knew then he had killed before." A single tear slid down Ioana's lovely cheek.

Her daughter whipped out a handkerchief and handed it to her mother.

Dumas wondered how many of those things she had in her purse. He'd previously seen at least two hankies used in exactly the same way—as emphasis. "Huh. You didn't say that earlier."

Ioana dabbed at her cheek.

Marya stepped closer and lowered her voice. "Chief Dumas, my mother is from Belarus. Her family disappeared, was killed or forced onto the streets. She escaped the worst kind of police oppression, but she has never forgotten."

He'd dealt with Marya before. When she'd come up to visit her mother, she'd requested permission to view evidence of the case that convicted her sister of murder and then sent her to prison—and death. What was he supposed to do? Uphold the honor of a former corrupt police chief? No, and since the moment he'd granted access, both in person and with scans and photos, it had been obvious Marya would clear her dead sister's name.

Dumas spoke through gritted teeth. "I can promise her justice from the people who work in my department."

Ioana proved she was listening when she transferred her hand to Dumas's arm. "Chief, if you only knew the joy I experienced when Zone arrived to save me. And when you and your officers charged in, it was as if justice itself had walked through my door."

Yep, Dumas was pretty sure he was being played.

"Really, Chief Dumas, please let me take my mother to the hospital and then home." Marya wasn't nearly the drama queen her mother had proved to be, but she was relentless. "This ordeal has been a nightmare."

On cue, Ioana withered into a chair.

Dumas said *again*, "All you have to do is accept a police escort who will take you to the hospital, then sit outside your home to guard your safety—"

"But am I not the victim?" Ioana lifted the handkerchief and dabbed at her damp eyes. "To have a law officer lurking outside my house, spying as if I had done something wrong. My neighbors will gossip. I'll be the center of unkind attention. I'll be reminded of my sad past in Belarus…"

Abruptly, Chief Dumas decided this wasn't worth it. The women weren't flight risks, so why was he insisting on correct police protocol?

The answer: because he couldn't figure out why it was so important to them *not* to have a police escort.

What were they hiding?

"You win. No police escort. Go wherever you want." He put his hands on his hips and leaned forward into Ioana's face. "As long as you stay within the Rockin city limits."

"Chief of Police, thank you. Thank you." She grasped the sides of his head, pulled him close and kissed him from ear to ear. "I promise I have no reason to leave. Rockin is the place where I established my family's home. I swear to return here tomorrow. Whenever you want! Then you may question me to your heart's content. What time do you wish me to arrive?"

Marya had already gathered their belongings. "Not too early, Chief. My mother is under stress and needs her sleep."

"Don't we all," he agreed.

When Marya's request to review the notorious Evelyn Jones evidence had come in, Dumas been curious enough to do his own review. A cursory examination showed him the case had either been the sloppiest police work in the history of the world or former Chief of Police George had deliberately sought a conviction. So he had granted Marya access to the files and the physical evidence. The family had suffered a grave loss; they deserved the truth.

Marya handed Zone her keys. "We'll catch a ride with one of the officers who will act as our escort to the hospital. Perhaps the officer will remain to take us home."

"And then not remain in front of our house as if we were bad people?" Ioana asked.

"Yes, Mama. Chief Dumas promised." Marya turned back to Zone. "When you're released—my car is the silver Ford Explorer in the lot across the street, spot number seventeen."

"Right. Thanks." Zone slid the keys into his jeans pocket.

Dumas spoke to Ioana. "Come about one tomorrow afternoon, and we'll talk."

"I look forward to it." Ioana fluttered her eyelashes at him, and she and Marya cleared the area in record time.

Officer Ivanov sauntered by. "Chief Dumas, better wipe that lipstick off your face. Pink isn't your color."

Dumas looked out at his officers to see smothered grins all around the room. He said loudly, "To heck with y'all. I've been played by less beautiful women."

42

HER MOTHER AND SISTER came home while Petie was in the bathroom.

Because, you know, a person could reproach themselves about shooting another human, and worry about the consequences of returning to the town where she'd been unjustly convicted, think about her years alone and whether they trumped her dedication to her family...but at some point, she still had to *go*.

When she came out and saw Ioana and Marya, she jumped so hard and fearfully she was glad she had just peed.

They hugged, and cried, then shut the curtains in Ioana's bedroom, huddled together on the bed and talked until dawn.

"Okay, listen." Marya removed her fire-engine red hoodie with *California Dreamin'* embossed across the back, and put it around Petie's shoulders. "You're going to be me. So wear this with the hood up."

Petie shoved her arms into the sleeves.

Ioana dug around in Marya's purse, then offered Petie Marya's cat-eye sunglasses.

"Right," Marya approved. "The sun's up and it's a little cloudy, but no one's going to think anything about seeing me in sunglasses except that I've gone Hollywood."

Petie slid them on her nose.

Marya continued, "You walk out to the end of the driveway. You do a couple of stretches. Probably none of the neighbors will notice because it's so freaking early. But there's old Mr. Gagnon who I swear has worn a dent in his blinds. If he steps out and says anything, you wave at him and start jogging. You run out of the neighborhood."

Petie nodded.

"Jog or walk toward the hotel. About halfway, take off the hoodie and tie it around your waist. Go right in the front door of the hotel. If anyone looks at the security recordings, they're going to see that you left yesterday and didn't come back until today...but nobody has reason to look."

To her mother, Petie said, "Was she always this bossy?"

"She's grown into the role," Ioana answered.

Marya ignored them. "If the desk people speak to you, tell them it's a great day for a run. Or whatever. You've got your room key?"

Petie patted her backpack. It weighed less than it had yesterday; her pistol had been taken as evidence.

But she didn't need it now.

Donald White was dead, and she should be feeling better.

She did. Really, she did. Except...

No. She did.

"Then you're set." Marya caught her in a fierce hug. "Don't worry about the future. Mama already set the chief of police on the trail of that bastard as a serial killer. Once he's revealed, by God I'll prove you innocent, and you can return to life."

"I haven't been dead," Petie said tartly.

"And buried in an Alaska fishing camp!" Marya answered.

"It wasn't that bad." Petie stumbled, trying to explain. "I learned a lot about myself, and I taught myself a lot about many things."

In Belarusian, Ioana said, "My language."

Marya looked between them. "What?"

In English, Ioana assumed command. "Evie, before you leave town—"

"Which she has to do promptly!" Marya interjected.

"—you come for Sunday dinner."

"No, she can't," Marya said.

Ioana ignored her. "I'll make pork stew and rye bread." She transferred her attention to Marya. "You can eat, too. I'll make *kalduny*."

Dumplings.

Marya clearly wavered.

Petie grinned. Marya loved *kalduny*.

"Come at four. No, three!"

"Mother, you have to go to the police station." Marya sounded as if she had gathered her patience.

"I'll be home in time to prepare dinner," Ioana said airily.

"We don't know how long Chief Dumas will keep you for questioning." Now Marya's patience was slipping away.

"He is a dear man. I like him very much."

"He's a good policeman, which means you can only push him so far," Marya warned.

"He is a good kisser."

Petie covered her mouth to hide her laughter.

"Mama, how could you possibly know…" Marya held out her hand in a stop signal. "Don't tell me. I don't want to know. I want to see Evie, too. You know I do. But having her remain in Rockin is risky."

"Three o'clock." Ioana kissed first Evie's cheeks, then Marya's. "Three."

43

"**DONALD WHITE IS DEAD.**" From her office in Quemada, Jeen Lee stared at the monitor, shifting her weight from foot to foot, in the White Crane Spreads Wings tai chi move.

Petie copied her motion, held the pose with less balance and grace, and spoke to the monitor on the Rockin Hotel desk. "He is."

"You have not been held responsible."

"No. Zone Jameson confessed. He's at the Rockin police station now, making his statement. In fact, he's been there all night." Petie shifted and performed the single whip. "The police chief is suspicious. But he has been unable to find contradictory evidence."

"You are free. What will you do now?"

"I don't know. Go back to the fishing camp until Marya settles my case." Petie lost her balance, staggered sideways, put both feet down. "I feel oddly unsettled, as if I've left something undone."

"Does it have to do with your blossoming relationship with Zone?"

"I didn't tell you about that." How did Jeen know?

"He confessed to a killing which he did not do. Unless he has strong feelings, no man does that for any woman."

"Zone is a part of my disquiet," Petie acknowledged.

Jeen sank toward the floor. "When all your being and consciousness strains for many days and years toward one goal, and that goal is achieved, it must be natural to feel unsettled. After finding my son, I feel that, too."

"Yes. I suppose you do." Centering herself, Petie sank also into the Snake Creeps Down position.

"What about your mother and sister?" Jeen asked.

"We'll try to form a family again."

"That is a noble goal, and achievable."

Remembering what her mother had said about why she'd protected Marya, and what she had believed about Petie, and how she had apologized... Petie agreed. "Right now, I'm going to meditate. I suspect this unrest indicates lingering issues."

"A good choice." Jeen rose and bowed to Petie. "May you find wisdom."

Petie rose and bowed in return. "May you find peace."

The flash of anguish in Jeen's eyes told Petie too clearly that for all her calm, the issue of her son and the time apart from him still left her shattered into a thousand pieces.

Jeen reached out to her monitor and turned it off.

Petie did the same. She seated herself in the middle of the hotel bed, crossed her legs and closed her eyes. She immediately sank into her meditation, into a deep, dark place in her mind where peace and strength waited to be plucked and—

Wake up!

Two words from Tuddy brought Petie to consciousness,

made her eyes open to face sunlight from the window and a sense of buzzing alarm. "What?" she said out loud.

With Donald's death, she'd put the bear in the closet. She couldn't see him, but what difference did it make?

He was only a stuffed bear. He didn't really speak, and she didn't really listen.

She got to her feet and pulled on her socks and athletic shoes.

She needed to get to her mother's house. Not because Tuddy had spoken to her but because...

Because why?

Because.

If she was leaving the hotel anyway, she should pack up her things before she went over.

No.

She should go *now.* She slung her backpack over her shoulder and walked into the corridor. As the hotel door closed behind her, she realized she'd forgotten her passkey. She should stop and grab one at the front desk and explain she needed late checkout...

No. Driven by an urgency she didn't understand, she got in the elevator and pushed the button for the garage.

She needed to be with her mother *now.*

44

PETIE PULLED OUT OF the hotel, stopped at a light and texted Zone.

> **Going to my Mama's a little early. You have to take that teddy bear away. More when we talk.**

The light turned green, and she drove toward her mother's at five miles over the speed limit, keeping an eye out for law enforcement, but sick with the need to get there before… before something happened. Before the worst happened.

She hadn't felt like this yesterday, going to unknowingly confront Donald White.

Why now? What was it that propelled her to get there and…whatever? Donald White was dead, shot twice, carried out in a body bag, lifeless in the city morgue. She knew that as surely as she knew something was very, very wrong. This felt like…like when Tuddy had sent her into the basement to discover the bodies.

This didn't make sense. Even if the worst happened, even if someone figured out the truth of what happened yesterday, Donald White was still dead, his crimes would be laid bare and her mother was safe.

When her phone rang, she jumped so hard her seat belt engaged and rammed her back against the seat. She fumbled with the controls of the rental car, trying to pick up. It rang twice, three times. Finally she clicked the right button on the console and said, "Hello?" She hadn't seen caller ID; she didn't even know who it was.

"Hello, honey. I thought I'd better let you know before you left the hotel that I'm not home right now." Her mother sounded breezy and assured, not at all like someone in jeopardy. "Your sister's at home sleeping in after her late night. I should be, too, but something is niggling at me."

Petie slowed down. "Something's niggling at me, too."

"Probably the same niggle. In all the blood and horror and trouble, I forgot about that cursed set of jewelry Derrick, or Donald, whatever his name was, gave me."

"Yeah?" Maybe that was what niggled at Petie. "Priceless jewelry shouldn't be hanging around."

"Right. I didn't think about it until Stacey called to see if I was okay. I told her the, um—" Ioana lowered her voice "—facts."

"The facts you told the police?"

"Those. Somewhere along the line, while we were on the phone, she complimented me on the bracelet and necklace I wore to the fundraiser. That triggered my memory, and I said, 'My God, that's right!' She asked me what I meant, and I explained they were still in my bedroom and I had to take them down to the police station at once." A long inhale of air. "Honey, she was horrified!"

Petie turned into her mother's neighborhood. The house

looked fine. No fire. No explosion. That damned teddy bear had upset her for nothing. "Because dangerous someones could show up at the house to grab the jewelry by whatever means necessary?" Maybe that was what Tuddy had warned about.

"Not that. Stacey said in her capacity as a member of the city council, she'd been quietly investigating the police department. Lately, stuff has gone missing—drugs, dear, and contraband—and she felt uneasy about taking the jewelry to them."

"That doesn't seem right. Not with Chief Dumas in charge." Petie pulled into her mother's driveway and sat with the car running. "Everything I've read about him says he's a good cop, runs a clean house."

"I thought that, too." Ioana sounded troubled. "I hate to think I was wrong about him. It goes to show you never know."

"I wish I could talk to Zone, hear his opinion of Chief Dumas."

"Chief Dumas has kept him there for so long, I imagine Zone's opinion is none too good." Ioana sounded indignant.

"Maybe. Mama, if Chief Dumas has doubts about the story of yesterday's shooting, you can't blame him. He has every right!"

"I suppose." Ioana sighed. "I hardly know the man, but I've known Stacey since her days at the bank. I trust her. You must, too, because Stacey said you told her who you are!"

"Not quite. She guessed, and I admitted it." Right now, Petie suspected denial would have been wiser. Following her own niggle of disquiet, Petie asked, "When you introduced Stacey to Donald White, did they seem to know each other?"

"Honey, Stacey's the one who introduced us."

"No. That's not right." The memory of her conversation

with Stacey in the hotel bar replayed in Petie's mind. "She said you introduced her to... Mama, where are you?"

"I'm headed to the bank."

"It's Sunday." Petie glanced up at the house.

Marya opened her bedroom curtains and waved cheerfully.

"It's okay. I'm using the side door, the one in the alley. Stacey's meeting me there. We're going to put the jewelry into my safety deposit box."

So wrong. This was so very wrong. Petie waved back at Marya, a frantic goodbye, backed up and headed downtown, accelerating past Mr. Gagnon and his picket fence at a speed that made him shake his fist. "Mother, Stacey doesn't work at the bank anymore. Stacey shouldn't have a key to the bank anymore, or the security code, or anything."

"You know Stacey. People trust her. I imagine they never took her key away."

This was it. *This* was what Tuddy had warned about. *This* was what Petie had feared. "Mama, don't go in."

"What?" Ioana raised her voice. "You're cutting out. You know how bad cell service is in this bank, all stone and iron and—"

Abruptly, something killed the connection.

Petie drove as fast as she dared to the bank.

45

ZONE SAT IN THE Rockin police chief's office, patiently answering the same questions over and over.

Yes, I shot him twice.

Yes, he was threatening to kill Ioana.

No, I felt as if I had no choice.

No, I had no idea his description matched that of a criminal wanted in other states.

Yes, those are priceless artifacts sitting on your desk, and in fact, if you have a safe, I'd suggest you stash them inside until someone from the MFAA arrives to retrieve them.

He'd been here long enough that he'd met most of the officers and even the dispatcher and noted that as Dumas tired, his Cajun drawl grew stronger and slower.

At last Dumas said, "It seems to me quite coincidental that you return to Rockin at the same time the man who might have killed your wife and child also returned."

Zone eased up off his tailbone to sit straight in the chair. "What do you mean? A young woman was convicted of their murder. That's what I know. What evidence do you have to think otherwise?"

"That young woman's sister applied to the Rockin Police Department to view the evidence pertaining to the trial."

Zone leaned forward. "She can do that? View the evidence? Can *anyone* view the evidence?"

Dumas pushed his reading glasses up on his nose and viewed the report on his monitor. "The request came to me. I saw no reason why not. She's been combing the evidence files from the time of the trial. When she visited Rockin, and via scans. She found issues."

"Issues?" Such a revealing word.

"Leads not followed, discrepancies and one partial fingerprint which was unaccounted for."

Dumas had all of Zone's attention. "Unaccounted for? Where was it found?"

"In your old home on Michele and Timmy Drive."

Zone clasped his hands and stared a demand at Dumas. "*Where* in my home?"

"On a picture frame."

"What picture frame?"

Impatient, Dumas said, "A photo of your son with his teddy bear."

Zone laughed softly. "Tuddy always took care of his boy."

"At the time, when my predecessor and her team ran that partial print, there were no matches."

"And now?"

"Other partials."

In a daze, Zone spoke without thinking. "My God. She's going to be cleared."

"*Who's* going to be cleared? The way I heard it, the young woman, Evelyn Jones, died in a landslide." Dumas peered at him over his reading glasses. "Didn't she?"

Not for the first time, Zone realized he had to step warily. Dumas had been polite, respectful. He'd assured Zone he was sure the killing of Derrick Green, alias Donald White, had been justified. He'd asked if Zone would mind staying at the police station, not as a prisoner, just so Chief Dumas could gather the evidence and ask him questions as they occurred. He'd had a cot brought in so Zone could sleep when he needed. Never had Zone imagined such a polite murder interrogation.

But Dumas was no fool; he'd been steadily working Zone over for hours, suspicious of the story that Zone and Ioana had recited so flawlessly. The pistol had presented problems, too. It was unregistered and untraceable.

Where did you get it?

In Anchorage. A guy in a bar wanted to sell it, and since I was coming back to Rockin, I felt the need for protection.

Why did you come back to Rockin?

It was time for me to set the ghosts to rest.

Did you know that, according to the manufacturer, the Ruger LC9s had been shipped to Quemada, way out there in the middle of the Atlantic?

No. Like I said, I bought it from a guy in Anchorage.

Among all the half-truths and lies, that much at least was true. Zone said, "If what you say about that fingerprint is true...someone knew the truth."

Dumas poured himself another cup of coffee. "You hungry? You want some more gumbo?"

"Thank you, it was great, but I'm gumboed out."

If Zone admitted now that Evelyn Jones was alive, the investigation into Donald White's death would start over from scratch. At best, everyone involved in the shooting would be charged with perjury, and Evelyn would be once again sent to prison. Even assuming the conviction would be overturned, this time she'd spend time behind bars.

Zone didn't know what he thought of his new and precarious relationship with Petie. He only knew the misery that had haunted his days had been suffered in equal parts by Petie, and she didn't need more punishment, more pain.

He needed to go at this from a different angle. "Do you have evidence that Evelyn Jones is alive?"

"If I had that, I'd be arresting her."

"That woman was convicted of killing my wife and son. If there's anything I should know—"

"That's not what we're here to talk about."

"You brought it up. There must be some reason for that."

Dumas took a breath, then let it out in a big puff.

A firm thump hit the chief's door. Officer Louis Ivanov peered in the side window.

"Come in," Dumas bellowed.

Officer Ivanov opened the door. "Sir, we have a pacer out front."

Dumas focused completely on the officer. "Who is it?"

"Marc Yazzie. Owns Yazzie Rentals."

"I remember him. On one of the darkest days of my life, I rented a cement mixer from him."

"Yes, sir." Officer Ivanov grinned. "But you got a good-looking patio out of it. He's been out there a good ten minutes, back and forth, back and forth, talking to himself."

Zone had no idea why this would be of interest, but in his sojourn in the building he'd met most of the officers and learned a lot about police work, and he figured he was about to learn more.

"You're sure he's not talking on some kind of fancy hidden mic to his cell phone?" Dumas said. "Happened one other time I went out after a pacer. Gosh darned embarrassing."

"No, Chief," Ivanov said. "Because he keeps pulling his phone out of his pocket, looking at it, shaking his head, looking at the stairs to the door, shaking his head, pacing some more. He's even managed to get up a couple of steps before backing down and starting it all again."

"I think I should go out and offer him our hospitality, don't you?" Dumas heaved himself to his feet, adjusted his belt and headed out of his office. At the last moment, he spun on his heel and pointed to Zone. "You are free to go. Get your stuff. Sign the papers. Stay in town. I'm sure I'll see you again." And he was gone, moving fast.

Zone stood and stretched. Even with his time on the cot, he'd been awake most of the night. He was ready to go… somewhere…and get some sleep.

Somewhere…where Petie was.

He wanted to tell her the ghosts were laid to rest. He wanted to make love to her. He wanted…he wanted to sleep in her arms.

"What was that all about?" he asked the officer.

"When we get a pacer, it means they've got something they want to tell us, but they're afraid to come in. Usually it's an abuse victim," Officer Ivanov said. "Then Chief Dumas has to coax them in. But he's got a way with hurt animals, all kinds."

"He seems like a good cop."

"The best. Not long ago, we had a pacer who killed his high-school girlfriend…killed her twenty years ago, and he wanted to confess. Showed us where the body was and everything. Cleared up a cold case." Ivanov got a troubled expression. "We'd seen him pacing before, but when Wretchen Gretchen was in charge, we didn't ever stick our necks out. Chief Dumas changed that."

"I gather by the accent and the gumbo he's from Louisiana?"

"Yep. We can't figure out what he's doing here."

Zone knew. It was the same thing that pulled him to live in a lonely outlook in Washington. "He wanted to be somewhere clear and cold."

The sociable officer looked startled. "Right." He scrutinized Zone as if he was a Martian. "Sure."

Zone's cell phone chirped in the pocket of his jacket. He dug it out and read the text from Petie.

Going to my Mama's a little early. You have to take that teddy bear away. More when we talk.

"Okay," Zone muttered. That was cryptic enough. He looked up at the sound of a man's voice, loud and excited.

"Listen. I can't believe I'm even here. I can't believe I'm even thinking this. She's not, you know… I mean, I really believe in her."

"'Scuse me, I'm needed out there." Officer Ivanov moved out in a rush.

46

"**WHO YOU TALKIN' ABOUT**, Mr. Yazzie?" Chief Dumas's voice sounded warm, calm, curious.

Zone stepped through the door and looked around the lobby.

Dumas had managed to herd Marc Yazzie through the outer door and into the waiting area. Dumas now stood between the dark-haired man and the door. Which was a good thing because Marc Yazzie looked wild-eyed and ready to bolt.

Officer Verne opened the security gate that led behind the counter and latched it open.

Officer Ivanov wandered toward the coffeepot located beside the outer door.

Zone realized other officers were moving into place behind Yazzie, acting as obstacles to retreat. Fascinating, like watching a play. Everyone here knew their role.

"She...she...she..." Marc Yazzie started backing up.

Officer Donatti bumped into him.

Marc jumped violently.

The officer apologized. "Sorry! I didn't see you there. Can I get you a cup of coffee?"

Marc stared at her as if she was speaking a foreign language. "What? Coffee." He rubbed his face. "Sure. I'd like coffee. I haven't slept more than five minutes straight since that reporter was shot."

Zone felt the buzz through his skin. The whole department went on high alert.

"Cream? Sugar?" Dumas asked.

"What?" Yazzie stared at him.

"In your coffee. Do you take cream or sugar?" Officer Verne asked.

Even that simple question seemed to excite Yazzie. "No! Black!"

Officer Donatti had a cup ready and shoved it into Yazzie's hand.

Yazzie took a sip. His eyes closed, and he sighed.

"This way, Mr. Yazzie." Dumas moved him through the security gate and behind the counter.

Zone saw the whole department heave a virtual sigh of relief.

Officer Verne slowly, quietly shut the gate so as not to startle Yazzie.

Yazzie stopped anyway and stared as if only now realizing where he was. His gaze slid past Zone without recognition, but he nodded to a couple of the officers.

They nodded back. One raised his hand in greeting. One called, "Hi, Marc."

They were making him feel at home.

In a genial voice, Dumas asked, "Mr. Yazzie, did you shoot Faye Miller?"

Marc Yazzie jumped. "What? Who?"

"The reporter."

Yazzie put the cup down on Officer Bailey's desk so hard coffee sloshed out on the paperwork there. "No. That's what I'm trying to tell you. I think *she* did!"

Officer Bailey jumped to rescue his work.

Dumas glared, and the officer subsided.

The huge room fell still.

"I supported her campaign for mayor. I keep her funds. That reporter, she heard us arguing about money."

"You and Stacey Collins were arguing about her campaign funds?" Dumas paced out the words.

"After Friday's kickoff fundraiser, I was stupid. I should have waited until we were in a private place. But I thought it was some kind of weird mistake." Yazzie appealed to the department at large. "I mean, there was a lot of money missing from the account."

"Can we back up for a minute, Mr. Yazzie?" Dumas brought Yazzie's attention back to him. "If Friday night was the kickoff fundraiser, how did Miss Collins have a campaign fund?"

"She was on the city council. She always has a campaign fund. She managed it herself before."

Dumas nodded and moved a few steps toward his office. "She's been embezzling from the funds she received to help her run for office?"

"No! Stacey wouldn't embezzle." Yazzie sounded shocked. "She's not that kind of person."

"What kind of person is she?" Dumas moved a few more steps toward his office.

Yazzie followed. "She wrote a check to that guy! I think he was blackmailing her about something!"

"What guy?" Dumas asked.

"That sleazy guy. That Derrick Green."

Someone gave an audible gasp.

A few of the officers looked at Zone.

It might have been him that gasped.

"Derrick Green was killed last night," Dumas said.

"I know. I'm so afraid that she... That Stacey..." Unable to complete the thought, Yazzie hung up on the last word.

"We have the shooter, Mr. Yazzie." Dumas came back and placed his hand on Yazzie's shoulder. "And it's not Stacey Collins."

"I know. I know." Yazzie rubbed his mouth, then pulled his fingers away and burst out, "I think she set it up. That second shooting. So she didn't have to pay him anymore."

"That's quite a stretch, Mr. Yazzie." Dumas glanced toward his office and did a head tilt to indicate Zone should move out of the doorway.

Zone moved.

Dumas made a shooing motion to Yazzie. "Why don't we go into my office and talk? You could explain why you think the candidate for mayor may have shot Faye Miller."

Yazzie shuffled toward the chief's office. "Because the reporter called me and said she'd overheard Stacey and me arguing, and I called Stacey and told her we were in trouble, and Stacey said to keep my mouth shut and she'd take care of it, and that night, Faye Miller was shot!"

47

THE PRONOUNCEMENT ELECTRIFIED THE department.

"Is she dead?" Yazzie looked at Chief Dumas with wretched, guilty eyes. "Is Faye dead? I can't stand it if she's dead."

"Last I heard, she's unconscious but holding her own," Dumas said. "Now, we really need to go to my office and—"

The phone in Zone's hand buzzed. He looked at the screen and read,

Stacey Collins has my mother at the bank. Tell the cops I need them now.

Evelyn Jones, the woman who had been convicted of a double murder, who had miraculously escaped and remained at large with no evidence of her existence... The woman who was now known as Petie said to hell with freedom and wanted the cops to arrive prepared to shoot because her mother was at risk.

"I'm coming!" Zone took off running for the security gate.

Dumas called, "Let him out!"

Zone spun and shouted, "Stacey Collins. At the bank. Holding Petie and her mother!" And he was gone.

"Petie? That woman who was at the fundraiser?" Officer Donatti frowned in confusion. "Who's her mother?"

Chief Dumas took over with the calm that characterized him. "Ivanov, get a call out to the patrolmen. They're needed at the bank. Lights and sirens, all speed. Proceed with care, please. Verne, let's make sure that Mr. Yazzie stays here in comfort."

Verne made a face. She'd drawn the short straw.

"I'm going to throw up," Yazzie said and ran toward the men's room.

"He's secure in there." Dumas walked toward the back door, moving fast. "Bailey, you're my driver. We're headed to the bank."

In a rush, Bailey followed, managed to get ahead, held the door.

The front-desk phone rang.

So did three cell phones.

Officer Verne already had her cell in her hand. "Chief, there's reports of shots fired in the alley between Big Dollar Deals and the bank."

"Of course there is. Officers and emergency personnel to the scene." Dumas corrected himself. "More officers and personnel. Victims?"

"Eyewitness reports of a body."

"Perp apprehended?"

"No. One or two people reported fleeing the scene."

"One or two?" Dumas sounded incredulous.

"Maybe one. Maybe two going in different directions."

"Video?"

"None yet."

Chief Dumas threw his arms in the air and bellowed, "What in heaven's name is happening in this town?"

48

FOUR BLOCKS AWAY IN the old town square, the weekend market was gathering steam. Empty cars lined the streets in all directions. With her window rolled down, Petie could hear an Irish band, voices haggling and laughing, and smell curry, tacos and cherry *vareniki*. It was early hours; a few people wandered toward the revelry, drawn by the music and the guarantee of fun and good eats, and so far, no one was returning to yield a parking space.

Petie could have double-parked, and maybe that would have quickly brought the police. But with her luck, they wouldn't listen if she explained her mother was inside a closed bank with the death-dealing candidate for mayor. They'd probably arrest her, and her instinct was to go in quiet and swift.

Or maybe it was Tuddy's instinct.

She didn't know or care. Right now, instinct was all she had. That, and the lug wrench provided in case she had to change a tire.

She turned down the alley between Big Dollar Deals and the bank, drove to the back and parked in the bank lot, in the same parking place she'd used all those years ago to deposit money for Donald White.

Habit was a bitch.

When she thought how cleverly Stacey Collins had played her, and how much she'd liked Stacey, trusted her...when she realized what Stacey intended to do to Ioana, she actually *wanted* to knock her into next week.

She dug around in the back of the QX60, located the tools under the third row seating, hefted the lug wrench in her hand—solid iron, it weighed more than a pound—and tucked the hook end into the back of her belt.

She ran down the alley, tried the side door.

It was locked.

She headed toward the front of the bank. Here between the buildings, it was dim and quiet, and halfway down she slowed to text Zone.

Stacey Collins has my mother at the bank. Tell the cops I need them now.

She knew she would need backup.

She heard footsteps ahead. She looked up and—my God! Matella came around the corner, dressed in jeans, a T-shirt, a short leather jacket and running shoes.

She walked toward Petie, her gait confident, her gaze fixed on Petie's face.

Questions flashed through Petie's mind like, *Where have you been since the flight?* And, *What bad timing.*

Although... Jeen had mentioned Matella was trained in martial arts. Maybe Matella could be Petie's backup?

Yes. Yes, she could. A break, at last.

Matella smiled, said, "Hello," and put her hand in her pocket.

Petie said, "Listen, Matella, I don't have time to explain, but could you—"

Matella started to pull her hand from her pocket.

Petie heard a step behind her: heavy, moving fast, somehow male.

Before she could turn, a pistol roared, the sound amplified by the narrow alley.

A bloody hole opened in Matella's chest.

Matella dropped to the ground.

She was dead. She was dead!

Not understanding, Petie whirled.

Pistol in hand, Miska ran past her, checked Matella for a pulse, then holstered his gun.

"What did you do?" Petie shouted.

Is he going to kill me next?

He pulled Matella's limp hand out of her pocket.

She clasped a small handgun.

"She was going to shoot you," he said.

"What?" Petie was incredulous. "Why?"

"Remember Copeland?"

Bradley Copeland, the guy at the camp with the big fish and the bigger bear. "What about him?"

"Zone Jameson came to the camp. He showed up ready to bring you in and said he'd received mystery texts informing him of your whereabouts. Hawley and I knew then someone was gunning for you, so Hawley sent me to make sure you came to no harm." Miska nudged Matella with his foot. "Copeland must have hired this piece to kill you if Jameson didn't turn you in."

"He's crazy!"

"Copeland? Yep, nutjob." Miska turned away. "Now, I'd

stick around to help you, but I'm not from around here, and I've just killed a woman. I have to get out of here."

She shoved him toward the parking lot. "Go on!"

He took off running. "You, too," he called back.

She ran the other direction, toward the street and the front of the bank. She didn't need to send Zone another text. With this shooting, the cops were going to be here real fast.

She burst onto the street.

The sidewalks were empty. If anybody had been near, they'd heard the gunshot and fled.

She ran up the bank steps two at a time and reached for the outer door, wondering if it was unlocked.

How about that? It was open, especially for her.

She slipped into the bank vestibule. She had somehow hoped this was a mistake, that it wasn't real, that her mother had been mistaken and the lost connection meant nothing more than building interference.

But no. The door was unlocked. The nightmare had begun. This was real. This was it. Stacey Collins had been Donald White's accomplice. Maybe she'd been his boss. Whatever her involvement, now she needed to deliver stolen antiquities to a buyer, and the police had impounded three of them.

By luring her mother here, Stacey was about to secure the most valuable pieces, the cabochon sapphires set by an ancient artisan in old, heavy gold.

Now all she had to do was kill the people who knew what she had planned.

The air in the vestibule between the outer and inner doors was still and quiet; this was a breathless place, a waiting place. Looking through the glass into the bank, Petie could see a single light that shone against the back wall.

But the lobby was shadowed, a place of unknown men-

ace. Somewhere inside, Ioana waited for rescue…and Stacey
waited to kill.

For ten years, Petie had anticipated this moment; to prove
herself as brave and strong *to herself.* Now she was afraid, yet
she opened the door and slipped into the shadowy depths of
the lobby. She waited as her eyes adjusted…

The lobby hadn't changed.

On the left, the teller cages marched in a long line of bulletproof glass and ornate, antique steelwork. On the right,
doors opened into dark, cavernous offices. The long center
carpet led to the bank president's desk. The only difference
from so long ago was that the old-fashioned, steel vault door
stood open.

Light shone from inside, and Petie caught a glimpse of
Ioana, sprawled facedown outside the vault. "Mama," she
whispered and took a step. And stopped.

One other thing had changed. Halfway down the length
of the bank, someone stood beside the coffee station, sip-
ping from a mug and holding a serious-sized pistol pointed
right at Petie.

49

"I REALLY WISH THIS wasn't necessary." Stacey Collins clicked the safety on her handgun.

A thousand responses flashed through Petie's mind: defiance, pleading, insults, and all wrong. She knew how to disarm a situation. Hawley had taught her.

Keep them off-balance.

"Coffee," Petie said in heartfelt thankfulness. "I left my hotel before I had my morning coffee. Do you mind if I...?" She gestured at the pot.

In the dim light, she couldn't quite see Stacey's reaction, but after a moment's hesitation, Stacey moved to one side and out of reach. "Sure." She gestured with her pistol.

In case Petie hadn't grasped the seriousness of the situation, Petie supposed.

She stepped up to the table where the twelve-cup coffee maker held center stage. She picked up a paper cup, inserted it into a cardboard holder, lifted the pot, licked her finger and touched the side of the glass.

She winced.

Good and hot.

She put down the cup, pulled the lid off the pot and peered inside like someone checking the level.

"I made it a half hour ago." Stacey sounded impatient. "There should be plenty."

"There is." Turning, Petie flung the contents of the pot at Stacey's face.

At the last moment, Stacey realized what was coming and tried to turn aside. No luck. The boiling stream swept her chest, neck, face. She screamed, dropped her mug and clawed at her face.

The handgun she carried wavered wildly, but she didn't drop that.

Petie leaped toward Stacey and kicked at the pistol. Not a good kick, not a solid kick, but the gun went off in a roar that echoed in the empty bank.

Petie thought she must be dead.

Instead, the bullet hit the glass over the teller cage and dinged a hole out of it.

So no, Petie wasn't dead. Not yet. And the glass was clearly bulletproof.

She fumbled for the lug wrench, tucked in her belt at the back.

Stacey punched her in the face right between the eyes.

Petie staggered back.

Somewhere, Stacey had learned to fight. Made Petie think she wasn't the only one with a record.

When Petie blinked the blood and tears from her eyes, she saw Stacey again held her pistol in both hands, pointed at Petie's chest.

Petie held up her hands. "Okay. Okay." *Misdirection, Petie. Misdirection. The cops are on their way.* "Um, listen. You don't work here anymore. How did you get in without setting off the bank alarms?"

"Oh, the bank," Stacey snorted derisively. "Mr. Terwilliger trusted me to install the alarm system. I know the overrides."

"Ah." Petie glanced again at her mother. No movement. Was she already dead? "You can't imagine you're so lucky that no one saw you come in and no one will see you leave."

"Of course not. Your mother asked for help. I didn't know why." Stacey fell into the role of surprised, upset victim. "It turned out her fugitive daughter, Evelyn, had returned to town and was threatening her, trying to steal her jewels."

The jewels Ioana had dropped when she fell. The sapphires sparkled, heartlessly beautiful, on the carpet beside her hand.

Stacey continued, "I tried to stop you from harming your mother, but you killed her."

Petie made the logical leap. "Afterward, you killed me."

"Precisely."

Petie was *so* sorry she guessed the whole scenario ahead of time. "How can you live with yourself? Ten years knowing you were an accomplice to a double murder?"

"I was not an accomplice," Stacey snapped, then drew a breath. "I needed the money to finance my campaign for the city council. I have only ever wanted to do good for Rockin."

"By killing a woman and a little boy?"

"Donald wasn't supposed to do that. He was supposed to clean out their valuables, bring them to me for sale and we'd split the profits. But he got greedy and Michele got smart." Stacey didn't sound in the slightest bit regretful. She was more matter-of-fact…about a gruesome double murder that had broken a family and convicted Evelyn Jones, an innocent, on a false charge.

Inspired by the memory of that long-ago bus ride to Rockin, and strange and talented Weezy, the painter, Petie asked, "Did you meet Donald at the state psychiatric hospital?"

Before Petie had even finished her question, Stacey shouted, "I was *visiting* my *mother!*"

The mother Stacey had used as an example of her tough early life. No one was supposed to think Stacey was unstable. They were simply supposed to think she'd risen above her past.

"How did your mother die?" Another random question that popped out of Petie's mouth from nowhere.

Stacey's eyes narrowed. "Aren't you clever." It wasn't a compliment.

So Stacey had killed before.

Petie glanced toward the teller cage where the bullet had dug its hole.

Of course she'd killed before. Norma had died not long after Petie left town. That old woman had been smart, and if she realized what Stacey had done and spoken to her about it…

"Can I please spend a moment with my mother?" Petie didn't have to fake the quaver in her voice.

"More tricks?" Stacey touched her own cheek and winced. "I can't get to the hospital until after I drop off the necklace. Damn you, I'm going to be scarred."

That's the least I owe you. "Please. Mama. Did you kill her?" Petie edged sideways, keeping her hands up and never showing Stacey her back—and the lug wrench she had tucked in her belt.

"No, I didn't kill her!"

"You intend to. Why would you wait?" *Shut up, Petie. You're getting panicked. Don't talk unless you can improve matters.*

"There's always a chance things won't go as well as I planned." Stacey spoke through gritted teeth. "People are stupid. They frequently fail to do the smart thing. They don't obey. If you'd brought somebody along and I was the only one in here with her, they'd know it was me."

"Of course." Petie had realized Stacey was a sociopath. But she was still methodical. "Is that why she's still got the necklace?"

"Right."

Petie edged some more, staying in the shadows at the side of the bank. "Please let me go see my mother."

"Go. What do I care?"

Petie ran toward Ioana's prostrate form, freeing the lug wrench as she went.

Stacey followed. "Why do you care about her? She left you alone in California juvenile detention. When you got to Rockin from California, you were afraid to tell her you were here."

Petie knelt beside her mother and pressed her fingers to Ioana's jugular.

The heartbeat was faint but steady. Petie wanted to weep with joy, then weep with fear. Blood clotted in Ioana's blond hair at the back of her head. She was alive now, but for how long?

Stacey was talking now, filling the time. "When you were on trial, she didn't come to be with you."

Petie cradled the lug wrench, eased her fingers around the cool metal rod, glanced back at Stacey. "I was always the rebellious child. My sister was younger, softer, gentler. Mama knew I was strong. Mama had a responsibility to Marya."

"*Marya.* That nosy little bitch. If not for her, you could have had your mother's love."

"I did have my mother's love." For the first time, Petie realized how true that was. For the first time, she saw herself as her mother saw her: strong, self-sufficient, a survivor.

She was going to survive this, too. She didn't want to kill anyone. But she would do what she had to do.

She glanced back at her mother. "I do have my mother's love, and I wouldn't trade my sister for any jewels."

"That is so touching it makes me want to vomit. Your sister's the reason I introduced Davey to your mother."

That stopped Petie, knocked her off-kilter. "Davey who?"

"Davey Brown. I met him when I visited my mother."

Now Petie remembered. Weezy had said that at the state psychiatric hospital, Donald's name was Davey.

"Your sister has been digging around in the records of the Jameson murder investigation and your trial. I figured when Davey killed Ioana, that would distract her but good."

Fury rose like a killing red tide. On one knee, Petie edged around, grasped the lug wrench and prepared to stand and charge—when behind Stacey, she saw movement.

The bank's front door eased open.

"What have you got?" Stacey asked in a furious rush. "What are you holding? Is that a gun?" She pointed her own pistol at Ioana. "Put it down. Put it down!"

"It's not a gun. But okay. Okay." Slowly, Petie lowered the lug wrench onto the floor beside the sapphires bound with gold.

"What do you think you are? A ninja?" Stacey's voice hit a high note. "When I've already got this in my hand?"

Petie focused on Stacey, on that countenance that had fooled so many people for so long. The scalding coffee had left her cheek and forehead swollen and scarlet, and one eye drooped as if the nerves had been damaged. Petie was glad of that.

Stacey was a monster. She might as well look the part. "I hoped I could save my mother."

"Let's dispatch that notion right now." Stacey's eyes narrowed on Ioana. She aimed the pistol.

With her free hand, Petie picked up the jewels that glinted on the carpet. She stood swiftly, without grace or forethought.

The eye of Stacey's gun steadied on her forehead.

"Such a fuss for something so small." Petie tossed the jewels into the air and caught them again, a simple motion that focused Stacey's attention. "Someone's coming for the necklace and the bracelet, or you wouldn't want them so badly. What about all the other pieces?" Petie was sure she was going to die, and she didn't know if she was stalling or if she was stupidly curious. "Whoever's coming must be coming for them, too. What's going to happen when you don't deliver?"

"They dealt only with Davey. Donald. They don't know I was involved." Stacey's breathing intensified as Petie tossed and caught, tossed and caught, each motion growing higher and less controlled. "I'll tell Donald's contacts I saved the jewels. They're worth more than all the rest put together."

"Of course they are. Too bad." Petie saw a man's form moving swiftly toward them on silent feet.

Zone Jameson. It was Zone.

Something in Petie's face must have given him away. Or maybe he made a sound she couldn't hear for the rushing of blood in her ears.

"Stay where you are." Stacey pointed the pistol at Ioana and half turned.

Hoisting the jewels in her fist, Petie shouted, "Catch!" threw them high in the air and flung herself over her mother's body.

It was the perfect gamble.

In a frenzy to protect the precious gems, Stacey snatched at the necklace, caught it. Snatched at the bracelet, dropped it. Realized she'd been duped.

She aimed at Petie and shot.

Pain ripped through Petie's hip.

Stacey steadied herself to shoot again.

Zone hit, low and fast, taking Stacey out at the knees.

They slid across the carpet.

Stacey's scream was agony.

Petie hoped Stacey's scalded skin had been ripped from her face.

50

PETIE WOKE AS EMERGENCY personnel transferred her to a stretcher. Everything hurt. Everything.

The bank was full of people, noise, lights.

In the corner, Zone stood, surrounded by police as he gestured and spoke. He continually glanced toward her and when he met her eyes, he threw her a kiss.

All around them, everything stopped.

People turned to look at her, then back at him.

Everything started again.

She wanted to ask him what that gesture meant, but movement was what brought her to consciousness. Agony rolled across her in waves. Feverishly, Petie asked, "Is she alive?"

"You bet, she's alive. But you should see her face. It's bad." The EMT hung the IV bottle from a stainless-steel hook on the stretcher beside her.

"Her face? What's wrong with her face?" Yesterday, Donald

White had hit Ioana, and her cheek and throat were bruised, but why did the EMT sound so horrified?

"She's scalded, and the trip across the carpet stripped most of her skin away."

Realization—and scorn—broke. "I don't care about Stacey Collins. What about my mother? What about Ioana Jones?"

"Oh. Her. She'll be fine. The blow to her head was vicious, but she came to consciousness as we put her in the ambulance. That's the most important thing, that she was awake and cognizant of her surroundings. Really cognizant. That woman can talk." The EMT put straps across Petie's chest and legs and tightened them. "This is so you don't roll off," he said. Then, "She asked about you."

"Did she?" Petie felt an upswell of love.

"She wanted to get up and take care of you herself." He signaled, and the stretcher started for the door. "We told her that you'd been shot but you were lucky. This wound is not life-threatening. The bullet didn't touch the bone."

She didn't like his almost-cheerful attitude. Not when she felt this bad. "Please don't tell me it's not serious."

"Gunshot wounds are always serious."

Glad to hear it, buster.

"On a scale of one to ten, how's your pain level?" he asked.

"Ten. Does it always hurt this much when you catch a bullet?"

"So they tell me." The stretcher rolled through the bank's front door and stopped at the steps. "I'm going to start a pain reliever now."

Petie subsided. Her mama was okay and asking about her.

Within the warm, comfortable joy of knowing her family was safe and together, Petie felt an ungodly joy in knowing Stacey had been scarred forever. After all, Stacey had changed Petie's face.

It was only fair Petie returned the favor.

51

THE PATH CUT THROUGH the middle of the vegetable garden at the old Jameson place. Last time Petie had seen it, when she was eighteen, the landscape had been covered with snow and ice.

Now it was September, the last days of light and warmth. Basil lifted green leaves to the sun. Tomatoes bloomed, set and turned that glorious ripe red. Beans climbed trellises and carrots dug their roots into the earth.

The weather service warned the first cold front of the season was bearing down on them. Petie believed it, for it seemed the world held its breath.

Or maybe it was her, going to talk to Zone Jameson after, um, leaving for a breather.

Her recovery had been painful. The reunion with her mother and sister had been postponed as Ioana and Petie recovered from their wounds. Yet Marya had hardly left their sides, and Zone…he'd been at the hospital every day.

She hadn't told him she was leaving.

He might not be too happy about her sudden absence or her lack of communication. She'd find out directly.

When she arrived at the old Jameson house, she knocked on the door to ask for Zone. Seeing the place again, she felt none of the twinges of horror she expected. The interior seemed so different, changed by the smells of cooking, a riot of shouting children and their two mothers.

The women had directed her out to the garden and the long row of potatoes. "You can't miss them," the petite woman said. "The plants look exactly the same as they do in *The Martian*."

How had the woman pegged Petie as the kind of nerd who watched *The Martian* over and over? And not for Matt Damon, either. For the science.

Also for Matt Damon.

Now Petie saw Zone kneeling with a pad under his knees. He'd placed the shovel on the ground beside him. He'd used a garden fork to loosen the soil around the potato plants and now carefully separated the potatoes from the earth and placed them in a bucket. His hair had grown out, and his beard was black and curly. He looked like the quintessential Alaskan outdoorsman.

Petie carried Tuddy in one arm.

She passed a bench that looked like a good place to sit, and think, and remember, and placed Tuddy there, sitting up, looking out through that shiny plastic eye. She smoothed the ratty fur on his head. "Make yourself comfortable."

And keep quiet. Since the morning he had sent her to rescue Ioana, he had been silent.

That was fine with her.

She stepped into the garden, over rows of plants to reach Zone's side. "Hello," she said.

He glanced up, adjusted the mat under his knees and went back to work. "Hello."

The issues between them were not easy.

Neither of them knew where they stood.

She said, "I suppose you wonder where I've been."

"I talked to your mother. She told me you went to the fishing camp." He sounded accusing, then neutral. "I was surprised, to say the least."

Mama said he'd shown up at the house, looking good, with flowers and candy, and when she told him Petie had left town, he dropped the f-bomb four times in a row. "I understand you had dinner with her and Marya."

"Your mother's a great cook." He sounded less prickly.

Note to self: even the memory of good food made Zone mellow.

"After I cleared it with Chief Dumas and I gave that reporter an interview, I went to Midnight Sun Fishing Camp to see what—"

He interrupted, "I was surprised you gave Faye Miller an interview."

"We had something in common, only she was hurt a lot worse. Stacey came close to killing her."

"Did Faye tell you exactly why?"

"She overheard Marc Yazzie haranguing Stacey about giving campaign money to Derrick Green. Faye looked over the list of Stacey's campaign contributions, but Derrick Green hadn't contributed. Faye called Yazzie and asked for an interview. He said tomorrow and called Stacey. Stacey called Faye and wanted to meet that night, and when Faye went to the meeting place—"

"Stacey shot her."

"In the back. Twice. Faye's lucky to be alive, and what with being unconscious and in the hospital, she missed all the excitement about the Donald White shooting and the crap with

Stacey Collins at the bank. Giving Faye the interview seemed like the right thing to do." Plus Petie liked Faye.

Zone rubbed his forehead with his wrist and left a dirty streak. "That explains a lot about the sequence of events. When Yazzie was at the police station, he wasn't exactly... rational."

"I can see why not. He really liked Stacey, and to think that she was a brutal—" Petie rubbed her forehead, too. The memory gave her a headache. "Faye got national coverage with that story."

"International."

"I never would have thought so many people would be interested."

"In a girl falsely accused and convicted of a sensational double murder, who escapes on the way to prison, hides for ten years, then comes back to bring the real killers to justice?" He got sharp and sarcastic. "You didn't think that would interest people?"

"Fine." She supposed he had the right to be sharp and sarcastic. "When you put it that way..."

One of the children, a girl about eight, arrived with a lawn chair and set it out beside Zone. "Miss Jones, Tall Mommy says you shouldn't be standing because of that lady who shot you."

Zone looked up and assessed her with his gaze. He might have been more sympathetic if he hadn't been so irritated.

"Thank you." Petie eased herself into the chair and watched the child skip back to the house. "Nice kids they're raising."

"Hell-raisers, the lot of them." He said it with affection. "The last month with them has been a revelation. It's been like all the years of Timmy's life at once."

"What a lovely way to think of it."

They smiled, looking at each other.

Their smiles faded.

They had never been friends. They hadn't really been adversaries. Grief and horror had united them.

And passion.

And justice.

"Anyway, it seemed like a good time to go back to the fishing camp." Sitting did help her hip. As the EMT had said, gunshot wounds were always serious, and she'd learned of the discomfort firsthand.

He bent back to his work. "I didn't realize you were going."

He didn't sound reproachful, but she felt guilty and flushed anyway. "At the hospital. The noise. The attention. People coming at me. Talking. Chief Dumas. My sister being the lawyer. You and Mama, taking the credit for the Donald White shooting. Chief Dumas not believing it, but he couldn't prove...whatever. He wanted to arrest me. I guess he didn't *really* want to, but I was technically a criminal and he should." Recalling the chaos made her chest tight. She felt dizzy...

"Inhale," he said.

She did. Better. That was better. "But the publicity. I had been exonerated to the max, and Chief Dumas was on the spot. I could give the interview, disappear and the worst of the fuss would have time to die down. Midnight Sun Fishing Camp—I had lived there so long, I felt homesick." She still felt homesick, but she didn't know for where.

"If you don't mind me asking—are you going back? To stay?"

Such a polite question put in such a mild tone, yet she watched as Zone used the fork to gouge deep into the dirt, turning it over and over although he'd already dug in that spot. "No. Hawley already hired someone to take my place. Meriwa. She's—"

"I know who she is. She drove me from the airport to the fishing camp."

"Ah." Petie waited, but he didn't say anything else. "She's good with people. She's competent with everything."

"He should have hired her sooner."

"Yes. Yes, he should have." But he hadn't because he'd had Petie. "She's got family in the area, so no worries about her being alone in the winter. She's a good replacement for me."

"How do you feel about that?" He sounded like a therapist.

"Weird." Therapist or not, it felt like a good question. "Hawley had already had my stuff packed and someone living in my cabin. When the season was over, he was going to send it."

"So no more fishing camp."

"No more fishing camp. He also had a paycheck for me. All my wages and the investments he made in my name, minus the social security and income tax."

Zone reared up. "And a whopping fine for not paying it!"

"He's been paying it all along, in my name, with my social security number." She laughed a little too hard. "He said as long as the money came in, the government wasn't going to squawk about me being dead."

Zone looked her in the eyes, and sounded fierce and indignant. "He took one helluva chance someone in the government wouldn't connect your name with the name of a convicted murderer and come after you, arrest you, put you behind bars."

She tried to lessen his outrage. "Hawley said in the government, the right hand doesn't know what the left hand is doing. I guess he's right."

Zone grunted, tossed the fork aside and dug into the dirt with his bare hands, as if he needed the earth to make him whole.

She understood. For people who had lived in exile, people who had lived on the edge, their needs were primitive and pure: live in the simplest way possible. "Anyway, the wages weren't much, but I never spent money except on online classes and books, and what with the investments—I got a nice check."

He leaned back and looked at her, unsmiling.

She clarified, "A really nice check."

"Good for you. What are you going to do with it?"

"I suppose I should travel." She didn't realize she sounded fretful.

"Petie, you don't have to travel if you don't want to." He was digging in that dirt, finding potatoes, being Zen. "You're not even thirty. Travel can come later. You can stay in the States. It's a great place. It's your choice. It's up to you."

It *was* up to her.

She appreciated the reminder. "I did travel. I also went to Quemada, then on to China to visit my grandmother."

He paused in his work. "That explains a lot. You were gone a long time for a visit to the fishing camp. Did you find her well?"

"She is very old." With some humor, she added, "And when it comes to tai chi, she can kick my ass. She welcomed me. She made sure the rest of the family also welcomed me. She wants me to go there to live."

He kept his gaze firmly fixed on his hands. "Will you do that?"

With slow grace, she reached out. Her fingers hovered over his hair. It was curly and so black, and she remembered the vitality that sprang from it when she had taken him into her arms and into her body.

He must have felt a disturbance in the air, for he swiftly turned, caught her hand, kissed it and bowed his head over it.

So she touched his hair with her other hand. "I like your face. I like it better when you're shaved."

"Then I'll shave."

Her world, so out of kilter, began to right itself. Life had taken so many abrupt spins lately, and she still felt uncertain. But maybe she could land on her feet.

"I live in a lookout in the Olympic Mountains," he told her. "It's beautiful there. In the winter, it's completely isolated. In the summer…it's still pretty isolated. But I keep busy. I think you'd like it up there. Would you come?"

"I'd like that. I can also keep busy."

"Would you like to get married?" he asked so matter-of-factly, as if marriage was the next logical move.

She didn't see it that way. "Someday. Maybe next summer, if we find we suit." She had to inject some sensibility into this discussion. "We really don't know each other very well."

"I got your hand dirty." He brushed at her fingers, then brushed his palms together. In a manner that made light of their history, he said, "We're joined by tragedy. I'd like to know if we could be joined by joy."

The sound rose from nowhere. From the air. From her brain.

Yes…

The hair rose on Petie's arms. She looked at Tuddy, his tattered fur, his one shiny plastic eye. "I'm never going to get rid of that bear, am I?"

"We could leave it for the kids here."

"Give someone a haunted bear? *No.*"

"No, I suppose not… We don't have to live at the lookout forever."

"Just until we figure out what to do with the rest of our lives?" she suggested.

"Right. Petie, I suspect we'll both do well far from the madding crowds."

"I think so, too." She rubbed her fingertips across her cheek. "I'm Evelyn Jones again. Evie to the people who love me."

He took her hand and held it. "Evie, I know of a good drive-in. Would you like to go get a burger?"

★ ★ ★ ★ ★

ACKNOWLEDGMENTS

A special thanks to Kie Relyea who took so much time and care to give me the facts about news reporting in these difficult times.

Thank you to Lennette Corwin who generously advised me on procedures for the tricky banking situation I created in *Wrong Alibi*.

Thanks to the art department who worked through so many iterations of the *Wrong Alibi* cover. Your dedication is amazing and inspiring.

Thank you to the editing department who saw the potential for a story about a TSTL young woman (too stupid to live) who transforms herself into a strong, smart female.

To everyone at HQN, as always, it is a pleasure and a privilege to work with you.